AS
YOU
LOOK

About the Author

Verónica Gutiérrez is a former community organizer, civil rights attorney, and corporate executive who was born and raised in Boyle Heights, the East Los Angeles neighborhood that her protagonist Yolanda Ávila calls home. She lives with her wife, Laura, in Los Angeles and San Francisco, where they provide mixology-lesson-themed fundraisers for their favorite nonprofits and host frequent gatherings for a close community of family and friends of all hues.

AS YOU LOOK

VERÓNICA GUTIÉRREZ

BELLA
B O O K S
2022

Bella Books, Inc.
P.O. Box 10543
Tallahassee, FL 32302

Printed in the United States of America on acid-free paper.

First Edition - 2022

Editor: Heather Flournoy
Cover Designer: Kayla Mancuso
Cover photo: Abel Gutiérrez

ISBN: 978-1-64247-344-5

PUBLISHER'S NOTE

Acknowledgments

I am grateful to so many people who have inspired and helped me along the way to completing this novel. Dr. Joella Castillo provided timely inspiration, encouragement, and tips regarding the juju and the publishing world, not to mention excellent chiropractic care and ergonomic advice that all writers should heed.

Lisa Cron's Story Genius workshop provided a fabulous jump start on the writing process. Excellent book coach Erin Lindsay McCabe from Jennie Nash's Author Accelerator program provided indispensable feedback and cheerleading. I could not have asked for a better book coach. Dawn Ius also provided a great manuscript review.

Beta readers are a writer's angels. My wife, Laura, provided great story feedback, initial copy editing, and so much more. Thank you, Love! My sisters and childhood reading buddies, Socorro Siqueiros and Laura Casias, read and commented on my earliest drafts, as did Alicia Moisa Duran and Daniel Flores Duran. Carla Peterman, Dr. Debbie Flomenhoft, and Barbara Nack provided additional welcome input. Laura Luna offered insights and resources that helped me develop several story lines. Dr. Marcus Eubanks provided much appreciated feedback and input on emergency doctor education and career progression, as well as concussion treatment. Juan Ramirez offered some insights on Taekwondo techniques. Nora Rohman provided much welcome insights on private investigators and the Bradbury Building. Any errors in these areas are mine. And then there's Heather Flournoy, my awesome editor, who helped pull it all together in the end. All of you are truly angels.

I am of course grateful to my family who provided so much material growing up that I hope you don't mind seeing composites of you in some of these, and future, characters. I love you all more than I can say, Laura, Socorro, Elsa, Ricardo, Martin, Beatriz, Gabriel, and Abel, but especially my parents Juana Beatriz and Ricardo Jesus who inspired in all of us a love of books, education, and a commitment to justice and our community of Boyle Heights. Thank you, Abel, for the photo shoot and the great picture on the book cover.

A special thank you to my crew, *The Lokas*, Luna, Eda, Barbara, Martha, Nancy, Kim, Angee, Judee, and Lisa: You all have provided much material, including some quotes, research leads, beta readers, and much inspiration and support. Thank you for building the community that inspired Yolanda Ávila's friends.

The strange year of the pandemic interrupted a year of Nifty Fifty celebrations but somehow still strengthened the bonds of another group of friends, the Roomies. Kelly, Trish, Debbie, and Amelia, thank you for welcoming me to your bubble and especially for being my default sisters-in-law.

And finally, Laura, you are not only the love of my life, but also the inspiration for Yolanda and Sydney's healthy relationship, "because there are enough broken people out there." Thank you for the life choices that have made our adventure possible, and for always making me happier. I love you!

Dedication

To Laura, thank you for sharing this
great adventure called life.

"Como te ves me vi; como me ves te verás."
-Dicho Mexicano

"As you look, I looked; as you see me, you will be seen."
-Mexican saying

CHAPTER ONE

Friday, 3:23 a.m.

I used to think dreams were just your brain rebooting for the night, not a big deal—until they were. Then I wanted them to go away, but they kept coming, wouldn't leave me alone. That may have been the biggest gift my mom ever gave me, but I didn't want to believe it for the longest time.

On this night, I woke in a cold sweat. Not the hot, hormonal one of my cycle. So, I knew the time without looking, but I checked anyway. 3:23 a.m. Again.

"*Chingado.*" I kept my voice low so as not to wake Sydney. I'd never understood how she could sleep through low-flying LAPD helicopters but startle awake at a creaking floorboard. She'd once explained it was due to her time in Afghanistan, but I thought it had more to do with growing up in LA. I stayed in bed and reached for the comforter, careful not to pull it away from her, and stared at the ceiling fan's faint outline in the dark.

What was that dream? And why had I felt faint at the end of it? That was new. I tried to recall if I'd ever felt that in other dreams, but nothing came to mind. After several attempts at a relaxation exercise Sydney had taught me, I gave up on images of my body melting and returned to my catatonic examination of the ceiling fan. *Wait, was that Joey melting in my dream? Was I remembering that right? Creepy!*

I was still trying to remember, when Sydney stirred ahead of her six o'clock alarm. She moaned from deep in her throat the way she always did upon waking and turned to kiss me lightly on the lips. I loved that she kissed me before getting out of bed. Now that she was an attending, her schedule at the hospital was more sane, the morning kisses more regular.

"Earth to Yolanda," she said when I continued to stare at the ceiling after returning her kiss. "Awake long?"

"Since three twenty-three."

"Uh-oh. The juju's back."

I gave her a noncommittal grunt.

"Be careful today, okay?"

"No worries, love. Just collecting on a Workers' Comp case and dropping by Dad's. You coming to happy hour at Mel's later?" Our group of Friday regulars would be at the Highland Park dive.

"Yeah, but don't change the subject. Promise me no heroics today, okay? No climbing into lockers and fighting off bat-wielding men." She smiled, propping herself up on her left elbow, but her eyes turned serious. She rested her head on her upturned hand, her durag sliding a bit off-center.

"I promise." I didn't want her to worry. I knew she was thinking of the last time I'd woken up at that time. That night, I'd brushed off an odd, claustrophobic feeling. But later, while on stakeout at a baseball field, I'd hidden in a utility shed to record and expose a fake shoulder injury. Some nosey Little Leaguer made me, and my subject took a bat to the shed. I got shaky video on my phone, timed my escape between swings, and got away with just a few scratches and bruises from a less-than-graceful, tumbling exit. Ace move by your friendly, neighborhood private eye.

"What else?" Sydney brought me back from the memory.

I yawned. "What do you mean?"

"A dream, a feeling…?"

"Just one dream." I sighed, knowing she wouldn't let it go. "I was browsing for a book for Joey's birthday. That's all."

"And then?"

"I said, that was all." I left out the part about Joey's image melting away. I wasn't sure of my recollection, and I didn't want to get into it anyway. Sydney connected these early morning wakeups to my mom because they'd started after her death. A few weeks earlier, Sydney had started pressing me to "work through these issues," but I didn't want to dredge up old regrets and nagging guilt.

"There's always more to these dreams, babe." I'd never liked that term of endearment before hearing it from her. I liked it fine, now. "So, then?"

"Well…I felt a little dizzy. Must've been cuz I was in the kids' section and kids have cooties." I hoped making light of it would get her to drop the subject. It didn't.

"Look at me," Sydney said in that soft voice that always got my attention. "Turn your head and look me in the eye."

I did as instructed.

"What else?"

"That's it. Just felt like I was losing my balance."

"And?"

"Are you interrogating me?"

"Trying to get you to remember all of it." She caressed the scar on my left arm and kissed me on the forehead.

"Okay, I'll play." I hoped to get the retelling over quickly so she'd leave me alone. "I was at Espacio 1839 over by the Mariachi Plaza. I was looking for bilingual chapter books. Everything's fine, and then I get a little vertigo when I move a dust cloth from the shelf…Funny, I just remembered that. Wonder what that was doing there." I stopped and looked at her, but she only nodded so as not to interrupt. "That's pretty much it." If I'd mentioned the image of Joey melting, she'd never let it go.

"How did the dream end?"

"Um…kinda like a movie. You know how things fade to black between scenes? Like that. Nothing special."

"Feel anything other than vertigo at the end of the dream?"

"Now that you mention it, maybe a little anxious. But, really, I think it's just cuz I haven't gotten around to getting Joey's gift. I've been so busy."

"I think maybe you should consider your brother's advice and at least give this stuff the benefit of the doubt."

"Aww, Syd, you know I'm not into Jesse's woo-woo stuff. Dreams are just your brain rebooting for the night. No. More like clearing your browser history. You click on 'clear' and you move on."

Sydney frowned, so I tried to explain. "Otherwise your brain gets clogged up and you...and you can't focus on what's important, you know?" My voice trailed off, Mom coming to mind. I squeezed my eyes shut and tried to block out the memory. Sydney picked up on it.

"Babe, look at me," she said again. She caressed the side of my neck with the back of her warm, brown fingers, a gesture I usually loved, but not so much today. I opened my eyes to meet her gaze.

"Can you repeat after me? Please?" She waited for me to nod.

"I did not kill my mother." When I hesitated, she insisted, "Say it. Please."

"I did not kill my mother," I repeated. *Why is she making me do this?*

"I am not responsible for her death."

"Why are you doing this?" My voice caught, and tears welled.

"Please," she said in a near whisper.

"I am not responsible for her death." Tears flowed. "You're lucky I love you, cuz now you're pissing me off. Okay?"

"I'm sorry." She held me tight. "And I love you. That's why I needed to hear you say it, even though your eyes tell me you still blame yourself." She ran her fingers through my spikey, bed-head hair and gave me a sad smile. "I'll let it go, but only if you promise to check in with Carmen on Joey, and talk to Jesse about it too, okay?"

"Okay." I held her close, confident there was nothing to the dream. Carmen would've called if there'd been anything up with Joey. She'd been my best friend since third grade, when we'd agreed to baptize each other's kids and be *comadres*. So far, being a godmother was enough motherhood for me.

"Okay, then." Sydney ran her thumb over my wet cheek. Her alarm sounded with its gently rising trill, and she leaned over to stop it before it reached the annoying level. "Gotta hit the shower if I'm gonna check in on the new residents. But promise me you'll be careful today, okay?" She gave me a peck on the cheek.

"Always."

She gave me another peck, this time on the lips, accompanied by a concerned frown, but she said nothing else and got out of bed.

I lay back with my forearm over my eyes and tried to block out the guilt and shame that engulfed me every time I thought of Mom's death. Sydney was right; I did blame myself. It was my fault. If I'd focused on what I'd already known at the time, instead of chasing a stupid dream, Mom would be alive today. I remembered it like yesterday.

The morning of Mom's funeral, I got a call from the Highway Patrol investigator. The man who'd run my mom off the road had been killed instantly when his car crashed into a freeway pylon. They'd had trouble identifying him because he'd used several aliases. Blood drained from my face at the mention of three names all too familiar to me—an identity thief I'd been tracking. I'd followed a stupid dream vision about his location, instead of the one real lead I had—a license plate that could have led me to him earlier.

"Stupid, stupid, STUPID!" I'd said over and over, pounding my forehead with my fist after that call. Sydney had tried to convince me that I couldn't have done anything to prevent the road-rage accident. That it was a freak coincidence. The guy had no way of knowing I had conducted Internet searches for him. But I wouldn't listen. I was numb with guilt throughout the funeral and went through the motions of accepting condolences without feeling anything. Sydney told me later that she was afraid I wasn't letting myself grieve. But how could I? I was too busy blaming myself. I vowed, then and there, to be done with this intuition and dream crap, and stick to the facts. If I'd done that, I would've traced the old license plate, found the guy, kept him off the road somehow, and saved my mother. She'd be alive. She was dead because I hadn't done detective work the way they'd drilled into us at the Academy a lifetime ago.

Maybe it was a good thing I'd left the LAPD. Maybe I wasn't cut out to be a cop after all. *No. I was a good cop. Damned good.* But that was before I'd been shot, long before all this juju stuff surfaced.

I fidgeted under the covers, antsy with guilt all over again. Sydney may get me to say otherwise, but I was never going to believe I wasn't responsible for Mom's death. I sat up and tried to slow my breathing, biting my lower lip.

"Syd," I called out when she stepped out of the shower. "Why'd you do that? Why'd you make me remember? I am not going to repeat that mistake. It will never happen again." I wiped a lingering tear.

"Babe." She stepped back into the bedroom wrapped in a towel, her smooth, dark skin glistening with moisture. "I just think the juju can help with the guilt."

I started to protest but flopped back onto my pillow when she continued.

"You know deep down that it wasn't your fault, but you won't acknowledge it." She sat beside me on the bed, her own scar— "my Taliban tattoo," she called it—highlighting her right biceps. "I just want you to be all of you, love." She placed her hand over my heart, her kind, brown eyes locked on mine. "I know I can't tell you how to grieve, but acknowledging anything—even this psychic stuff—has gotta be better than that unjustified guilt. It's been almost a year."

I knew she was trying to help, but the psychic thing was a step too far.

"Please. I am not psychic. And even if I had some…what do you and Jesse call it? Psychic intuition? It could never be reliable.

It's just a distraction." I sat up again and hugged her. "No, love, don't worry—this juju stuff's not for me. Besides, it would never hold up in court. I'd be laughed off the witness stand. Nah…If Mom's death taught me anything, it's that we shouldn't let the juju get in the way. And it won't. I'll call Carmen now. You'll see. Joey's fine."

I dialed Carmen on speaker and heard road noise when she answered.

"Hey, *mujer.* Off to work already?" I tried to sound unconcerned, calling her "woman," one of the terms we used for each other.

"*Buenos días, comadre.* Have a deposition downtown. Gotta get in early and kick some butt. My client waited until last night to tell me about another witness. Can you believe it? *Chingado.* What's up?"

"Um, just checking in on Joey's party tomorrow." The little white lie couldn't hurt. "What time should we be there? What can we bring?"

"Ah, you've turned into your mother, Yolanda." I felt her smile through the phone. "She would never arrive to a party empty-handed."

"No Ávila would. What can I say?"

"Well, now that you mention it, how about your potato salad? Or Sydney's awesome mac and cheese? Either would be fine. Say one o'clock? Joey'll be getting hyper before the party and you and Sydney are so good with him."

"Carbs and entertainment for a six-year-old. You got it. Good luck with the depo."

"*Gracias, mujer.*"

We hung up, and I raised my eyebrows at Sydney, feeling justified. She gave a curt nod.

"You'll still be careful today, right?" she said, standing up.

"Absolutely!" I jumped out of bed, pretending to feel much better about the rest of my day. I knew it would take most of it to shake off the resurfaced guilt. I'd done it before. All it took was concentrating on my work, keeping busy. The thought made me feel a little better—perhaps prematurely.

CHAPTER TWO

Friday, 7:00 a.m.

After Sydney left for work, I showered and made some final edits to yet another Workers' Comp fraud report for an insurance company client. More and more of these cases were coming in, and I was beginning to understand why Workers' Comp reform had become a hot political issue in California. It certainly didn't hurt my business, so I wasn't as concerned about the politics as were Carmen and her labor union clients. A few more of these insurance company cases and I might start looking for a place to hang a shingle instead of working from home. Then I'd be more established and out from under the cloud of my short-lived LAPD career.

I delivered my findings to a happy client in West Covina. I would close out the case altogether after the inevitable police reports and court testimony, if necessary. But, for now, I patted the check in my pocket with satisfaction.

On my way back to Boyle Heights, I was glad I was early and would have a chance to talk to Jesse before our "after-school snack," a Friday tradition Mom had established when I was in high school—an attempt to hang on to some family time as we got older and Dad had the flexibility at work to drop by. Now we did our best to indulge Dad on those days.

Inching along the westbound 10, I thought I'd make the conversation with Jesse a quick one, because we both knew where I stood on letting dreams dictate our actions. He insisted I was in denial about psychic messages. And when I said I just didn't want to think about it, I got a lecture on some philosopher who equated avoidance with denial. I wasn't looking forward to resurfacing the argument, but I'd promised Sydney, and now my good mood diminished along with the sunlight behind a dirty dishwater sky. June gloom had set in early, and a fire raging in Griffith Park only made the air quality worse. Like everyone but the firefighters, I wished for the cleansing Santa Ana winds as I crept along in traffic.

The midafternoon traffic toward downtown was almost as heavy as the early rush-hour traffic heading away from it, unusual, even by LA standards. Either there was an accident ahead or I was caught in one of the traffic waves emanating from the fire two freeways away. I switched my satellite radio from Mexican boleros to classic rock. The Rolling Stones are better for dealing with bottlenecks. An electronic freeway sign flashed ahead, too far away to make out the message. Something about the fire, no doubt. Creeping closer, I could make out the traffic picking up again after the sign.

I was about to curse the slow readers and the high-tech distraction when I read the Amber Alert: "CHILD ABDUCTION—SILVER JAGUAR" and a license number. Well, at least the Jaguar made it sound more like a custody dispute than a pedophile case. Pedophile kidnappers don't usually drive Jags. The news had been reporting on a serial kidnapper taking little boys in the desert county east of Los Angeles. He hadn't ventured into the LA area as far as I knew. And like most of my friends, I hoped he wasn't Black or Latino. My stomach tightened, something other than a pedophile and fear of resurgent hate crimes nagging at me, but I couldn't put my finger on it. I switched the radio to an all-news station but didn't hear anything about the Amber Alert before reaching Dad's house. My brother's beat-up Honda Civic blocked the driveway. He was reaching the porch steps when I pulled up to the curb and lowered the passenger window.

"Road hog!" I shouted.

Jesse turned around, glanced at his car, and smiled. My twenty-six-year-old brother, younger than me by four years, was home from school. Sometimes I wondered whether he went to class at all. Who would have time to do that and be involved in every political cause on the Eastside and on UCLA's Westwood campus?

"You should move your *carcancha* up the driveway before Dad gets home. Ditching class again?" I stepped out of my good-as-new, green Subaru Forester. I hadn't wanted a black car, but dark green looks black at night and is ideal for nighttime surveillance.

Jesse ignored my suggestion but stopped at the porch steps.

"Friday. No class. Jesus observes the Sabbath." He used the English pronunciation of his given name the way he sometimes did to mess with people on campus. "Jewish, you know."

"The Sabbath doesn't start until sundown, you ding-a-ling," I teased in the corny way we'd both picked up from Dad.

"So, I'm a few hours early. But who can tell with all the smoke?" He looked up at the sky, then turned back to me as I approached. "You're early too. What's up?"

"Just being a good *hija* checking in on her father," I lied. And before he completed his eye roll, I added, "Actually, I was stuck in traffic and needed to pee real bad."

"Nice to know we're a convenient potty break on the great road of life."

"Hey, at least I'm on the road while you're still stuck in park as a professional student."

"Who says I'm stuck? I'm well on my way to becoming the most renowned philosopher of our time." He held his head high, right hand on his chest in mock superiority.

"Well, in your own mind, anyway. At least you've got the hair for it." I tousled his dark, unruly curls. I envied his and

Mom's curls as much as he envied my and Dad's straight hair. I was proud of my brother, even though he could be a bit strange at times. Not more so than any other philosophy graduate student, I supposed.

Moving ahead of him, I unlocked the front door, put my keys and phone on the small foyer table inside, and headed for the restroom. Our father was still at the mechanic shop he managed and wouldn't be home for another hour or so. He'd go back to work later and close the shop at eight o'clock.

"Hey, I do need to tell you about something real quick," I called over my shoulder, "but let's surprise Dad and cook something ourselves."

"Hey, let's not surprise him and order out for something edible."

When I returned to the living room, Jesse was on his way out the door. He responded to the question in my eyes with, *"Carnitas Michoacan."* My brother sometimes spoke in shorthand, but I understood. He was going three blocks to Whittier and Soto and would be back with a bag of *carnitas*, chopped cilantro and onion, salsa, and fresh, hot tortillas—all the fixings for perfect tacos. Just as well. The only fresh thing in the refrigerator was probably Jesse's beer, or Dad's milk. After setting the table, I put on an old Nora Jones CD and lingered over the family pictures on the fireplace mantel. One of them was of Mom and me at my Academy graduation.

I wiped dust off the glass with my finger, pausing over Mom's image. She'd tried to be supportive of my career, but her concern for my safety had always been a source of tension between us. She was relieved when I left the department, but only after very supportive indignation that "the *cabrones* will regret losing" me. Her protective maternal instincts outweighed everything.

Mom battled similar contradictions when Sydney and I moved in together the year I left the LAPD, and again when we got married without telling anyone but our witnesses. We hadn't hesitated after the US Supreme Court legalized gay marriage in June of 2015. Like most gay couples in California, we remembered the 2008 legal window when sixty thousand

Californians wed before voters took away the right. In the end, Mom had approved of the idea of our marriage before the US Supreme Court had, if only because she thought it was good to have someone "take care" of me, especially a doctor, when I left the department. She'd become even more supportive as our national politics turned less civil and more hateful.

When Jesse drove up again, I remembered I'd put my phone on silent during my meeting with my client and had forgotten to switch it back. I picked it up and saw that I had messages. I dialed my voice mail and heard Carmen's voice as Jesse came in the door.

"Yolie, where the hell are you?" Carmen never called me Yolie; she preferred Yolanda. Something was wrong. "I need your help. Joey's missing!" The skin on the back of my neck went cold as I visualized the Amber Alert I'd just seen. "Call me at home. God, where are you?" My jaw tightened at the desperation in her voice. The voice mail icon on my phone indicated two more messages. I called Carmen without checking them. Jesse turned back from the bags of food as I dialed.

"What's wrong?" The look on my face must've given me away, but I didn't answer because Carmen picked up, her voice loud in my ear.

"Oh, god, Yolie. It's about time! Where've…Joey's missing. I know that *cabrón* has him, so I tried to teach him a lesson with an Amber Alert, but the cops just picked him up and he says he doesn't have him. I bet he's at the house in Rosarito or the cabin in Big Bear. But god, I don't know, Yolie. I need your help!" She said everything in one breath before I got a word in. I pictured the petite "dynamo," my dad's name for her. Wild, dark curly hair made her seem taller than her five feet, three inches, but she looked even taller when upset.

"Carmen. Stop. Breathe." I tried to stop her before she rattled off again in incomprehensible sobs.

"Carmen…" I tried again. To Jesse, I whispered, "Joey's missing."

"Go." Jesse handed me a Styrofoam shell with a couple of tacos he'd hurriedly put together, deep concern etched on his face. I took the food automatically, knowing I wouldn't eat it. "Call me as soon as you know more." He placed his hand on my shoulder and looked me in the eye. "It's not good, Yolie," he said, his voice a hoarse whisper.

I ignored him. "Carmen, I'm coming over. Be there in fifteen."

I hated when he did that. How did he know how bad it was? I rushed out the door and tried to shake off his foreboding. But my mind went back to my dream.

Shit.

CHAPTER THREE

Earlier Friday, 7:25 a.m.

On his way to school, Joey looked out the back seat window, wishing Mom and Dad would get back together. He usually liked to see the changing storefronts along Sunset Boulevard and guess what kind of business was coming in. But today he barely noticed them, his thoughts on his family. The adults all told him he needed to be a "big boy," except for *Nina* Yolanda. His godmother always told him it wasn't his fault and said that adults sometimes needed a break from each other. She said it was okay to be mad and sad, and to punch his pillow and even cry if he wanted, because adults did that too, sometimes.

Joey only cried at night when nobody was looking. He didn't tell anyone but his *nina*, and she said it was okay and never told on him.

He wished *Nina* would tell Mom and Dad to stop fighting. One of his friends at school said this separation thing was what happened before his parents got a divorce. He didn't want Mom and Dad to get a divorce. He wanted things to be like before.

But these days, he liked staying over with *Nina* Yolanda and Sydney more than with Mom or Dad. They didn't treat him like a baby. They asked him what he thought about stuff and really listened. The only other adult who did that was Mrs. Goldberg, his kindergarten teacher.

Dad asked him about stuff too, but usually stuck to school or the building models in his office. It was fun playing with the models, but *Nina* and Sydney always wanted to know if he was okay, and what he thought about things.

The other day, while watching an old *Aladdin* movie, Sydney had asked him if he had any wishes. Joey had only three. He wished Mom and Dad would get back together, he wished he had a puppy, and he wished he could rewind life.

"Rewind life?" Sydney had asked.

"Yeah, so, like when you have a birthday party, you can have it over and over again."

Sydney had smiled at that and said, "You're a big thinker, Joe."

Sydney was the only person who called him Joe. He liked that. He couldn't remember everything else Sydney had said, but he did remember something about rewind people being better than fast-forward people. Joey wasn't sure what that meant, but he thought maybe his parents were fast-forward people because they seemed to want more and more from each other—and from him.

"Why so quiet, Joey?" Dad asked at a stoplight, looking at him in the rearview mirror.

"Just thinking about rewind people and fast-forward people."

His dad smiled and wrinkled the space between his eyebrows in the mirror before turning back to the road.

"You're a weird kid, Joey, but in a smart way, I think." Joey thought it was Dad's way of being nice. He was fun lots of times, especially when they played chess and soccer, but Dad thought he was a little kid. He was going to turn six tomorrow—he wasn't a baby anymore. But Dad sometimes came through for him too.

"Dad, you're gonna drop me off at the church so I can walk to school, right?"

"'Course, big boy." His dad smiled at him. "And don't forget, your mom's picking you up after school."

"I know, Dad." Joey groaned. He hated having to go back and forth between his parents. Of course, he didn't tell anyone except his *nina* and Sydney. He stared out the window until they pulled up in front of Saint Martin's.

"Okay, then." His dad always let Joey walk across the front of the church and go into the schoolyard through the gate on the other side. Mom wouldn't like it and would never do the same, but Dad was cool about it. Besides, it was only a few feet. They were a bit earlier than usual because Dad had to get to the office for some emergency, but that was okay. He'd wait in the schoolyard until his friends got there.

His dad's cell phone rang as Joey got out of the car. By the time he'd pulled on his backpack and turned to wave goodbye, his dad was already on the call, waving and driving away without looking back. Joey watched the car almost hit a tiny black puppy. It scampered behind a dumpster in the alley next to the church. Joey ran after the dog and into the alley to catch it on the other side of the trash bin.

When he bent over the puppy, a big hand came over his face, covering his nose and mouth with a wet cloth. A strong arm trapped his arms at his sides and lifted him off his feet.

Joey kicked as hard as he could.

He opened his mouth to scream, but all he got was a gross chemical taste in his mouth.

The white cloth squeezed tight over his nose and mouth. He tried to fight, to wiggle free, but the arm had a good hold on him. The more he kicked, the stronger the hold.

And he couldn't breathe.

His eyes opened wide.

He was so scared.

He tried to bite, but just got more of the nasty-tasting stuff in his mouth.

Something warm ran down his leg at the same time that a sharp prick stung his left arm. Before he could wonder what it was, his legs and arms got heavy. All he could see was a white van in front of him. Then just the door handle. Then just a small, white dot before everything went black.

CHAPTER FOUR

Friday, 3:15 p.m.

On my way to Silver Lake, I raced through side streets, avoiding congested freeways. I wound my way around the Mariachi Plaza at First and Boyle, waving an apology to a rail-thin violinist I'd cut off at the curb. Then I headed west, past the northern edge of downtown along Sunset Boulevard. The Jaguar in the Amber Alert and that nagging feeling I'd had made sense now. Luis, Carmen's estranged husband and my *compadre*, drove a Jaguar. Carmen had said she'd reported him, but she'd also said Luis claimed not to have Joey. I hoped the kidnapper in the news had not moved west.

I tried calling Sydney to let her know, but she didn't pick up. We had a code. If she didn't pick up it meant she was busy. If I called right back it meant it was important, and she'd return the call as soon as she could. But I didn't have time to call again. I wanted to know more about the desert pedophile's profile and knew who could help.

I dialed Sheila Robinson, a private investigator I'd partnered with a few years ago on a housing discrimination matter. We'd hit it off posing as prospective renters. Sheila was a middle-aged African American, single mother of two teenagers who had moved her family from Birmingham, Alabama to Chicago— "too cold"—then to California, thinking that less racism would mean greater opportunities for her children.

"Just my luck, the only place I could afford turned out to be California's version of Alabama—better weather and racism with good teeth," she'd said as we worked a case against an apartment management company in the desert county east of Los Angeles. They'd coded applications from Black renters with smiling emojis to reject them. Sure enough, they rejected her application and accepted my nearly identical one, with an inferior credit score. Sheila answered the phone on the first ring.

"Robinson. If you lost it, I can find it. How can I help you?"

"Sheila, it's me, Yolie."

"Child, why you been a stranger? When are you and that sweet wife of yours coming out to the desert for some good pie? Better come out before it gets too hot to bake."

"I'll ask the wife. But I have an emergency and hope you can do some snooping around for me."

"You name it, I'll do it." God, I loved the woman.

"My godson's missing. You've met Carmen, his mom. She and Luis are separated now, and she thought he had Joey, but the cops picked him up and he says he doesn't."

"Oh, my lord! The poor boy. And his parents. They must be going crazy with worry."

"I'm sure they are. I'm on my way to Carmen's now. I didn't mention it to her, but I thought of that kidnapper you guys have on the loose out your way. Any chance you can get a profile on him? I mean, more than what's been in the news?"

"Oh, my god, I hope he didn't head your way. Let me see what I can find out and get back to you."

If anyone could get information out of her contacts, Sheila could. I thanked her before hanging up.

Carmen's home was tucked away on one of the narrow, hillside streets in Silver Lake west of downtown. Some of the young couples who lived there liked to call it the Eastside, to the irritation of actual East LA and Boyle Heights natives like my brother. Carmen's hillside lot didn't have the much-coveted view of the 100-acre reservoir from which the neighborhood took its name, but she was proud of her gardening and decorating skills. I never would've had the vision to create the warm and homey place she had in what first looked like cement cubes piled on top of each other.

I'd helped her bring the huge clay planters from near her beach cabin in Rosarito, south of the border, and watched as she planted flowering succulents, bougainvillea, and climbing roses along balcony and staircase walls. In little over two years, the cold, industrial structure had been transformed into a cascading garden of fuchsia, white, and green. Jesse, in one of his New Age moments, had recommended burning sage, saying the positive energy she'd created wasn't enough to overcome the negative energy he perceived in the hipster community. Carmen had laughed it off. As I approached her street now, I wondered if there might not be something to my brother's New Age babble.

I couldn't turn onto Carmen's cul-de-sac because it was already packed with police vehicles. I wound my way farther up the hill and squeezed between two huge SUVs that had never seen an unpaved road. The sight of the patrol cars made me queasy, not a feeling I'd expected. I hadn't dealt with the LAPD much since leaving the department and I didn't look forward to it now.

The six-year-old memory of escalated retaliation still made my stomach turn. It had come in response to a complaint I'd made about overzealous arrests. A Valley councilman had requested a crackdown to stop drug runners from Rampart coming up to his district. My colleagues had picked up some good kids I'd been cultivating as contacts and had not appreciated my criticism at roll call. Anonymous threats started showing up on my locker. I'd miscalculated when I reported the notes to Internal Affairs. The retaliation grew beyond the occasional cold shoulder and culminated with officers ignoring my calls while I chased a wanted suspect. No one responded until I started taking fire. And even then, it was in response to calls from another patrol unit. Were it not for my Kevlar vest, I would've taken one in the chest. I'd been lucky to escape with an ugly bruise below my clavicle and a flesh wound on my left arm. After filing another complaint against the non-responding officers identified in the internal review, there was no going back. At Carmen and Sydney's urging, I'd sued instead.

I thought I'd left that episode behind, but my apprehension reminded me that I hadn't. For a moment I wondered if the feeling was related to the vertigo or anxiety in my dream, but it felt more like nerves than wooziness. I put the uneasiness out of my mind. I was there to help Carmen.

Two patrol officers I didn't recognize leaned against the hood of their unit when I approached on foot. They looked at me as I climbed stairs winding around the garage, but they went right back to their conversation before I got to the door. I posed no threat in my jeans, sneakers, and an untucked, white button-down.

They were probably complaining to each other about the sergeant wanting them there only to give an appearance of "appropriate response." If Luis didn't have Joey, he no doubt had called his childhood buddy, Councilman Manny Martinez, who would have made calls to the department to request special treatment. It would've been no sweat off the politician's back. And, after all, one never knew when, or how, such favors could be repaid. Martinez had been a Valley councilman's chief of staff when he'd pushed for the aggressive policing that resulted in my departure from the department, so I didn't care for the guy, but I hoped he could be helpful now.

I let myself in without knocking, all eyes turning to me as I took in the scene. Lieutenant Lawrence Peak, whom I'd last seen at his deposition in my case, looked over expectantly. He leaned against the kitchen island at the edge of the open-concept living room, his eyes narrowing upon recognition. If he was here, someone had definitely called the brass. Carmen rushed toward me with open arms. Two other suits, a man and a woman, seemed relieved by the distraction. Carmen had obviously been badgering them with questions they couldn't answer.

"Yolie!" More trouble. Carmen thought I was more of a Yolanda and only called me Yolie when she was feeling emotional and vulnerable, usually after a couple of drinks. But she was quite sober. "Finally, maybe you can help me get some information that makes sense." I hugged her and noticed Peak's eyes narrow even more, if that was possible.

"I'm sure they're doing the best they can," I said.

"Oh, pleeeease, Yolanda." She rolled her eyes and regained some of her customary sense of authority. I knew she was about to ask why I bothered to stand up for my former brethren, but I interjected before she could heighten the tension in the room.

"They have to work with the FBI on this, Carmen." I led her back to the sofa. "They'll find him together. But let's sit down so you can fill me in."

The strain on her face softened a bit as we walked to the sofa. The two suits breathed easier too. I extended my hand and introduced myself. Detective Ralph Conroy seemed pleasant enough. Detective Carrie Lan raised an eyebrow and glanced at Peak when she heard my name. I wondered which version she'd heard: the one about the dyke who went on a crusade against the department, or the ambitious Senior Lead Officer who thought she was better than her colleagues. I hoped she'd heard the one about another woman's career derailed by men who'd forgotten that they were there to protect and to serve.

Lan was a tall, some would say big-boned, woman. Obviously in good shape but would never be called svelte. I thought her name might be Vietnamese, but her build reminded me of Sydney's best friend, Kevin Park, a Korean American doctor whose family still owned the corner store and upstairs apartment on the block where Sydney and Kevin grew up. Lan probably looked slightly older than her age. She was all business, but in that personable way that tall women acquire from years of putting people at ease with their height and size. She had the kind of naturally firm handshake that some try too hard to imitate.

By contrast, Conroy had the look of a guy who'd always been thought younger than his age. He had a crescent-shaped scar on his chin that he probably thought helped him look older or tougher, but his short, sandy-blond hair and slight build made him look anywhere between twenty-five and fifty. The only indication that he was on the older side was the hint of gray at his temples. Crow's feet appeared at the corners of his eyes only when he smiled—the kind that Sydney would say were a sign of happiness rather than aging. To me, he looked like a middle manager trying to fit into the executive suite and failing in his untailored suit.

Peak nodded a greeting. He looked on with an air of detachment, but I knew from experience that he didn't miss a beat. He was a good detective in his late fifties, with the dignified air of African American men of an older generation. He'd been passed over for promotion more times than he would admit, but he hadn't become cynical as much as simply resigned. It was tough seeing him almost give up because he'd been one of my mentors in the department.

At the Academy, I'd thought he'd seen a bit of himself in me and had meant well when he'd told me to be more reflective and less gung-ho if I wanted to make detective—think before acting, before speaking up. It was probably good advice which I had yet to master. I still respected the man, but neither of us had overcome our disappointment in each other over what he'd called my "job action." Still, something he'd once said had provided encouragement when I'd decided to become a private investigator.

"Even while stuck in your car drinking cold coffee on a stakeout," he'd said, "it's only you and the target. Your wits against his, like a chess match where everything else disappears. There's nothing like it, as long as the brass and civilians stay out of it."

I turned to him now at the memory.

"I'm a friend of the family, Lieutenant." I raised my palms, trying to put him at ease. He responded with a slight nod.

Carmen and I sat on her cream-colored leather sofa. I remembered when she'd bought it. She'd made Luis take their old, black leather couch when they'd separated because she'd never liked it. The new one was beautiful and comfortable, but I thought it impractical with a kid in the house. Detective Lan brought over two bottles of water and offered them without a word. Carmen and I thanked her but held the bottles unopened as we settled in.

"Okay, *mujer*," I said. "Can we start from the beginning?"

Conroy and Lan exhaled in unison and sat back on the matching chairs across the also impractical, glass coffee table. Peak remained impassive but leaned forward slightly. I guessed they hadn't made much progress and would take whatever help I could provide.

Carmen opened her water bottle, brought it to her mouth, and swallowed before taking a deep breath. "I'm so glad you're here." I squeezed her knee, encouraging her to go on.

"Luis had Joey for the week. I was supposed to get him back for my week today. You know the arrangement." I nodded in acknowledgment, and Carmen continued, "Well, when I went to pick him up at school, he wasn't there. Luis and I fought on the phone a couple days ago. He wanted to keep Joey for his birthday this weekend. But there's no way I was going to start giving in on that shit. He's kept him for other weekends since we separated, just to get back at me, but he always has Joey call and tell me that he wants to go to the beach house in Rosarito, or Luis's cabin in Big Bear, or Disneyland, or some other bribe. God, I hate the way he manipulates him. The *cabrón* doesn't even have the balls to tell me himself. I told Joey to get his dad on the phone and I let him have it." By now, she was talking fast.

"Well, this time I said, '*¡Ya basta!*'" Carmen gestured with her hands in the air. "When I went to get Joey, the school told me he'd been absent today. *¿Te imaginas?*"

No, I couldn't imagine getting that news, but said nothing so that she'd continue.

"I tried calling Luis but I couldn't get ahold of him. His intern told me he was going to Rosarito after a stop downtown and didn't know if he had Joey. So, I figured he'd taken him. *¡Pero ya me tenía harta!* Enough is enough! I called the police and reported a kidnapping, because that's what it was. I wanted the cops to stop him, you know?"

Conroy and Lan edged a little closer in their seats. I pictured Luis's silver Jaguar. So, the Amber Alert had been about a custody dispute after all, but now it was about much more.

"He was stopped all right, but now he says he doesn't have him. I don't know what to think. He has to have him. Joey's teacher said he didn't go to school today…" She trailed off before regaining her voice. "He has to have him!" Her anguish told me she feared the worst but didn't want to voice the possibility.

Conroy leaned forward. "Ma'am, have you talked to your husband at all today?"

I could tell he was good with victims and witnesses and wondered how different he might be with suspects.

"No. I never reached him, but you told me what he said."

"Where's Luis now?" I asked, looking from Carmen to Conroy and back. The detective responded.

"He's downtown. They held him for questioning at Headquarters after stopping him coming out of the City Hall garage about an hour ago."

Oh, great. The image Luis most wanted to portray was that of a squeaky-clean developer for the people, and the cops detained him outside of City Hall. I had to hand it to Carmen on that one. But this was not good. The Luis I knew would've copped to keeping the kid right away and tried to explain it all as one big misunderstanding. Anything to avoid a scene.

"And he says he dropped Joey off at school this morning?" I turned to Peak. Again, he only nodded. I'd heard enough and turned back to Carmen.

"Okay, Carmen. If Luis doesn't have him, these detectives and the FBI will find him." I tried to reassure her, rather unsuccessfully.

"He has to have him, Yolie."

"We're checking the cabin at Big Bear, Mrs. Ochoa," Lan said.

"The FBI is?" I asked.

"The San Bernardino Sheriffs," Peak said.

I turned back to him and away from Carmen, and mouthed, "And the FBI?"

"We're working this case, don't worry about it." He sounded more annoyed now, but I didn't want to alarm Carmen. I couldn't believe they hadn't called in the FBI. That's the general protocol when a kid might be taken across state lines. A potential trip south of the border would call for them as well. And their resources would certainly help. Peak was probably writing it off as a spousal dispute. I had to get downtown where Luis could tell me more, because the straight line that Peak's lips had disappeared into told me I wasn't going to get more from him. But I didn't want to leave Carmen, who now held her head in her hands.

Just then, my dad and Jesse walked in. Jesse went right up to Carmen and knelt in front of her.

"We're going to find him, Carmen," he said in that earnest way of his. "Don't worry, we're going to find him."

Carmen broke into sobs again and hugged him. Then she stood and embraced my father for a long time as he murmured *"mija"* into her ear. He didn't have to say more. Carmen had always seen my dad as the father she wished she'd had. Her own father had left when we were third graders, but the family had been better off without his drinking and beatings. She'd managed the psychological trauma of the abuse by taking up Taekwondo at the Boyle Heights Recreation Center—*"El Hoyo"* to those of us from the neighborhood—and she'd kept it up, earning a black belt before law school.

On the wall behind her now, she proudly displayed her white, green, brown, and red belts in a framed box my dad had made for her. It was a testament to their special bond. Carmen had asked him to give her away at her wedding and he'd been honored. Both told the story less often after Sydney and I got married, thinking that it somehow pained me to not have had my dad do the same for me. But there was no way we would've done the "chattel exchange," as one of our queer activist friends called it. No, in fact, I was glad that my dad had had the experience because no way would I ever be married in a church. He loved Carmen as a daughter and now he wanted to make everything right.

My dad looked at me over Carmen's heaving shoulder and pointed with his chin, first to Jesse and then to the door. That signal was all I needed. Jesse saw it too, and we both walked outside and out of earshot.

I looked at Jesse and could tell he was trying to keep himself calm with his hands in his pockets. He started tentatively. "Okay, Yolie, I know this stuff creeps you out." I felt him willing me to listen and knew he was about to tell me he'd had some kind of psychic message that would help find Joey, but I really didn't have time for his nonsense.

"I need to go talk to Luis. I don't have time for this shit. Time is everything right now. If he went missing this morning, we're in trouble." I kept my voice low. "But if anyone saw him later, we might have a better chance of finding him before he gets hurt." I started to go back inside to tell Carmen that I'd be back, but Jesse reached out and grabbed my shoulders. He looked at me so intently that I had to stop.

"Just listen to me for a sec. When you were on the phone with Carmen back at the house I got this feeling I haven't had since that pervert grabbed me at the *jamaica*. You remember?" Of course, I remembered. He'd been five years old at the time of the Salesian High School carnival. He was traumatized by the attempted kidnapping, wouldn't let go of anyone's hand for a month after that, even though the pedophile had been caught immediately, thanks to an alert family friend who'd spotted Jesse with the stranger. I'd felt responsible because I was supposed to have been watching out for him when we went to the restroom. After that, I rarely let him out of my sight whenever we left the house. He still reminded me how annoying that was years later as a preteen.

"It was awful," he said now. "It was exactly that same feeling I had way back then. My legs got weak. I almost peed in my pants. And I wanted to cry so bad. It scares the shit out of me. It wasn't just a memory, Yolie. It was so real. The only difference was some nausea that I don't get. But he's out there. He's out there and he's scared."

"And now you're scaring me. But none of this helps. I gotta go. Let me go." I started to turn away again, but he held me tighter.

"There's something else." He loosened his grip when I grimaced, but he had my attention. "Colors again. Red and white. It's only a partial image, but the white is like a circle on a red background. I don't know what it means, but Joey is someplace with that image."

"*Chingado*, Jesse. I have no idea what you're talking about." I pushed him away and went back inside where my dad had taken my place on the sofa.

I told Carmen I was going to talk to Luis and would be right back. Peak asked if one of us would stay with Carmen tonight and my dad said he would. Peak's lips tightened again, like maybe that was the wrong answer. I was on my way out the door when I heard Peak tell Carmen that he'd call if they had any news. He hurried down the stairs and called to me before I made it to the street, Lan and Conroy on his heels.

"This is official LAPD business, Ávila. Stay away from it."

"Sure, as soon as you make it the FBI's business too. What the hell are you doing waiting on that with the Riverside kidnapper out there?" I gestured with my hands, drawing the attention of the two uniforms.

"I know these folks, Peak," I said in a lower voice. His cell phone rang. "That's my godson who's missing." He ignored me and turned away to answer his phone, but I continued, "I'm going to talk to his father. If he says he doesn't have him, he doesn't have him, and you're wasting your time in Big Bear."

I turned and ran to my car. I didn't think he'd heard me because he'd put his finger to his ear and had said two "Yes, sirs" before I'd finished. As I rounded the corner to my car, I caught a glimpse of him angrily pocketing his phone. So much less satisfying than shutting an old flip phone or banging a receiver on its cradle.

I was out of earshot and couldn't hear what he said to Conroy and Lan, but I hoped he wasn't going to create problems for me downtown.

When I reached my car, my phone rang. I answered it, pulling away from the curb.

"Honey, my contacts at the sheriff's don't know much," Sheila said over the car's speaker, dispensing with any greeting. "And they're likely to know less as time goes on."

"Why's that?"

"It looks like the FBI is taking over the Riverside kidnapper case. Seems the kidnappings each occurred closer and closer to the Arizona border, so they're calling in resources from over there too."

"Well, hopefully that means the guy didn't come this way, but it doesn't make me feel much better. Any word on what kind of vehicle he's using?"

"Nothing on that. They haven't been able to find any witnesses either. It's just the kids disappearing on their way to, or from, school."

"Shit." My stomach tightened. "Joey may have disappeared on his way to school."

"Holy Jesus. Has the FBI been brought in?"

"No. That's just it. The cops seem to think this is a custody dispute." I explained what I'd learned from Carmen and described my exchange with Lieutenant Peak.

"Well, I let my contacts know about Joey. I'll call one of them back. Maybe she can ask the FBI to call the LAPD."

I wanted to hug her through the phone.

But shit. Luis has to have him.

CHAPTER FIVE

Friday, 4:30 p.m.

The rush hour had really hit now. Fortunately, I was going against traffic back toward downtown and made good time. I didn't know what to make of the fear and dread that Jesse had described, but I hoped it had nothing to do with the Riverside kidnapper. And I couldn't help but wonder about my dream. Jesse had mentioned nausea, and I'd felt dizziness. Were they connected? Had we felt the same thing? *Shit.* Whatever it was, it only served to make me anxious, a distraction I didn't need. I reminded myself to remain calm and focused.

When I arrived at the ultramodern building with the underwhelming name of "The Police Administration Building," I was struck with how much cleaner it smelled than the old Parker Center. And I wasn't given the brush-off I'd expected. The guy at the desk in the holding area didn't recognize me.

I asked for Luis Ochoa and was told that he was with his lawyer. I wouldn't be able to see him until after that. Okay, I got the brush-off after all. All I could do was wait.

While I did, I thought about Jesse again. He had this idea that Mom's death had opened him up to psychic abilities. Everyone deals with grief in their own way. And I didn't discourage his exploration into an area that even he admitted might lead nowhere. Sydney encouraged it more. I figured it had to do with what she called "near-death moments of grace" in her medical and military experience. I found Jesse's take more entertaining than profound, especially when he tried to help with "leads" on some of my cases, more like suggestions so general as to mean nothing. But he was starting to worry me. He wasn't going to bring Mom back. No amount of juju would do that. He just had to let go and deal with her death.

I checked the time on my phone. Again. A few minutes—more like an eternity—later, Andy Stewart, Luis's business partner and best friend since college, walked out of the holding area. I'd always liked Andy. Slender and fit in a tailored, charcoal-gray suit, he looked like he was walking out of a *GQ* ad. He was average looking without a beard, but the nicely trimmed one he sported now highlighted the twinkle in his hazel eyes. His dark brown hair was in the early stages of salt-and-pepper that makes men look "distinguished" and women "old." Yes, I liked Andy just fine. We were best man and maid of honor at Carmen and Luis's wedding. And we were Joey's godparents. He saw me and came right over.

"Oh good, they called you." Andy greeted me with a hug and a kiss on the cheek.

"We don't have much time. The longer a kid's missing, the lower the likelihood of finding him. The LAPD hasn't even called in the FBI yet. I need to talk to Luis to see what he knows, but they won't let me in."

"He'll be right out. We had Manny call and raise holy hell." He smiled. I knew I was biased, but to me Manny Martinez was just another slick ribbon-cutter who couldn't be counted on to deliver for the community unless there was something in it for him. Still, I was glad he was being helpful in this case.

"Luis was pretty worked up in there," Andy said, giving me a knowing look. "You can imagine. I had to calm him down, but Manny's call helped."

"I'll bet. Glad you were with him."

"You know how it is. Brother's keeper and all." Andy turned up a corner of his mouth as if it were no big deal to help his friend. And Luis was indeed like a brother to Andy, who'd grown up an only child in a dysfunctional family. I knew Andy was drawn to Luis's family life and was more disappointed than I was when our friends separated—the only time I'd ever seen him nearly come to blows with his friend, disgusted that Luis hadn't tried harder to mend things with Carmen. Otherwise, he was a steady influence on Luis's mercurial moods. And this was definitely a big deal.

When Luis walked out of the holding area, he looked sick to me. He wore a wide-eyed scowl of desperation that turned to determination when he saw me and rushed over.

"We need your help, Yolanda." He never called me Yolie either. "The bastards kept me in there wasting time. They thought I had Joey until Manny called and read them the riot act. We need your help. This is what we have to do. I want to hire you to work with the cops to find my son. They don't believe I don't have him. We need to—"

"Dude." I stopped him before he rattled on too long. "You're not paying me to find my godson. Sit your ass down and tell me what you know so that somebody can find him." We were about to sit on the metal bench I'd indicated, then I thought better of it and motioned him and Andy outside. Out of earshot of any officers, I peppered Luis with questions.

"Damn, you sound like the cops." And then he glanced at Andy and looked down, embarrassed. He knew how much I'd hated leaving the department.

"No offense taken," I said. I'd gotten what I needed but wasn't happy about it. Luis had acknowledged the argument with Carmen two days ago, but he'd sworn he'd kept to their custody agreement. He'd dropped off Joey in front of the church as he always did because Joey thought he was too old to be driven onto the school grounds. It was less than sixty feet to the school gate. Luis had waved goodbye and his son had waved back, and that was the last he saw of him.

"I should've taken him all the way in." He brought his hands to his face and ran them through his jet-black hair, adding to his uncharacteristically rumpled look. Luis had always been a sharp dresser, but his expensive, beige linen suit hung from him in a wrinkled heap. "I know Carmen will hate me even more now, but you gotta believe me. There's no way I would've dropped him off like that if I thought he'd come to any harm."

"I know. But we have a problem here." I glanced at Andy for support. "You didn't see anyone, and it looks like Joey never made it to school."

"I should've stayed and watched him go in," he repeated. He brought a hand to his mouth, his worried eyes shifting from me to Andy and back. "Don't you think I've been kicking myself over and over for that? But I was rushing to get to the office. My mind was on those fuckin' last-minute changes to the specifications for the Boyle Heights project," he said more to Andy than to me. Then, turning to me, "They're due on Monday."

"I thought you were going to the beach house in Rosarito."

"Rosarito?" He squinted in confusion.

"That's what your intern told Carmen."

"What?" Then, with realization coming over his face, he added, "No, that's next weekend." I couldn't help but think that the fight with Carmen over Joey was just to gain points with the kid. I knew Luis loved his son, but he was probably relieved to have the time to work on his big deadline.

"Go back to Carmen's, Luis. Maybe the cops will know more by now."

"Where are you going?"

"To the school. I'll check in with you at Carmen's if I learn anything."

"No, Andy and I'll go with you."

"Look. I know what I'm doing. Go to Carmen. You'll only be in the way with me. And even though you two stubborn *burros* would disagree, you need each other right now."

"She's right, bro," Andy said. "Let's get you to Carmen's. We'll see about getting the cops to release your car later."

I could've kissed Andy. Instead, I thanked him and told them I'd call. They didn't ask about the Riverside kidnapper, and I didn't want to bring it up and add to Luis's distress.

On my way back to Silver Lake and the Saint Martin Elementary School, I couldn't help but think about my dream again. Nothing in it signaled anything about a kidnapping, but I did wonder about the white cloth and the dizzy feeling. Then I kicked myself for dwelling on it. *Get your head together, Yolanda. Focus on finding Joey. You can't afford to get sidetracked by a stupid dream. You can't let Joey get hurt while you run down useless bunny trails. Not this time.*

CHAPTER SIX

Friday, 6:00 p.m.

I tried calling Sydney again from my car, but she still didn't pick up. I was about to leave a message when a boy about Joey's age darted onto the street from behind a satellite news van. I hung up and slowed down, my heart racing. It was a good thing it was still light out. I wouldn't have seen him otherwise.

Two more satellite news vans were parked across the street from Saint Martin Elementary School. Several police cruisers lined the school side of the street. At least the cops had arrived before the media. Channel 9 was interviewing Lieutenant Peak, with the church steps as a backdrop. Neighborhood parents and kids watched from a distance.

I had planned to get a look around and maybe talk to a few people, but Lieutenant Peak's presence blew that idea. He wasn't going to let me talk to anyone and "interfere" with his investigation. I'd have done the same if I were him, but I needed to know what had happened. I drove around the block, parked one street over, and walked back through the alley next to the church where Luis said he'd dropped off Joey.

By the time I reached the church, a group of officers and detectives, including Detective Lan, had moved to the alley entrance. Damn, I wasn't going to get much done here. Not that there was much to do. The only thing in the alley, other than typical debris, was a remarkably clean dumpster. No graffiti and no markings other than the Waste Management logo, but it didn't look new either. Someone in the neighborhood had good influence over the taggers to keep them from this prime canvas, which also meant someone was watching the neighborhood. If I'd had time, I would've waited until the cops left before I snooped around, but I couldn't afford to wait.

I caught Lan's eye and I beckoned her over with a head tilt. I didn't want to appear on the sidewalk only to be shooed away by Lieutenant Peak. Lan approached, and I pointed to the dumpster.

"Someone's keeping the taggers in check. Any idea who?" I wasn't sure if she'd be willing to provide any information. Lan said nothing for a couple beats. My shoulders dropped in disappointment. Then she surprised me.

"Mrs. Lopez. Green house, two doors down across the street, according to the principal." Then she whispered, "Don't let Peak catch you here."

"Thanks. I know." I hoped I sounded grateful. "I know you guys are doing your best, but you can use help, can't you?"

"Not much to find here. You may want to focus on the father while we run through perv scenarios." I knew she meant well, but I cringed at the easy reference to pedophiles. She pulled out her card and handed it to me. "Here, call if you come up with anything."

"Thanks. Really." I pulled out one of my own cards and gave it to her. "You too." But I knew she wouldn't call unless they'd found Joey.

Detective Conroy called over, "Lan, Peak's asking for us. Back to the principal's office." He looked surprised when he saw me but didn't say anything else, and only lifted his chin in greeting. I took that as a good sign and figured I could come out and talk to people while Lieutenant Peak was occupied.

Giving them time to leave, I stepped closer to the dumpster. A wave of vertigo hit me—not unlike the dizziness in my dream. I shuddered involuntarily, then shook it off, scolding myself for losing focus. *Think, Yolanda. Don't feel. You can't trust random feelings, but you can trust what you see and what you hear.*

I looked toward the departing officers to get my bearings and refocus on questioning potential witnesses. After a deep breath, I walked across the street to Mrs. Lopez's house. It was one of those bungalows that had survived the stucco period of the seventies and still had sage-green wood siding. The tidy yard had well-tended rose bushes, succulents, and a chicken-wired section with herbs, all among mismatched paving stones and bricks. What really stood out was a small, handmade cement grotto under a loquat tree. It held a cast statue of the *Virgen de Guadalupe*, the kind sold roadside at the Tijuana border crossing. The yard had "Mexican grandmother" written all over it.

I was about to open the gate when I heard a mother scold a kid on the porch next door. "You're coming in now and that's it! I don't want the same thing happening to you that happened to Joey." I looked over and saw that it was Gabriel, one of Joey's friends, with what appeared to be his mother and a teenage sister who went into the house. I couldn't remember his last name, but I waved and walked over.

"Hi, Gabriel. Remember me? I'm Joey's *nina*." The shy six-year-old nodded and looked down at a puppy in his arms, but his mother responded as I'd hoped.

"Hi, I'm Alicia Mendoza." She gave me a sympathetic look as I approached. I introduced myself and asked if I could speak with her and Gabriel. She invited me in and offered a soda, which I declined. I took the high-backed chair she indicated, and she and Gabriel sat on a couch opposite me. I reached over and handed her one of my cards.

"I'm helping look for Joey." It was true, but I didn't want to say I was working directly with the police. That would only piss off Lieutenant Peak. "Have the police been by yet?"

"No," Alicia said, "but we just got home from getting Gabriel's sister at band practice. We heard about Joey just before we left. Any idea what happened?"

"Not much. Joey's dad dropped him off in front of the church across the street, but the school told his mom he was absent today."

"Oh, my god." Alicia raised a hand to her mouth. With her other hand she pulled Gabriel closer in a one-armed hug. The kid winced and the black puppy squirmed in his arms.

"Apparently, it happened very quickly around seven thirty this morning. Did either of you see or hear anything? Squealing tires? Anything?" They both shook their head, but then Gabriel glanced up at his mother, as if thinking.

"*Mijo*, did you see something?" Alicia asked her son.

"No. But when I was looking for my shoes, I seen a van across the street."

I brightened. Finally, a lead. "Now think hard, Gabriel, where exactly was the van and what can you remember about it?"

"All I seen was that it was white."

"All I saw," his mother corrected.

"Where was it?" I asked.

"In the alley. Parked behind the big trash bin."

"Facing the street or facing away?" Gabriel's eyes turned toward the ceiling, thinking before he spoke.

"I seen…" He glanced at his mother and corrected himself. "I saw the back of it, so I guess facing away?" It was a question more than a statement, but that was good enough for me.

"Anything else about the van that you remember?"

"I think it had orange writing on it?" Again with the question.

"Like a rental van?" I asked.

Gabriel shrugged.

It was all he could remember. Most adults don't remember make and model, let alone a six-year-old.

"That's really good, Gabriel," I said. "This might help. Can you make sure you tell the detective who will come to ask you more questions?" He looked at his mom.

"We'll do that," she answered for both.

"What time did you go to school?" I turned to his mom for the answer, but Gabriel spoke up.

"Five to eight."

His mother looked up proudly. "We've been learning to tell time."

"Was the van still there when you walked to school?" I asked. His mother held him tighter. He winced again and shook his head.

"But I found Chulo in front of the church." He smiled and held up the puppy.

"This morning?" I asked.

"On the way to school," his mother said. "My daughter already named him, so I guess we'll have to keep him."

Shit. Pedophiles sometimes use puppies to lure children.

"Did you see Chulo near the van this morning?" I asked Gabriel. He shook his head.

"You don't think…" Mrs. Mendoza stopped herself from voicing what we were both thinking. Her eyes widened when I cocked an eyebrow and nodded, hoping I was wrong.

"Okay, I'm going to call the detective to come over and speak with you, okay?" Gabriel and his mother looked at each other as I dialed Lan's number. It always helps to provide information if you want information. Lan answered in hushed tones and said she'd be right over. I thanked Gabriel and his mother, and went next door before risking a run-in with Lieutenant Peak.

Mrs. Lopez was much younger than I'd expected. Midthirties at most. I complimented her on her front yard when she answered the door.

"Oh, that's my mother-in-law's doing," she said with a smile. But her smile faded when she glanced at the police cars and news crews over my shoulder. "I hope they find that little boy soon."

"That's why I'm here," I said. "I'm Joey's *nina*." She gave me the same look her neighbor had and gestured for me to enter. The living room was more Mexican-grandmother-meets-Ikea, with doilies everywhere, a *Virgen de Guadalupe* print over the fireplace, and knickknacks filling every shelf of a modular entertainment hutch, a thirty-five-inch TV in the center. We sat on the clear-vinyl-wrapped couch.

"Is your mother-in-law home?" I asked.

"She went to Mexico to get her new dentures, but she comes back tomorrow, so I need to remember to water or she'll kill me." She smiled again, but a look of concern came over her face when she remembered why I was there. She hadn't seen or heard anything, but I asked if she or her mother-in-law were responsible for keeping the street graffiti-free.

"Not me." She shook her head. "My mother-in-law. I think the taggers are afraid of her," she said and huffed. "She doesn't let 'em get away with calling themselves 'graffiti artists.'" She made air quotes with her fingers. "Knows most of them from when they were little *esquincles* and knows all their tags. If she saw one of them anywhere near here she'd go directly to them and make them clean it off. She once caught a guy stealing a battery from our neighbor's car. The guy ran away, but his friend came to apologize and reinstall the battery the next morning. She made him go get the guy who had taken it to reinstall it." She shook her head in wonder at the memory. So did I.

"Your mother-in-law sounds like my mom." The memory tugged at my heart. "Let me give you my card. I'd be interested in speaking with her if we don't find Joey by the time she gets back. And I'd like to speak with some of the taggers she's keeping at bay. They might've seen something. A long shot, I know." I thanked the younger Mrs. Lopez and walked back across the street. As I did, I saw the investigative trio in the Mendoza living room. Fortunately, Lieutenant Peak had his back to me and didn't see me walk over to the school.

I passed the alley with no queasiness this time, and followed what should have been Joey's steps across the front of the church and into the schoolyard.

The hallways of Saint Martin smelled like the ones I remembered at Santa Isabel—a faint odor of baloney and a stronger smell of pine-scented floor cleaner. In the principal's office, I looked out the window and saw the adults on the playground keeping a close eye on the few kids left in the after-school program. But I didn't learn anything new. Joey had been marked absent and hadn't been seen at school all day. Not good.

I needed to speak with Luis and Carmen again and tell them about the white van.

In the corridor, a janitor spread more floor cleaner with a mop. The strong smell triggered a memory, like smells sometimes do.

Six-year-old Jesse, and I, had just arrived at Uncle Bobby's apartment building on St. Louis Street, a couple of blocks from school. It always smelled of the same pine cleaner. But when we knocked on his door, we heard shouting. It sounded like Bobby, and it sounded like he was in trouble. Jesse and I looked at each other and tried to open the door, then banged on it. The shouting stopped at the sound of our banging, and then the door flew open. Bobby's new girlfriend, Sandra, stormed out with a tall man I didn't recognize. They knocked me to the floor and the man picked up my brother by one arm like a rag doll and threw him out of the way. They ran past us and out of the building. It happened so fast. Then, everything moved as if in slow motion. I rolled over to get my bearings and saw Jesse sitting against the wall opposite the door, wide-eyed and still. We were both in shock, unable to cry. That came later. Still speechless, we glanced at each other as we both got up and faced the open door. We held hands and entered the apartment quietly, taking tentative steps.

"I found him. I found Sandra's brother, but I couldn't find the money," Bobby sputtered from where he lay in a fetal position on the floor amid debris from an overturned table—unlit candles, cards, beads, and various colored stones. He held his stomach with one hand and his jaw with the other. His collar was torn away from his shirt, and a red welt was growing darker on the left side of his face. I turned to Jesse when he began to whimper and held him tightly, holding back my own tears. This was no time to cry.

"We need to call 911, Bobby," I said as I continued to scan the mess.

I still remembered what the responding officer had told me when she and her partner appeared at Bobby's door. After Officer Leal had established that Bobby was our uncle and that

Mom would be there soon, she asked if we were ready for some questions. Jesse and I nodded.

"Now, the way this works," she explained, "is that I get as many facts as I can about what happened. Do you know what facts are?"

When we stared at her blankly, she said, "Facts are only those things you see or hear. They can be things you smell, or taste, or can feel by touch, but not things you just think may have happened. Okay?"

"Like the five senses?" I asked. We had studied them in science class the week before.

"Exactly!" Officer Leal beamed. "We'll combine what you tell me with what your uncle Bobby tells Officer Jackson, then we'll see what we can do. Okay?"

I nodded again and repeated what I had heard and what I had seen as best I could. She smiled when I told her that I had not smelled or tasted anything, but that it did hurt when I got knocked over. Jesse said that it hurt him more when he was thrown against the wall. I overheard Officer Jackson ask Bobby, "Now, did you see that with your own eyes, or was that a vision too?" He wasn't making fun of him, but it sounded like he didn't believe him. Officer Leal asked me for a detailed description of Sandra and the man with her, and I did the best I could. She thanked us and asked if we wanted a glass of water while we waited for them to ask Bobby more questions. We both declined and remained seated on the couch as instructed.

When Mom arrived, Jesse and I ran to her as she dropped to one knee to hug us both.

"What happened?" she asked with a worried frown. Jesse and I both started talking at once, but Mom looked up to Officer Leal, who had come over to us. She explained that there had been an assault and battery and that the assailants had taken all of Bobby's cash.

"Your junior detectives here gave us a good description of the assailants," Officer Leal said, smiling down at us. I felt heat rise from my neck to my face and blushed with pride. I felt confident Officer Leal was more likely to find Sandra and the man than Bobby was with his colored stones and crystal ball. Mom sat with us while the police finished. When they left, she could barely contain her anger.

"I can't believe you would let this happen, Roberto!" she said in Spanish through clenched teeth. I'd never seen her so angry. "I told you this was not something to toy with!" I don't remember everything else she said because Jesse and I had covered our ears. We knew we weren't supposed to say some of the words Mom was saying. She wouldn't let Bobby get in a word edgewise. And that was the last time he babysat. He took to drinking more and more after that, until the night he stumbled in front of a bus. Mom hadn't forgiven him, but she was pretty torn up when he died, kept saying the *"brujería,"* or witchcraft, had gotten to him and that we were not to follow his example.

I shook off the memory when I got back to my car. Another reason to stay away from the juju. I needed to get back to Carmen with a clear head, but first I wanted to head back to my place to get my gun. A kidnapper is someone you should take seriously. Back on the road, I caught sight of a beautiful sunset in my rearview mirror, courtesy of the Griffith Park fire. The chamber-of-commerce sky didn't match my mood. Three boys were missing in the desert county to the east. My stomach turned at the thought of Joey being a fourth victim. But then I tried to remember any cases involving a pedophile renting a car. I couldn't think of any. Maybe it wasn't the same guy. Maybe it wasn't a pedophile. But was I just being hopeful?

CHAPTER SEVEN

Friday, 7:20 p.m.

When I got home, I realized I'd forgotten to call Sydney again, but then I saw her car in the garage as I pulled in. Once inside, I recognized the music at the end of Sydney's yoga video—the one Joey sometimes tried to keep up with. I pushed the thought aside and put Jesse's uneaten tacos on the kitchen counter, wondering how long the onion smell would linger in my car.

Then I paused to admire Sydney sitting in the lotus position, in shorts and a sports bra. A slight sheen of perspiration covered her nearly flawless skin, the jagged scar on her right biceps nearly matching the one on my left arm. Healthy curves were the envy of several of our friends. Nothing bony about her. But the smile that filled her whole face was what I loved most. It telegraphed a serene self-confidence and a playfulness at the same time.

She looked up, standing, and gave me that smile now.

"Welcome home, babe."

Carmen had known I was in love with Sydney even before I did. She'd said that Sydney's smile was the only thing she ever saw that could turn me into mush. Not even holding baby Joey in my arms did that to me.

I walked to her with a sad smile, hoping I'd be able to hold him again.

Carmen had introduced us when I was still in the LAPD and Sydney was a resident at County General. They were sometimes Taekwondo sparring partners, both black belts, but they had first met through Sydney's mom who worked with one of Carmen's labor union clients. Sydney still kept long hours, but at least her schedule as an attending was more normal now than back when she was a resident and constantly sleep-deprived. That time, accompanied by my trials with the LAPD, would have tested anyone's relationship, but I thought it strengthened ours.

I wrapped my arms around her and held on for an extra beat. I needed her calming energy.

"What's wrong?" She cupped my face with her hands and kissed me softly.

"Oh, love. I'm so glad you're home. I thought you'd still be at the hospital."

"I'm sorry. You called earlier, didn't you? I just remembered. I was tied up, but I got done with the new residents early. What's wrong?" she asked again.

"Joey's missing." My throat caught.

"What?" Her wide-eyed concern now matched my own.

"He never showed at school today after Luis dropped him off. I came back for my gun." I motioned us upstairs. "But I need to get back to Carmen's before it gets too late." My throat caught again. I could tell Sydney anything without having to do the "level-headed cop" bit, but we didn't have time to be emo, as the kids would say. She followed me to the bedroom.

"I'll come with you and you can fill me in on the way."

"Okay." I was so grateful. I needed to talk over what I'd learned so far and Sydney was my best, and most reliable, sounding board. She never sugarcoated her feedback. "I can get you a donut with that," she liked to say whenever I bucked at her "truth-telling." She hurried into the shower while I went to the safe in the bedroom closet. I took off my white shirt and put on my shoulder holster over a white tank. I needed to get a less bulky, magnetic hip holster—maybe after my next case paid. I pulled out my nine-millimeter Glock, checked the magazine, and holstered it. I made a mental list of the items I knew I had in my car—flashlight, lockpicks, handcuffs—the usual upgrades to a well-stocked earthquake kit. "You forgot the kitchen sink," Sydney would say whenever we loaded up the Subaru for a road trip. And thinking of that, I pulled out a hunter's knife in its ankle holster and strapped it to my right calf. Sydney walked in from a quick rinse as I pulled my jeans leg over the knife.

"I hope I never have to fix anyone you use those things on."

"Just hope you never have to fix me up." I kissed her on the cheek, and she hurried to dress.

We were out the door and on our way to Carmen's in no time. Avoiding rush-hour freeways, I filled in Sydney on the day's developments as I drove. Near Dodger Stadium, when I got to the part about my visit to the alley, I hesitated. I wasn't sure I wanted to share what I'd felt by the dumpster.

"You're not telling me something," she observed. I tightened my lips and kept my eyes on the road, feeling her eyes on me before I responded.

"How do you do that?" I said, finally glancing at her.

"Just tell me. What happened in the alley?" I loved that she knew me so well, but at that moment it annoyed me too.

I turned back to the road. "I just had a bit of vertigo when I got near the dumpster in the alley. That's all."

"Vertigo? Like in your dream?"

I sighed and tried not to roll my eyes. "I knew you'd go there. That's why I didn't want to mention it."

"Look, don't you want to use everything at your disposal to find Joey?" She placed her hand on my leg as I turned west onto Sunset Boulevard. "Please don't ignore this."

"That's just it, Syd." I couldn't help raising my voice. "How many times do I have to say it? It is not going to happen again.

Not this time. Not ever." My hands tightened on the steering wheel, skin taut over white knuckles.

In my peripheral vision I caught her pursing her lips, thinking. She finally spoke at a stoplight.

"Okay. I know this is all stressful and you need to focus, so why don't you let me think about it?"

I frowned at her.

"Are you patronizing me?"

"No…No! I only meant, you can tell me about the juju stuff and let me think about it while you focus on your work."

"I hate it when you're so reasonable." I turned my eyes back to the road. "Fine. Yes, it was like the feeling in the dream."

"And remind me again, how did the dream end?"

"Like a movie, fading to black." My eyes widened. "You think he could have been drugged?"

"Don't know, but…" She put out her left palm. "A white cloth? A fainting feeling? Fade to black? Could be, don't you think?"

"I didn't see a white cloth in the alley."

"Doesn't mean it wasn't used."

"I don't know how you do that, but I think I'm glad you do." I glanced at her again as I started up Carmen's hill.

"Do what?"

"You bring up juju connections like Jesse does, but when you do it, it doesn't sound so crazy. I didn't bring up the dream with him because I had to rush over to Carmen's. He started with those color visions and I had to cut him off. He wasn't making any sense." Sydney waited for me to go on. "But I guess I also wanted to avoid another lecture about being in denial."

"Maybe you are." I gave her a side-eye, and she added quickly, "But that doesn't mean you need to dwell on the dreams either. Look, I'm not a budding empath like Jesse. I swear he reminds me of that corpsman we lost to the IED. 'Always getting messages,' he used to say. Jesse can't help his feelings. All I can use is logic. It doesn't mean anything without proof, and I know you don't want to be distracted, but you can always keep the possibility in the back of your mind in case you come up with facts that support the messages, don't you think? Maybe Jesse and I can put our heads together on it."

She had a point, but I couldn't afford to speculate about wacky dream interpretation. I'd leave that to her and Jesse. Maybe that would get him and his juju stuff out of my hair too.

"Okay," I said. "Just promise me one thing?"

"Sure."

"When you talk to Jesse, don't pull me into it. I really need to keep my head clear."

"Okay, as long as you talk to Jesse about it after all of this is over, if not before."

"Fine. But for now, leave me out of it. And, thanks, love." I squeezed her thigh as we arrived at Carmen's street.

CHAPTER EIGHT

Friday, 7:50 p.m.

Joey woke up feeling drowsy. And like he was going to throw up.

So sleepy. Where am I? It's so dark.

He squeezed his eyes shut and curled into a fetal position to relieve the sick feeling. He vaguely remembered waking up earlier and drinking milk. It was all fuzzy.

But then he felt tape covering his mouth.

His eyes shot open.

He was breathing fast. Couldn't see.

Joey reached for the tape. His hands were tied in front of him. His ankles were bound together too.

I'm tied up!

He tried to scream for help, but the tape was strong. No sound came out.

Joey got his hands to his face but some kind of rough cloth covered it. He tried pulling it away, but it wouldn't come off.

What is that? I can't see!

Joey's heart pounded. He cried and didn't even try stopping himself.

He grabbed at the material again. It was some kind of hood over his head, but he couldn't take it off. He thrashed around, trying to get it loose. The hood caught on his neck. Something was tied around his neck. He pulled at it, but it wouldn't budge. He took in quick breaths through his nose. But he couldn't get enough air. It was hard with his mouth taped shut. He swallowed between sobs and that seemed to help. He stopped thrashing and sat up. He needed to calm down and figure out how to get this thing off.

Joey blinked. It was harder to breathe now.

It's so dark.

He grabbed at the hood again, but it still wouldn't move. The rope around his neck held it in place. And the hood smelled like hay, or like those sacks *Abuelita* Rosa brought to picnics for three-legged races.

Joey tried to pull the rough material up between his neck and the rope, but it was too thick, and it scratched his neck. It hurt, but he kept trying. He realized now that it was tape around his wrists too. That made it harder to pull off the hood.

With each pull, the pressure on his neck made him gag. He thought he might throw up inside his mouth, but nothing came up.

Think, Joey. Think.

Then he heard a door squeak open. It sounded like metal. *A car door?* He didn't dare move an inch. He held his breath, trying to listen for any movement.

Heavy breathing nearby.

Joey tried to back away from the sound.

He tried to get up, but his legs were shaking, and he fell back on his butt.

The heavy breather kind of laughed.

"Hold it, kid, you ain't going nowhere." A man's deep voice.

Joey felt something pull at his waist and realized a rope was tied there too. He said nothing but could hear his own breathing now, louder than the man's. He tried to make out a shadow through his tears and through the hood, but still couldn't see anything.

"You can be a good boy and make this easy, or you can make it hard," the man said. "Up to you."

Joey kept quiet. Scared. More scared than when he was grabbed in the alley. So scared that he couldn't move. He tried, but he couldn't.

A loud phone rang and Joey's whole body jumped. He heard the man answer the phone with a, "Yo." Then the man shouted.

"Are you shittin' me?"

Joey cringed and tried to back away from the man again. He brought his bound hands to one side, to whatever he was sitting on—a blanket on a hard surface. He tried sliding back but couldn't move much.

Then he heard the squeaky door slam shut and everything shook. He must be inside a truck.

No. A van.

He remembered now. He saw a van door before everything went black. He must be inside the van. He sat still in the dark, listening for any noise outside, and heard another door slam somewhere outside the van.

Joey tried the hood again, his hands shaking, the tape cutting into his wrists. The rough material scratched and hurt his neck again, so he lifted his arms and tried pulling it from the back and over his head in the motion his dad used to take off his T-shirts. This was hard. The material still scratched, but not as much as before. His arms ached, but he had to keep trying, keep pulling. He stopped to catch his breath and managed to get on his knees and bend forward. It was easier that way. He was so focused on pulling that he had stopped shaking, stopped crying.

Finally, the hood came loose from the back and hung down in front. Joey took a deep, deep breath, and let it out. The air almost smelled fresh. He blinked down at the material, his heart pounding. An image came to him of Juan Diego kneeling in front of the *Virgen de Guadalupe* with a poncho full of roses. His friend Gabriel had played Juan Diego in a church procession. *Is this what the poncho was made of?*

Joey reached up to the tape on his mouth, looking around. It was a van all right. And duct tape. He was sweating, but he felt cold, and like he might throw up. He had to get the tape off.

This is going to hurt.

He pulled carefully at the edges of the tape and tried standing up to look out the front windows. It was dark, but it looked like a garage. A messy one, with lots of shelves and junk on them. Joey hopped closer to the driver's seat to get a better view of the garage. The rope around his waist wouldn't let him go any farther. He stood there, pulling at the tape on his mouth, but he was shaking again.

It's so cold.

Then he saw something familiar. He stopped shaking. On the near wall of the garage hung a red flag. His mom had one like that framed in her office. People carried those flags at marches he went to with his mom and dad. *What is one doing here?*

But before he could think more about it, before he could finish taking the tape off his mouth, Joey heard a door slam in the garage again.

CHAPTER NINE

Friday, 7:50 p.m.

My dad and Jesse were still with Carmen when Sydney and I arrived. Luis and Andy were there too, and they all looked up when we walked in.

"Nothing," I said. Sydney silently hugged Carmen and then Luis. "Or maybe something at the school."

"What?" Carmen and Luis said in unison, turning to me.

"One of Joey's friends saw a white van in the alley next to the church this morning. It's not much, but the police are on it."

"Is that it?" Luis asked, impatience in his voice.

"At the mouth of the alley."

Luis shook his head, thinking. "I don't remember seeing a van, but I was in a hurry."

"Well, that's all we have for now, but…" Before I could finish, the door burst open and a portly guy in jeans and a baseball cap rushed in. A more slender man, in jeans and a long-sleeved T-shirt, entered behind him with a slight limp. Luis moved forward and hugged the first man.

"Luis, Carmen, I just heard," the big man said. He was a Latino about my dad's age and build but with a paunch that strained at the union logo on his gray T-shirt. "I'm so sorry. Is there anything I can do? We can have our guys canvass the neighborhood with flyers."

"Thanks, Tony. That's a good idea," Luis said before introducing Tony Gonzalez to the rest of us as "a friend from the building trades." Tony introduced his union buddy, Rudy.

"Clients of yours?" I asked Carmen.

"No," she said in a clipped tone, not bothering to hide her dislike of Tony. She frowned at him. "I don't represent the building trades." I stared at Tony, wondering about her reaction.

"What about the white van, Yolanda?" she asked.

"What white van?" Tony asked.

"That's it. Someone saw a white van near Joey's school. The police are looking into it, but I don't know if they have any more information yet."

"Well, we gotta do something," Tony said. "I can get some guys to drive around, see if they can spot it while others canvass the neighborhood. Can we put together a flyer, Luis? I'll call the hall and get some brothers to meet us at the school."

"Let's get to it." Luis seemed relieved to be doing something. He moved with purpose to the computer nook in the kitchen, calling back, "Carmen, let's call Lieutenant Peak and see if we can coordinate with the LAPD." This really meant, "Carmen, you call Lieutenant Peak." She would normally resent it, but she dialed the phone in speaker mode anyway. I had to agree it was a good idea. If they kept busy at this, they would feel like they were doing something productive.

"Lieutenant," she said when Peak picked up. "We want to put together some flyers and canvass the neighborhood."

"Good thinking. It'll help free up patrol officers for a wider search. Just make sure the flyer is simple, with a good picture of your son. Try the one you gave us."

"Okay. Any update on the white van?"

Peak paused a beat.

"How do you know about the white van, Mrs. Ochoa?" Carmen glanced at me.

"I just heard from the neighborhood," she said, covering for me.

"Well, we don't have anything solid, but it does appear that there was a moving van in the vicinity this morning."

"A moving van? You mean a rental van?"

"Yes, according to the crossing guard and another witness," Peak said. "But we don't have anything more at this time. We'll be updating the Amber Alert and will keep you posted." They both hung up.

"What kind of rental van?" Tony asked. "Did they get a license number? I can get it to our guys."

"No." Carmen shook her head in disappointment.

"I'm sure they're hitting up all the rental van places right now," I said. "They'll come up with something soon." I hoped I was right. Carmen walked over to Luis at the computer to pull up Joey's picture.

"I'll get my guys to round up canvassers." Tony stepped outside with his phone.

Jesse came up to me and whispered, "I don't like that guy."

I shrugged. To me, he seemed harmless, the kind of guy who granted favors to make himself look important and to get favors in return. But Carmen didn't like him either, probably because he was an opportunist. Still, I was glad he'd keep Luis and Carmen busy, but Jesse went on. "That red-and-white thing is becoming clearer now, Yolie. It's on some kind of cloth, like a curtain." Before I could protest, he added, "I know, it may not be anything, but that's all I'm getting right now. That, and that Tony guy gives me the creeps."

"Go tell Sydney," I said to get rid of him. "You two work the psychic angle while I do the detective work."

While Jesse and Sydney conferred, I kicked myself for not thinking about interviewing the crossing guard. I had to focus, but being this close to the emotions around Joey's disappearance wasn't helping. Jesse was starting to give me the creeps too—or at least his psychic insights were. I was sure he was projecting the feelings he'd had during his own near-kidnapping as a kid. The thought of Joey being scared like that, and the idea of a child predator taking him, was too much. I needed to think, but there were too many people around. Then I had an idea.

When Tony returned from his call, I turned to Jesse, Dad, and Andy.

"Guys, why don't you take Tony and Rudy over to the school to meet the union folks."

"Sounds good. Rudy and I are in his car," Tony said, "so it'll be good to get more cars to split up for canvassing."

I was glad for the political campaign experience of union activists. Most people would not yet know about the van, so the door-to-door activity could surface new information.

"Great." I took out a couple of my cards and wrote Lieutenant Peak's number on them. "Here's the LAPD number to call if you or the canvassers get any leads. Call Lieutenant Peak right away and then call me." My dad and Tony took the cards.

"You're with me," I said to Sydney. I needed to talk to Carmen and Luis, but I wasn't sure I'd be able to keep them in one place and preferred that they not be alone in case I needed to leave. People under stress don't always make the best decisions, and Sydney's calm demeanor would be helpful.

Luis and Carmen came over with several copies of the flyer—one side in English and the other in Spanish. "MISSING. Joey Ochoa. CHILD ABDUCTION. Suspect likely driving white rental van." It also listed another LAPD number Lieutenant Peak had offered for tips. The letters were all in bold red and black with a large picture of Joey in the middle. It was good, simple, and to the point.

"Okay, let's go," Luis said.

"Actually." I braced myself for an argument from him and Carmen. "Let's let the guys go to the school with the flyers. They can make more copies there and deploy the canvassers that show up. I need to ask you some questions about other possibilities."

"What do you mean?" Luis objected. "We've answered enough questions. Now we need to go find Joey."

"That's right. Let's go." Carmen surprised me a little by siding with him.

"Look, guys." I stopped them. Jesse took the flyers from Carmen and silently walked to the door with my dad and Andy.

The union guys followed. I watched them leave, then turned back to Carmen and Luis.

"Here's the thing. In cases like this, everyone jumps to conclusions about what happened. I don't think we want to make the mistake of leaving any stone unturned. And you two are the only ones who can help with this." That did it. They both sat when I gestured toward the sofa. Sydney brought over a notepad from the computer nook.

"Okay, now." I took a deep breath and let it out. "In cases like this, it's easy to assume there's a child predator, but I'm not so sure. The rental van may or may not be a good lead, but if it is, it raises other questions. Child predators don't usually use rental cars." I'd never heard of such a case. "They're usually desperate, sick men who use their own cars. Their impulses aren't normally conducive to the planning it takes to rent a car. So that raises other possibilities."

"Ransom?" Luis asked.

"Maybe."

"But we already told the cops—we don't know anyone who could've taken him," Carmen said.

"The cops were focused on a theory that Luis had taken Joey," I explained. "They'll come back to this other line of questioning because there's been no call for ransom. But we can't wait."

They listened as I explained the need to look into all of their acquaintances who may have felt slighted recently. Nothing was too insignificant at work, or Joey's school, or among friends. Carmen represented unions, and Luis worked on development projects that were more controversial than he'd like to admit. There were always winners and losers in those worlds. Someone was bound to hold a grudge.

"Let's write these down," Sydney suggested. "How far back do they have to go?"

"Let's start with three months," I said. "But it sometimes takes a while for people like this to get up the nerve, so we may have to go back further. Now, think. Who would hold a grudge? Want to get back at you for something. Make you hurt."

Luis and Carmen wanted to cooperate, but they were both drawing blanks. I encouraged them to not overthink it.

"Okay, who will benefit from Joey being taken?"

"Well, I'm not getting any work done for a while," Carmen said.

"That's it. Let's try that angle. List all the cases and projects you guys are working on right now and the people who would benefit from losing you two for a while."

"But I have a lot of open cases."

"And we have quite a few projects in the works," Luis added.

"Let's start with those on which you, personally, are spending most of your time."

"That's easy," Luis said. "The one thing taking up all my time is the Boyle Heights mixed-use project."

"My most active case is a new union certification," Carmen offered.

We dug in to both of those. Union certifications were especially touchy because any effort to unionize involved bad blood between workers, between workers and management, and sometimes between competing unions. Carmen's case seemed to have all of these. Her union client was stepping on the turf of the city's most powerful union to organize administrative assistants, mostly women. Both were strong unions, but usually stayed in their own lane. Carmen was taking on Leon James, the long-haired labor leader who was uniformly disliked and feared by his peers. But Carmen wouldn't speculate about union wrongdoing.

"Leon wouldn't do something that stupid," she insisted. "He's been successful for his members because he's smart and politically ruthless, but he's not a thug. None of the unions in LA are run that way. Those old stereotypes are long gone."

I listened but gave her what I hoped was my best I-can't-rule-it-out look.

"We have to consider it. I understand what you're saying, but I really think we have to check out every possibility."

Carmen's largest union client was headed by a popular, thirty-year-old, charismatic Latina—not your traditional union boss—who was often underestimated by her opponents. But I wasn't so sure others were immune to the stereotypes. And I couldn't help but note the similarity between Carmen's defense of unions and my own conflicted defense of law enforcement when I saw Lieutenant Peak in her living room earlier. Of course, I didn't mention it.

"My mom may have some insights on Leon," Sydney suggested. "I can call her." And with that she stepped into the kitchen to make the call. It was yet another thing I loved about Sydney—the way she kept her head in the game. I hadn't even thought of Mrs. Garrett, so was glad that she had. She could fill her in while I explored more with Luis and Carmen.

"Okay," I said to Luis. "How about you? What's keeping you most busy?"

"Well, nothing as controversial as Carmen's work. I do have the MTA project in Boyle Heights," he said, referring to the Metropolitan Transportation Association. "It's a mixed-use project above the Metro station. I have some stiff competition from the usual guys, but we all just got some last-minute spec changes yesterday that are due on Monday."

"What kind of changes?" I asked.

"Nothing big. Some aesthetic and landscaping details. Happens every once in a while, when the bids are close and the staff want to cover their butt by picking the most good-looking project. Not hard work, but really critical at this point."

"So, all the bidders are working over the weekend to modify their submissions?" I asked. Luis pursed his lips, nodding. "Any idea how the bids may line up, or who supports them?"

"I don't know." Luis frowned. "Some of the building trades are usually aligned with Barrio Homes. They go way back, but Tony Gonzalez is helping me with them."

"Is that normal?" I asked. I caught a slight eye roll from Carmen.

"He's a kind of broker between the unions and developers," Luis said.

"And elected officials," Carmen added. "He uses his political muscle to sway politicians on public projects." Disgust dripped from her voice.

"All unions do that," Luis said with a dismissive wave of his hand. "It's how they maintain power." Carmen was about to argue, so I interjected.

"Back to this project, please?" Carmen leaned back and crossed her arms.

"Well." Luis glanced at her then turned to me. "The Metro project is more private than public, but the union-friendly MTA board will insist on union concessions. It's a win-win for Tony. Whoever gets the contract will have to deal with him, and he will have the political backing to get concessions for his members. But we've worked together in the past and understand each other. That's why he's helping."

"Could he or his members gain by having one of the other bidders win?"

"Doesn't make sense." Luis shook his head. "They're out canvassing the neighborhood, for Christ's sake! And other bidders are too busy working on their own plan modifications."

I wasn't so sure. It hadn't escaped me that Tony had shown up out of nowhere. To me, he was like the first witness at a murder scene—automatic suspect. But I let it go for the moment so that we could continue.

"Tell me about the other developers anyway."

"There's two," Luis said. "Barrio Homes and Las Casas Builders." I was familiar with both from growing up in Boyle Heights and from Jesse's activism. Their founders were activists back in the Chicano Movement of the sixties and seventies, but I couldn't remember who ran them now.

"Don't they have different leadership styles?" I asked, vaguely recalling Jesse's comments about them. Carmen was the one who responded.

"The founders' kids and grandkids run them now. They're more business savvy, but Barrio Homes is old-school and still relies on mobilizing grassroots support and funding junkets to curry favor with politicians."

"They just provide political cover for the politicians by drumming up local support," Luis said. He sounded a bit defensive. "We have to do that too, sometimes."

I remembered now that Jesse and his friends took exception to the sometimes-shady histories of both developers and didn't trust them. But Luis used the same rationale as Carmen to discount any wrongdoing.

"The old way was to win favor with politicians, or to strong-arm them, to get favorable decisions," Luis said. "Today, it's all based on merit."

"And political cover," Carmen added. She wasn't going to let him get away with the contradiction.

"Are you telling me that Barrio and Casas are both above paying bribes or taking advantage of whatever might give them a leg up?" I asked.

"Not bribes," Luis asserted. "If they do anything, they have the older guys try to guilt politicians into doing them favors, remind them who was there for them in their first campaigns. But that's an old, ineffective way of doing business."

We all tend to downplay the warts of our own, I supposed.

"How about kickbacks?"

"Well, maybe with the small unions." He eyed Carmen, as if anticipating a negative reaction, but she surprised both of us.

"Some of the smaller unions still operate more politically than anything else," she explained. "They rely more on calling in chits for early political campaign support. They think that they have more political muscle than they do and offer to *help* in exchange for exercising it. They're the Ferengi of the labor movement." I knew she referred to the wheeling-and-dealing aliens on *Star Trek: The Next Generation*, one of our old favorites.

"They think they're being so subtle and smart but they're so fucking transparent. It's no different than the poverty pimps," Carmen added, using the same term Jesse used for nonprofit leaders who lined their pockets with money meant for community programs.

"I still don't understand how people like the Garcias can live in mansions," she said. The prominent family controlled a couple of social service nonprofits on the Eastside and hosted lavish political fundraisers at their home. But I knew she referred to nonprofit housing developers as well.

"So, Tony's union buddies and/or the developers *could* be involved," I concluded.

They looked at each other with worried frowns, but both shook their heads and wouldn't offer any more helpful suggestions. I wasn't going to get more from either of them, so I finally said, "Look, I know this line of thinking sounds impossible to both of you, but stranger things have happened. And you never know what invisible motivators may be out there, so can you at least try…for Joey's sake?"

They tried to focus, both frowning in concentration when Sydney returned with phone in hand, her mom on speaker.

"Carmen, Luis, I'm so sorry," Mrs. Garrett said. "I'm praying for you."

"Thank you, Eleanor," Carmen responded for both. It still felt weird to me that Carmen called her by her first name. As her daughter-in-law, I couldn't—not to her face anyway. "Sydney said it's a Black thing," I'd tried explaining when Carmen had asked me about it once. Sydney had simply smiled. I turned to her now.

"Tell them what you just told me, Mom," Sydney prompted.

"Okay," Mrs. Garrett said. "Sydney mentioned you're looking into possible union connections. That could mean some rogue element that probably runs just below the leadership level— guys with their own ambitions. There could be some unrelated power struggle if you really want to look at all angles." I could see her bias. She was part of the leadership in her own union, so I tried to get her to think it through some more.

"We were talking about Carmen's work challenging Leon James," I said. "Or the building trades taking sides on Luis's development project."

"Well, Leon…" she said, thinking. "He's pretty powerful. He's an asshole, but he's our asshole, like we say. He wouldn't have to stoop to this level. He has too many other ways to apply pressure. I'd bet he's targeting the women organizing for the union certification. Will try offering them something we can't— like indexing salary increases with the members he already represents. But he can't take the women for granted anymore."

"How about the building trades?" I asked.

"Those are several unions, but Tony Gonzalez is probably the strongest business manager among them, even though he was only recently elected. Again, I don't see leadership being involved, but they have lots of turnover over there. My best contact passed away last year, but I can ask around about their internal politics if you'd like."

Sydney looked at me and I nodded.

"That might help, Mom," she said into the phone. "Just be subtle."

"Like I don't know how to do that, baby?"

We all chuckled. She had not arrived at her position as the number two person at her union without knowing what she was doing.

"Still, let's all be careful and keep this between us. Don't even tell Tony," I said to Luis. I was about to mention Leon James as well, when Luis's eyes grew large. I realized, with a sick feeling in my stomach, that someone—Tony—had come in the door. Rudy, my dad, Jesse, and Andy entered behind him.

"Don't tell me what?" Tony asked.

"Nothing," Carmen answered before any of the rest of us could react.

"Oh, come on," Luis said. "It's nothing, Tony. We're just going through scenarios that may involve someone taking Joey due to some grudge or to interfere with our normal business, nothing about you."

Shit. I knew he was trying to help, but he was making matters worse. I'd have to be more careful. If everyone knew our theories, we'd compromise the investigation. Fortunately, we were interrupted by a knock at the door. Jesse went to open it and let in Lieutenant Peak and Detectives Conroy and Lan.

"Can we have a private moment with you?" Lieutenant Peak said to Carmen and Luis. "Perhaps out on the patio?"

"I want Yolanda with us," Carmen said. The determination in her eyes told him she wouldn't take no for an answer.

"So do I," Luis agreed. "She's Joey's godmother and needs to know what we know."

"Fine," Peak said in a tone meaning my presence was anything but. He turned to the rest of the room and added, "You all stay here. I'd like an update on anything you might have to report from your canvassing." They all gave various signs of acknowledgment, but Tony headed to the front door, raising his cell phone to signal that he was stepping outside to make a call.

Long shadows spilled onto the patio when we stepped outside. It would be dark soon. Sure enough, Peak was interested in the same line of questioning that I was, about anyone who might have a grudge against the family. We filled him in on our thoughts so far, and he looked on, impressed or annoyed, I couldn't tell. I suggested checking the homes or whereabouts of some of the developers or union officials.

"You do, do you?" Peak asked. I guess he wasn't that impressed after all.

"Yes." I crossed my arms, ready for an argument. He ignored me and turned to Carmen and Luis instead.

"We need more to go on than speculation," he explained. Then, turning back to me, he added, "You know that, Ávila."

"How about starting with Tony?" I suggested. "He's been especially helpful and seems to really want to stay on top of the investigation. I'm afraid he overheard part of our conversation and may suspect he could be a target," I confessed. Peak's jaw flexed, but he contained himself and spoke in a low voice that I found more menacing than if he'd yelled at me.

"Ávila, I tell you, you have to stay out of this case," he said through his teeth. "You're even more interested in this investigation and now you're coming very close to compromising it."

Damn. He might be right, but I sure as hell wasn't going to admit it. Then I had another thought.

"Fine, I'm out of here." I backed away. "But don't drop the ball on the grudge angle."

He glared at me as the others looked on, glancing at each other then back at me and Peak. The only thing I had in mind was getting to Tony Gonzalez's home before Tony got suspicious. It was just a hunch, but I had to start somewhere, and that was as good a place as any. On my way through the living room, I noticed Tony was still gone and asked about him.

"He's making a call outside," Rudy said from his position on the sofa.

I went up to Sydney, who was getting an update on the canvassing from Jesse, my dad, and Andy. I pulled her away and gave her a peck on the cheek to hide my whispered, "See if your mom can get Tony's home address. Text it and don't tell anyone." Then I turned to my brother.

"Jesse, you're with me. You can fill me in on the canvassing." What I really wanted to know was how Tony had behaved while they were out together.

Tony stepped inside as Jesse and I reached the door. *Damn.* I'd missed overhearing his phone conversation.

"Any news?" Tony asked.

"Nope."

"Where are you going?" he asked.

"Have some errands to run. Catch you later." I'd tried to sound unconcerned, but worried that I'd come off lame. *Errands? Really?* I rushed out the door, avoiding further conversation, Jesse at my heels. But he grabbed my elbow and stopped me when we reached my car.

"It's a UFW flag, Yolie."

"What?"

"The red background with the white circle. I got a fuller picture just now. It's a solid white circle with the black eagle in the center. The UFW flag."

Tony. Most Latino union activists in California had a United Farm Workers flag, or wished they did.

"Get in." I shook my head and unlocked the car before checking for Sydney's text. I hoped I wasn't running down a rabbit hole as the evening sky darkened along with my mood.

CHAPTER TEN

Friday, 8:00 p.m.

When Jesse and I reached my car, I checked for Sydney's text. Her mom had come through with Tony's address. *Thank you, Mrs. Garrett.* Tony lived in Eagle Rock, the trendy neighborhood that hipsters and *chipsters*—Chicano hipsters—were gentrifying, or "*gente*fying," as Jesse would say. It was home to Occidental College, whose claim to fame was Barack Obama's enrollment for two years, but students on the small campus kept mostly to themselves among postwar-era, Spanish-style and craftsman homes. It wasn't far from Silver Lake, so I knew we could make it in fifteen minutes.

"So, how'd Tony do while distributing flyers?" I asked Jesse, starting the car. "Anything suspicious?"

"Naw." He kept glancing back at Carmen's house. "We split up and took opposite sides of the street, but other than his heavy breathing, I didn't notice anything. He moved a bit slower than the rest of us. Had to stop and give instructions to the union guys who showed up. Plus, he's out of shape, and Rudy has trouble walking fast. But..." He hesitated.

I looked at him, then back at the road, knowing what was coming. I wrinkled my nose and pursed my lips as if smelling overpowering cologne. His psychic visions had grown that distasteful.

"Just hear me out, okay?"

We both braced ourselves for something he needed to say as much as I didn't want to hear it. "The flag…" I couldn't help but let out a groan. But Jesse grew more animated, turning toward me at a stop sign. I let him get it out so we could move on. "I tell you, it's the UFW flag, Yolie." His seat belt strained over his shoulder as he turned to me. "I swear, it came to me just now when we ran past Tony. Joey is somewhere with that flag, and I think Tony has something to do with it. There's gotta be a connection. He's a union guy. Bet he has one of those flags at home." He sat back again, staring out the front window as I drove.

"Are you finished?" I asked. He nodded, staring into midspace now—seeing the flag, I imagined.

"Look, we're going to Tony's. But this is not about your visions. It's about basic detective work. You may be right. He may have a UFW flag, but so do lots of folks. You have one. Carmen has several, and I think even Sydney's mom has one. No, we're headed to Tony's because he did something that doesn't fit with his personality. He made two phone calls out of earshot, both times after hearing about something we'd just learned." I raised a thumb on the steering wheel. "First, when he learned about the van. I know he called for canvassers, but he could've made other calls." I raised my index finger. "Second, he made the call right after he overheard me talking to Luis and Carmen about focusing on people holding grudges. But here's the thing," I said turning to Jesse at a stoplight. "The dude is a blowhard. He swoops in like a hero to help, and to get credit for his efforts, but then he disappears to make phone calls? Why would he do that? Why wouldn't he let us hear what he has to say so we can all be impressed with how important he is? I don't get it. That's why we're going to his house."

The light turned green and I turned back to the road. Then I added, mostly to myself, "That and the fact that we don't have any other leads." I drove on, lost in my own thoughts. Tony had to be involved somehow. His behavior didn't make sense otherwise. Did he make those calls to warn whoever took Joey? *He'd better not be hurt.* I wasn't sure what I would do if he was.

It was dark when we arrived at Tony's street, lined with tall jacarandas almost ready to bloom with their purple flowers. Tony's house was newer than most on the block, if you could call nineteen seventies construction new. Unlike the older bungalows and craftsman homes, it had an attached garage. The garage door was open, but no cars in sight. There were no lights on either. We approached the garage cautiously, but both of us stopped and stared wordlessly at the UFW flag on a side wall, then at each other.

Damn. Jesse had it right, but, to his credit, I didn't get an "I told you so." I was glad he was more focused on looking for Joey.

"It smells like spray paint," Jesse whispered. "Spray paint and…" He sniffed. "Piss?"

"Sure does." I also kept my voice low. "Don't touch anything. Why is the garage door open?"

We took in what we could of the garage in the light from a streetlamp. Nothing out of the ordinary, other than a coffee can with urine that Jesse pointed to on the floor. Strewn next to it were some rope and a mover's gray quilted blanket. The blanket appeared to block the garage door's safety motion detector. That would explain why it was open. Ours wouldn't close sometimes due to the occasional spider web. But a discarded rope and blanket were not a good sign, unless Joey had somehow freed himself. My throat tightened as I considered what it would mean if the kidnapper didn't need them anymore. I shook off the thought and pulled my sleeve over my hand to try the door to the house. It was locked, so I rushed back to the car and got my lockpicks.

"Where'd you get those?" Jesse whispered again, a little surprised.

"The I Spy Shop near Fisherman's Wharf," I said, working the lock. "Came with a lesson too." I'd never had occasion to use them but was glad for the impulse buy and quick lesson last year during a rare getaway weekend with Sydney. After a Neighborhood Watch guy threatened to call the cops when he saw me practicing on our front door, I switched to the inside door to the garage. This lock was similar.

I felt the tumblers fall into place and the lock give way.

"Yes." I cheered softly.

I pocketed the lockpicks and turned to Jesse with a finger on my lips. I pulled the Glock from my shoulder holster and motioned him behind me before entering. We stepped in quietly and made our way quickly from room to room. There was no sign of Joey, or anyone else, other than the typical mess of a bachelor. *How much pizza can one man eat?* Then I spotted a peanut butter and jelly sandwich and a glass of milk on the kitchen counter. My stomach tightened again—a kid's meal. Uneaten. I didn't want to think what that could mean. A more thorough search would help nail Tony, I was sure, but I'd leave that to the cops. I needed to find Joey.

"Damn, I hope we're not too late," I said, heading back to the car. I started the engine and called Detective Lan to fill her in, suggesting they hold Tony and get a warrant to search his house. Detective Lan thanked me but said Tony and Rudy had left shortly after Jesse and I had.

Fuck. He's trying to get away. I was sure that Peak would blame me for spooking him when he overheard me talking to Carmen and Luis. I'd deal with that later. I drove as if on automatic pilot.

"I messed up, Jesse," I said, staring straight ahead.

"What do you mean you messed up? Now we know it's Tony. We just have to find him."

"Now he knows he's a target." I shook my head. "I got careless, shared too much. Let him overhear me talking to Carmen and Luis. And now he's gone, his car's gone, and so's Joey. Shit!" I slammed the steering wheel with the heel of my palm.

"What do we do now?"

"Hope the cops put out an APB and update the Amber Alert. Shit!"

"We'll find him. You'll see," Jesse said with more confidence than I felt. "If I got the flag right, maybe I'll get another message."

I sighed. "I was hard on you about the flag, Jess. I'm sorry." When he didn't respond, I glanced over at him.

Jesse's head leaned back, his eyes closed. *Is he in a trance?* He seemed to be trying to conjure up another vision. Okay, maybe his vision of the flag was accurate, but I still thought it didn't mean anything—until after we saw it—but didn't say so, lost in my own thoughts again. Was Tony working alone? He couldn't have gotten home ahead of us. There had to be someone else.

"Where are we going?" Jesse asked, his eyes suddenly open. I hadn't realized until then that I'd turned onto Monterey Road as if heading home.

"Damn," I said and turned back toward the freeway to head back to Carmen's. *Get your shit together, Yolanda.*

CHAPTER ELEVEN

Friday, 8:00 p.m.

"Okay, kid. Dinnertime!"

Joey jumped at the booming voice and blinked at the sudden light from the back of the van. He raised his taped hands to shield his eyes. The duct tape stung on his wrists where he'd pulled at it when he took off the hood.

The man put down what looked like a glass of milk and a plate, but Joey couldn't be sure. His eyes were still adjusting to the light.

"Hey, how'd you get that off? Turn around!"

Joey obeyed, turning back toward the front of the van as best he could with his ankles still bound. He looked at his wrists, wishing he'd gotten the tape off his mouth so that he could bite through the tape to free his hands.

"You don't look at me. Understood?" When Joey did not respond, the man repeated, "Understood?"

Joey nodded. Now he wished he'd gotten a better look at the man, but he'd been mostly in shadow.

"Okay, then."

Joey heard metal banging on metal and then the man spoke again.

"You use this to piss."

Joey started to turn, but the man stopped him with a shouted, "Don't look!"

"So, this is the deal, kid," the man said in an accent Joey thought he'd heard on TV. "After I close the door, you eat. But first I gotta make sure you ain't up to no more shenanigans. Close your eyes."

Joey did as he was told and trembled as the man climbed into the van and came up behind him. He brought his bound hands to the loose tape on his mouth.

"Well, you got some of that tape off. You can get the rest of it off to eat. But one peep outta you, and you get a gag and no food. Got that?"

Joey didn't move, so the man grabbed his hair and pulled his head back.

"Got that?"

Joey grunted his agreement.

The man let him go and stepped out of the van. He slammed the doors shut. It was dark again, but not as much as before. The man had left the garage light on. And at least he hadn't put the hood back over his head.

Joey pulled at the duct tape over his mouth, faster this time. His upper lip stung. His heart beat fast again. Joey glanced at the sandwich on a plate, but he didn't want to eat—he wanted to get out of there. But he had to pee too. He crawled over to the coffee can by the back doors and knelt to undo his pants. His pants had only one button and a zipper, but he had trouble with his hands taped together. He bit at the duct tape. It had been bound in several layers, so he had a hard time at first. It took forever. When his teeth finally cut through the tape enough to let him cross his wrists, he stopped. He really had to pee. He crossed his wrists and used one hand to undo his pants. It took him a while, but he did it. Just in time. When he'd finished, he pulled up his zipper, didn't bother with the button, and went back to biting at the tape. He was making progress when the van door opened again.

So close!

"Turn around!" the man ordered.

Joey obeyed again.

"Not hungry? Suit yourself." Joey was too scared to respond. The man's phone rang again.

"Are you fuckin' kidding me?" This time he was angry. At first, Joey got scared again, thinking the man had seen the torn tape on his wrists. But the man kept talking into the phone. "No, not me. You, you twitchy fuck! You're the target, not me." He paused. "That's it, I'm calling it. I dump the kid now. I'll take the van a coupla blocks away, but that's it. You get your car at the airport. We never met." He ended the call and stepped into the van.

"Okay, kid. I guess you get to go home earlier than planned, but I'm gonna gag you." He was talking faster than before, seemed nervous. Joey cooperated so the man wouldn't tighten the bandana too much. He coughed a little at the gag, and the man loosened it a bit. He fake-gagged some more and the man loosened it again. Joey was surprised that his trick had worked.

The man took the plate and milk from the van, not bothering to close the doors this time. Joey looked out into the garage for anything he could use to cut the tape at his ankles, but all he saw was the garage door. He crawled toward it to get out of the van, but the rope around his waist held him back. Then he heard a door open and footsteps. He turned to look out the front windows and saw the man carrying a duffel bag over his shoulder. He moved beyond Joey's line of sight and Joey heard a car door open and close. Then he heard a marble shaking inside a spray can and a hiss before smelling paint. The man moved to the other side of the van and spray-painted some more. When he'd finished, he came back to Joey.

This time, Joey turned around without being told and tried to hide the torn tape on his wrists.

"I gotta wipe down this van and get rid of it," the man said, "so I gotta move you. I'm gonna strap you down in the back seat of this other car and I need you to be good. The sooner we get out of here the sooner you see your parents. Got it?"

Joey nodded. *My parents?* His eyes teared up again, hoping he could believe him.

Then the man spotted the torn tape on Joey's wrists.

"Fuck," the man said.

He grabbed rope from one of the hooks in the van and cut it with a sharp pocketknife.

"Close your eyes."

Joey did, and the man tied the rope over the duct tape. Joey tried pulling his wrists apart, as much as the torn duct tape would go, so that he could still have some wiggle room inside the rope. When the man finished, Joey slumped his shoulders, disappointed. The rope was tighter than he'd hoped.

The man moved fast but didn't seem so worried about Joey seeing him this time. Still, Joey avoided eye contact. He saw him only from behind as the man gathered blankets and rope from the van floor. He was wearing a blue tracksuit and had brown hair. With the bundle in his arms, the man crouched close enough to Joey that he could smell cigarette smoke on him. He tossed the bundle onto the garage floor and turned toward Joey with the knife. The man moved closer, the smell of beer on his breath. Joey closed his eyes again.

Please. No!

But then the man jumped out of the van.

Joey felt a tug on the rope around his waist. The man cut it away. Then Joey felt himself being lifted in the man's arms. Joey peeked and saw an open car door. It looked like his mom's Jeep Cherokee, but white instead of red, and the back was loaded with boxes of what looked like tools, wooden sticks, and paint cans. Mom's car was never that messy.

"Keep your eyes closed."

The man sat Joey down in the back seat of the car and looped a seat belt through the inside of Joey's elbows and behind his back, pulling his arms against his sides before clicking the buckle. The seat belt was not too tight, but the man must have noticed.

"Damn, need more rope," he said, moving away. Joey took the opportunity to look around and saw the outside of the white van for the first time. It had lots of fresh, black, sloppy graffiti. He couldn't read what it said other than the letters "P/V" and "C/S." He didn't know what those meant, but he'd seen them on graffitied walls.

The man returned with a blanket and tossed it over Joey's head, tucking it in behind him.

"That'll work. Good thing you're short."

At least it wasn't the hood again. He felt the man pulling at the seat belt, tightening it, probably with more rope.

"Now I gotta wipe down the van and ditch it," the man said. "Don't do anything stupid."

Joey wanted to test the slack on the seat belt, but he was afraid to move. He heard the man come back to the jeep and open the front door, then a grunt.

"I'll be right back, so be good." The man sounded nervous again before slamming the jeep door. Joey heard the van door open and close, an engine start, and the garage door opening before the van drove off. Joey waited to hear the garage door close, then he didn't waste any time.

His wrists were still tied in front, but his arms were now held back by the seat belt looped behind him and through his elbows. If he touched his chin to his chest, he could reach the gag. When he did, Joey realized he could pull it down, but he left it in place, fearing the man would come back and tighten it more like he had his hands. The rope around his wrists hurt, but he was more worried that he couldn't run with the duct tape around his ankles. He wiggled and pulled until he managed to move the seat belt a little farther out of the bench seat. The rope gave a little too. But it was getting hot under the blanket. He rocked back and forth but couldn't move more than a few inches. He tried twisting to unfasten the seat belt but couldn't reach the buckle. If he could just reach the hand brake in front of him, he'd be able to pull and loosen the seat belt even more. He tried rocking some more when he heard the garage door opening.

Joey leaned back against the seat and sat still. Then he heard the man curse and stomp, like he'd tripped or slipped. The car moved with the weight of the man getting in. He breathed hard. He must have run back from wherever he took the van. He wasn't gone long and could not possibly run fast, so he probably didn't go far. Then the car started and moved.

Joey could see his own feet and the hand brake from under the blanket.

"Won't be long now, kid."

As they pulled out of the garage, Joey lifted his legs a little and peeked under the blanket again. He saw the man's cell phone on the front passenger seat. His dad and *Nina* Yolanda had phones like that. *Nina* had taught Joey how to make an emergency 911 call on it. If he could reach it, he could call. He had to be careful, but the man drove fast and took turns without braking. The junk in the back made a racket moving around. The jerking back and forth helped Joey twist and reach for the seat belt buckle, but he was thrown forward when the man braked suddenly. He was thrown backward when the car took off again. This kept happening, so they were probably hitting stoplights or stop signs.

Joey tried the seat belt again. It had loosened some with all the movement, and Joey was able to reach the buckle. The rattling junk in the back masked the sound of it clicking loose. He almost shouted in relief but bit the gag instead. Joey leaned forward and reached for the phone. He got close but fell back as they climbed a steep hill and bounced hard over what felt like speed bumps. Joey almost fell sideways but caught himself. The phone fell between the front seats next to the parking brake. Joey reached forward again when the car leveled off. He almost had the phone, but the car suddenly bumped up and down. They weren't on a road anymore. The blanket slipped off with all the shaking. Just before the car came to a stop, Joey had the phone in hand. He hid it under the blanket as the man got out of the car and opened the back hatch to pull something out.

Joey didn't move for a second. Then he heard some metal banging outside of the car and the man grunting. Joey loosened the gag as best he could, his heart pounding. He steadied himself and the phone on the seat and hit the Emergency Call icon like

Nina Yolanda had taught him. He breathed hard, nervous and scared. *Don't let him see me.* The 911 operator answered before the man realized his phone was missing.

"My name is Joey Ochoa," he whispered. "I been kidnapped."

"Where are you?" asked the operator.

"In a car like my mom's, but white." He lifted his head to look around. "Hey, this is the soccer girl field."

"Do you know where?" the operator asked at the same time that the man shouted, "Fuck!"

Joey was about to say, "In Debs Park, where my *nina* takes me hiking," but the man grabbed the phone and ended the call before he had a chance.

"That was bad, kid," the man said and retied the gag, tighter this time.

CHAPTER TWELVE

Friday, 8:30 p.m.

I turned toward the freeway and back to Carmen's house. Then I turned to Jesse.

"Let's call Sydney," I said. "See if her mom knows what kind of car Tony drives. No, Luis. He would know." I handed my phone to Jesse so he could dial while I drove, but my phone rang first. Jesse answered it and Carmen's voice came on loud over the speaker.

"He called!" she shouted. "But he got cut off." I pulled over before reaching the freeway. "He's somewhere out there, but we can't figure out where. Near some soccer field."

"Carmen. Are the cops there?" I tried to stop her before she rambled on too long. Time was not on our side. If Joey got caught making the call, the kidnapper could have hurt him. I didn't say it aloud, but I knew the cops would be thinking the same. "Let me talk to them."

Detective Lan came on the line. "He called 911, but all he said was that he was in a soccer field."

"What were his exact words?"

"In a car like my mom's, but white," she said. "Hey, this is the soccer girl field...And then he got cut off." I knew exactly where that was.

"Debs Park." I glanced at Jesse and put the car in gear. "We're three minutes away." I turned back to Monterey Road. Joey and I had named the spot in the park where a little girl ran soccer drills with her dad.

"There aren't any soccer fields in Debs Park," Detective Lan said. "Just hiking trails and a picnic area."

"Stop!" I shouted. My heart pounded as I sped to the park entrance, my voice picking up speed too. "The soccer girl field is the name Joey and I gave the round field behind the main picnic area. It's up the trail behind the housing projects where those two girls were killed a few years ago." My heart dropped at the memory, but Lan stopped and listened. I described the location and its four access points from the picnic area, the street, and hiking trails.

Inside the park, I hit the speed bumps and careened up the steep road to the picnic grounds. I'd considered approaching from the trail behind the projects. That would be the escape route I would choose if I were trying to get away on foot, but Joey had said he was in a car. The paved road made the most sense. Detective Lan agreed and repeated much of what I said to Conroy, who radioed for assistance. We arrived at the parking lot in less than two minutes. I squinted, willing my eyes to adjust to the darkness. I could use the spotlight from a police helicopter, but it was probably another three minutes away if one was available. Sydney sometimes joked that realtors should include "Five minutes from gunshots to helicopters" in their marketing materials. It would be accurate.

"There!" Jesse pointed at a white Jeep Cherokee bouncing through the grass without headlights. It started to turn away just as it came onto the parking lot, but I sped up, turned my wheels to the right, and rammed it. Hard. My head hit Jesse's. Hard. We bounced off each other and I hit my head again against my window. At least the airbags kept us from bouncing against the windshield. It all happened in slow motion.

"Are you okay?" I said, not sure I was myself. Jesse blinked. A bit dazed, but conscious.

"Stay here." I shoved Jesse's airbag aside to reach the handcuffs in my glove compartment, my adrenaline pumping. I stumbled out of the car, a little unsteady at first, but drew my gun and managed to get to the jeep where a beefy white man seemed just as dazed as Jesse. I frantically scanned the inside of the car, but Joey wasn't in it.

"Where is he?" I yanked the door open, pointing the Glock at the man's head. A rush of heat rose from my chest to my throat at the proximity of lethal force. The once-familiar feeling is never something you can get used to.

"Huh?" The man turned to me slowly, blood trickling from above his eyebrow. His head bobbed a bit as he tried to wade through a torn airbag and lumber out of the car.

I wasn't going to get anywhere with him. I holstered my gun and grabbed the helpless man's hands. He barely struggled. I handcuffed him to the steering wheel and took the key from the ignition. He wasn't going to get away, but I didn't want to risk an engine fire. The car tilted to the right as if it had a broken axle. My car probably hadn't fared much better.

I lurched, more than ran, across the picnic area to the soccer girl field.

"Stay and wait for the cops," I shouted back at Jesse, who had staggered out of my car. "Tell them I went this way."

I regained my footing and bolted to the narrow opening between the picnic area and the round field beyond. Drawing near, I shouted for Joey, cursing myself for leaving my flashlight in the car. The only response I heard was my voice echoing off the hills and something scurrying in the bushes along the path. I reminded myself that small animals sound huge in the dark. I shouted again. This time I heard metal banging on metal.

"Joey!" I yelled again, and the banging increased. It was coming from the abandoned bathroom up ahead. I knew it had two gated doors on opposite sides of a hexagon-shaped structure. I couldn't see anything in the first one I reached but heard more banging and a muffled cry from the other. I rushed to it and my heart leaped when I saw Joey's bound hands gripping the bars of the gate. He stopped the rattling when he saw me and gave out another muffled cry. Through the dark I could see his eyes open wide, tears on his cheeks, a bandana gagging his mouth. I tried the gate but saw that it was held shut with a chain and a padlock.

"You're okay, *mijo*," I soothed, squeezing his fingers with mine through the gate. "I'm here. You're okay. Turn around, *mijo*. I'll take off that gag." He hopped to turn his back to me, his ankles bound together. *Damn!* I had some trouble working through the bars but loosened the bandana enough so he could pull it down, spitting and coughing.

"*Nina!*" he shouted, hopping back around to face me. I almost cried with relief, but I held back my tears, wanting to calm him instead, needing to hold him.

"I'm here, *mijo*." I squeezed his fingers again. "You're gonna be okay." I pulled the knife from my ankle holster and cut the rope from his wrists and the duct tape at his ankles.

"Help is on the way and we'll get you out of here. But let's call your mom and dad first." I dialed Carmen's cell phone. The sound of the siren in the background told me she was in a patrol car and on her way. Then I blinked at the sudden daylight from a helicopter hovering above. I shouted over the helicopter noise.

"I have someone here who wants to talk to you, *comadre*."

CHAPTER THIRTEEN

Saturday, 5:00 p.m.

"How can you deny it, Yolie?" Jesse turned to me as I dug into Joey's *tres leches* cake. The birthday boy himself played outside with an extra bounce in his step, proud of his quick thinking and call to 911. Other than minor bruises on his wrists and ankles, a little raw skin on his upper lip, and some scratches on his neck, he seemed fine. But furtive glances toward his mother telegraphed a need for reassurance and safety. I was sure it would last for a while. Today, he didn't seem to mind her frequent hugs in front of his friends. And he held them a little longer than usual. At least he looked better than Jesse and I did with our matching black eyes and arm bandages. The black eyes must've come from butting heads. The airbags broke skin on our forearms. Neither of us realized it until the police officers asked the paramedics to take a look at us after tending to Joey and the kidnapper. Other than the bandages, sore necks, and slight headaches, we were fine too.

Jesse continued, counting on his fingers, "Number one, you dream about Joey. Number two, in your dream, you touch a white cloth and feel faint, just like Joey before he passed out from what we now know was chloroform. Right, Sydney?" He turned to my wife for validation.

"Actually," Sydney said in her Doctor Garrett voice, "that was probably meant to disorient him and give the kidnapper time to inject him with a sedative. Chloroform only works that quickly in the movies, but it does explain Joey's nausea."

"Whatever." Jesse turned back to me. "And you feel faint again in the alley where Joey was taken. Three, you feel anxious in your dream. That alone should have told you something was wrong. Four, I feel the same fear Joey feels when I learn he's been kidnapped. And, hey…now I know why I felt nausea too. That's five. And six." He folded all of his fingers except his thumb. "I see the same things Joey sees when he sees them. I mean, the UFW flag? Come on. Oh, and seven…" He slapped his forehead in recollection and immediately grimaced in pain. "I felt Tony was a creep from the first time I saw him." He finished by crossing his arms and lifting his chin, self-satisfied. I polished off my cake and eyed what was left of the peach cobbler Sheila had brought.

"Look, I'm not saying all of that means nothing. It's just that none of it helped, and it could've resulted in bad detective work if we'd focused on it."

"I don't know why you won't accept that maybe Mom is sending us signs, Yolie," Jesse said in a quieter voice, staring at his hands. "The flag was so obvious. And what about the last coincidence?" He looked back up at me. "You said you drove as if on automatic pilot, but we ended up near Debs Park—near Joey. Don't you think that maybe you were guided there?" His eyes pleaded with me to believe what he believed.

I shook my head, but Dad was nodding too. That pierced my heart. *Him too?* I tried to let them both down easily, speaking to Jesse.

"Listen, I know this matters to you in a different way than it matters to me. But all of it only makes sense after the fact. I was lost in thought and wandered toward home. Who hasn't ever done that? It was just a coincidence that we ended up near the park. As for Tony, I didn't go to his house because you had a vision of a flag. I didn't even know we'd find one there. Like I told you, I went because it bothered me that he kept making calls out of earshot." I cocked my head to make sure Jesse was listening because he'd looked down again. Then I added for the benefit of those not in on our earlier conversation, "If he'd been trying to help, don't you think his ego would want us all to be impressed by the call?" I wasn't sure why I wanted to convince the others, but I did, especially Dad. "Plus, neither of us got anything on Tony's friend, Rudy."

Jesse looked up again. "Because he didn't have anything to do with Joey?"

"I don't know. I have to think he's involved somehow. No one's heard from him either. Did he skip out when their plan went sideways? Is he with Tony? And where's Tony?"

The kidnapper had confessed. Tony had contracted Gary O'Neil after meeting the bartender-cum-mafia-utility-man at a union conference in Atlantic City. He had described Tony's motive as an attempt to keep Luis occupied to give someone else—he'd claimed he didn't know whom—an edge on some business. But that was it, an intended distraction. O'Neil hadn't offered anything that would help us locate Tony or Rudy, but with their names and pictures all over the news they wouldn't get far. I still didn't get what was in it for Tony. Luis had said that Tony couldn't lose, no matter who won the bid for the Boyle Heights housing development. It didn't make sense.

"Someone'll spot them soon, I'm sure," Sheila said. She offered me the last of the cobbler she'd seen me eyeing and put an arm around Carmen, who leaned into her. Carmen's mom was outside on the patio with the kids, so I was sure she appreciated the motherly gesture. I savored another bite of peach heaven, thinking I'd earned the calories with all the stress and running around.

Luis bent down and rested an elbow on the table, his droopy eyes close to mine.

"You gonna find out who he was helping?"

I pulled back from his beer breath, but he continued, standing up straight, or as straight as he could.

"All I know is, if I find that fucker before the cops do, he'll wish the cops had found him first." He punctuated his statement by pantomiming a left hook and swayed a little, buzzed.

Carmen peeled herself away from Sheila's arm and placed a hand on Luis's shoulder.

"He'll wish you'd found him before I did," she said.

"You may be right, babe." Luis raised his beer bottle in a toast toward Carmen's framed Taekwondo belts. I'd once asked her why she didn't display her black belt, but she had explained that a belt is not displayed when it is still in use. It would join the others when she earned a second-degree black belt. Carmen glanced at the frame along with the rest of us but turned back to Luis with a frown. She wanted him to stop drinking. I'd seen this movie before.

"No worries, *mi amor*. Andy's taking me home."

Carmen rolled her eyes, further annoyed at the long-expired term of affection, but she turned to Andy and mouthed, "Thank you" before going out to the remaining kids on the patio.

Andy gave a reassuring wink, but an upturned corner of his mouth told me he was just as weary of Luis's act as the rest of us. I was glad Joey hadn't witnessed the tension between his parents. He was busy chasing Chulo outside. Joey and Gabriel had agreed to "shared custody," because Joey had found him first and his dad's building didn't allow pets. Carmen had chafed at the term, but Sydney had suggested it was a sign of Joey coming to terms with his parents' separation.

"What?" Luis asked when our eyes followed Carmen and then turned to him.

"Come on," Andy said. His hand replaced Carmen's on Luis's shoulder. "We should get going. We still have a long day tomorrow to wrap up that proposal."

"I'm fine." Luis shrugged off Andy's hand. *How could he still be so oblivious to Carmen's feelings?* She wasn't a prude, and had no problem with people drinking, but getting drunk was something else. Luis had to know it reminded her of her father and his violence. Luis never got violent as far as I knew, but after so many years together, I would've thought he understood her better. And I hoped he appreciated Andy for taking care of him.

Sheila, Sydney, and I glanced at each other, and I took the opportunity to change the subject, addressing Sheila.

"So, you think you can help with some of these calls I'm getting?" Since the news coverage last night, my answering service had received multiple calls for business. I had yet to get to them, but Sheila had offered to help.

"Sure," she said. "Just let me know when you want to go over them."

"I think you'll really need some office space now," Sydney said. I brightened, but I couldn't help feeling guilty that Joey's kidnapping would somehow benefit my business.

The party was winding down, so I offered, "Well, we should start cleaning up. After last night, I'm sure Carmen and Joey will need some rest." It was still early, but I was tired too. We'd all been up late with police and news crew interviews, but the adrenaline had long since worn off. I looked out toward the patio, where Carmen stood holding Joey in a one-armed hug, his own arm around his mother's waist, his head nestled into her side. We'd all have to be there for him, but I was glad he'd come to no greater harm.

But maybe he wasn't the one I should've been worried about.

CHAPTER FOURTEEN

Sunday, 11:00 a.m.

"I don't know, love. I think I agree with Jesse. There are just too many coincidences," Sydney said, taking Jesse's side. We were at Las Adelita's, the Figueroa Street dive named for Mexican revolutionary women, going over Joey's ordeal yet again, this time with our friends, Roxanne Piedras and Clara Gonzalez. The four of us met there regularly on Friday nights, or with a larger group of friends on Sundays during football season. We'd missed Friday, but it felt good to make up for it this Sunday, maintaining some semblance of our routine.

Some of us had ordered the owner's famous *chile verde chilaquiles*, others the *menudo*, while the music switched between Motown and Mexican ballads. The jukebox and small televisions were more old than they were retro, so only a few hipsters and *chipsters* congregated there, leaving room for lots of us longtime locals. We tried to keep the secret cocktail menu a secret, ordering "so-and-so's regular" whenever we wanted to try someone's favorite. Mel, the owner and our friend, customized drinks for most regulars with an alchemist's touch. No matter how hard we tried, none of us could replicate them at home. He'd only smile and say it was all in the technique, not just the ingredients. Now I looked forward to my Bloody Maria with his homemade mix, mezcal instead of vodka, and a smoky, *gusano* salt rim.

"I don't know why I tolerate your kind," Mel teased, handing out drinks with tattooed arms. "Half of you aren't drinking, and now you're giving my place the kind of 'color' I don't need with that street-fighter look." Jesse and I both mocked him by putting on our sunglasses.

"You don't drink either," I said to Mel's back as he returned to the bar. "And you seem to be doing just fine." I raised my sunglasses back on top of my head and winked at his suitor, the ever-patient Brissa at the bar. They looked at each other and blushed but said nothing.

"Hmm." Sydney lowered her voice and leaned over her Diet Coke. "You think they'll finally get together?"

"Who knows with those two." Roxanne, a Frida Kahlo doppelgänger minus the unibrow, had introduced them. "But we should celebrate them next time we have the whole gang here if they keep blushing like that." We'd known Mel since he was Melvia, before he transitioned, and we all smiled at the budding relationship.

"Mel and Brissa, sitting in a swing…" Roxanne singsonged a toast with her *Guavosa*—prosecco and guava purée. Jesse clinked his beer glass with her champagne flute.

"To Sticks and Stones, the Mexican Yentas," he said, offering his own toast. He'd given Roxanne and Clara the nicknames when they'd first met. "Roxanne Piedras?" he'd asked back then. "Your mom named you Rox Rocks? What's your middle name, 'Stones'?"

And with one look at Clara's lanky, five-foot-ten frame he'd declared, "And this *palo* must be Sticks." Sticks and Stones had stuck as the couple's name ever since. They were indeed matchmakers, responsible for introducing several couples among our friends, including Mel and Brissa. Roxanne was in her third career, a high school English teacher, after giving up on corporate public relations—"too soul crushing"—and community organizing—"too poor." Clara was a career public servant, the number two person at the City Clerk's office. We'd met during an investigation of a city council staffer for extortion of Korean small businesses and had bonded over our shared disgust at the cultural opportunism that had made it possible. Roxanne had claimed we'd bonded over our spikey hair.

"So, what's next?" Roxanne asked, getting back to Sydney's comment. "Any more clues from the juju?" But before I could respond, she continued, "You know, my mom used to see friendly orbs all the time, but the eye doctor told her they were just floaters. She was so disappointed." Everyone else laughed, but I cringed, feeling exposed to ridicule even among good friends. Roxanne caught my reaction and hurried to add, "No, really, *mujer*, I believe in this stuff, big time. You just gotta be open and let it come to you."

"She's definitely a believer," Clara agreed. "You've seen her altar. She's not hedging any bets." They smiled and nudged each other. It was true—Roxanne's home altar had as much religious iconography as it did witchcraft and Eastern meditation paraphernalia.

I relaxed a bit and sipped my smoky, tangy cocktail before responding.

"I got nothing," I said. "Just glad I relied on good ol' fashioned detective work to find Joey." Sydney's pursed lips told me she didn't agree with my dismissal of my dreams and Jesse's visions, but it was Jesse who spoke up.

"I don't know. I still think your dreams and the messages I got meant a lot."

"I agree," Sydney tried again. "I wouldn't write them off as meaningless."

I wasn't interested in a protracted discussion of the juju, even though Jesse had experienced a "hit" with the flag. I was about to change the subject when my phone rang. The caller ID flashed Carmen's name.

"Hey, *comadre*! Come join us at Mel's."

"Yolanda," she said, her tone serious. "I need you to come pick up Joey." I sat up. My expression must have given away my concern because everyone stopped to look at me. "The police are taking me in for questioning. They say someone killed Tony Gonzalez last night."

"Holy shit!" I covered the phone. "Tony's been killed," I whispered to the table. "The cops are questioning Carmen." A couple of gasps, and all frowns locked on me. Back to Carmen, I said, "We're on our way." Sydney and I got up, but Clara stopped me.

"Let me know if you need a contact at the coroner's," she offered. "I have a friend who works there."

I squeezed her shoulder in gratitude and turned back to my phone as Sydney and I rushed to her Audi at the curb. The broken axle on my car meant I'd have to replace it.

"What happened?" I asked Carmen.

"Apparently, that's what the cops want to know too." In the car, I put the phone on speaker. "They're doing me the *courtesy* of waiting for you to come get Joey," she said with obvious annoyance. I understood she couldn't say more in front of the police.

"Who are the cops with you?"

"Some detectives named Elton Chan and Henry Rios." She sounded like she was reading from their cards. "From Robbery-Homicide."

My antennae went up. I didn't know Chan, but I remembered Rios as an ambitious know-it-all. He'd been among the officers who sat at Langer's Deli while I took fire five years ago. And he was the one I'd suspected of taping the "Die dyke bitch" notes on my station locker. *How'd that asshole make detective?* He must be the one behind taking her in instead of questioning her at home. A red blush of anger rose from my neck to my face. Sydney must've remembered his name because she glanced at me and squeezed my thigh as she drove.

"I know you know this, but don't say any more until you're with your lawyer." I didn't want to alarm her, but I also didn't want her to say anything else, even to me, while the detectives were there. "We're coming around Dodger Stadium. Stay calm. Be there in five minutes."

"Thanks."

After we hung up, I Googled "Tony Gonzalez found dead" to see if any news sites were reporting on him. I scrolled through unrelated death notices before landing on a short blurb posted by a local news station. It mentioned that his body had been found in Griffith Park by an early-morning dog walker, but not much else. I was sure a feature story would follow.

Before we reached Carmen's street, my phone rang again. It was Andy Stewart.

"Hey," he said when I answered the phone, still on speaker. "Luis asked me to call you. The cops brought him in for questioning. Looks like someone killed Tony, and they suspect him."

"They're taking Carmen in too."

"Oh, shit."

"Sydney and I are just getting to her house to get Joey. Please let Luis know he's with us." Then, hearing the horn of a diesel truck in the background, I asked, "Where are you?"

"Outside the Northeast Police Station." I hoped more senior detectives from downtown would take over soon, due to the publicity around the case. More experienced detectives were less likely to rush to judgment like I suspected Rios and his buddies at the Northeast Station had. But maybe he also knew downtown would step in and was accelerating his investigation before the big guys took over.

"Why aren't you inside with Luis?" I asked.

"This is serious. We called Berto." Roberto Nuñez was a former federal prosecutor—now criminal defense lawyer—who'd been Luis and Andy's roommate at USC. "I tried Carmen, but obviously she didn't pick up. Can you let her know?"

"Sure. But what happened? All I could get was a small blurb online about someone finding the body."

"What did it say?"

"Only that Tony's body was found by a dog walker near the pony ride at Griffith Park." I vaguely remembered hearing news that the ponies had been evacuated due to the fire on Friday. It had been contained by Saturday morning, but the park was still closed to the public while fire crews completed their mop-up to prevent reignition.

"Anything else?" Andy asked.

"Nope. But what was Tony doing there?"

"And how did he die?" Andy asked, following my line of thought.

"And when?" Sydney added.

"I don't know, but I dropped Luis off at home after Joey's party. He said he was going right to bed, and I'm sure he did. He'd had a lot to drink."

Sydney and I said nothing to that, but glanced at each other knowingly. We'd both seen how drunk Luis was.

"And Carmen was home with Joey," I said. "No way she'd leave him alone after his ordeal." I remembered her holding him close and Joey smiling when she'd said he'd be sleeping in her bed last night.

"Shit, we really need to find that Rudy guy," I said, mostly to myself, before hanging up.

My phone buzzed with texts from my answering service. The new business inquiries continued to come in through the news cycle. They might spike again with news of Tony's death. I felt guilty again for feeling good about the strong validation of my work, especially now that Carmen and Luis needed help. I'd have to get together with Sheila soon and refer some cases to her, or get her started on them for me until I was free. I didn't know how long I'd be tied up.

Before getting out of the car at Carmen's house, Sydney turned to me.

"You didn't have any dreams about Carmen or Luis, did you?" Normally, I'd chafe at the question, but didn't this time.

"No, I didn't."

Carmen opened the door immediately when we knocked and greeted us each with a hug. Over her shoulder, I saw Henry Rios sitting on the sofa, his arms spread over its back, his suit jacket fanned open, and his right ankle resting on his left knee. The prick had a smirk on his face that made me want to slap him. He'd obviously made himself at home as an intimidation tactic. Joey wasn't in sight. Carmen must've sent him to his room so as not to alarm him.

Detective Elton Chan stood up from one of the white chairs and seemed about to greet us, but stopped when Rios spoke.

"Well, well, Ávila. Fancy meeting you here."

Fuck you, I thought. Instead of voicing it, I said, "Why are you harassing this woman? There's no need to take her into custody just for questioning. You know that, and so does Lieutenant Peak." I was glad I hadn't taken off my sunglasses. He would've loved seeing my black eye.

"I'm working this investigation, Ávila." He stood, but blinked. I took that as a bit of concern at my name-dropping. He didn't need to know that I could hardly call on Peak. He brought his hands to his belt buckle, then let them drop to his sides. Muscle memory from wearing the uniform. I guessed he hadn't been a detective very long. Then he looked at Carmen.

"Ma'am, is there an overnight bag for your son?" Carmen didn't respond other than to give him a cold, hard stare that made me proud. And a little intimidated. Apparently, she had the same effect on Rios because he began to backpedal.

"I mean, just in case you're held overnight," he said before crossing his arms over his chest to regain his authority. "We've been more than patient and need to get going."

Carmen gave him a look that would have withered most men, but her cell phone rang before she could respond. She raised a finger to hold off Rios and turned to me.

"It's Stan." He was the managing partner at her law firm. She listened for a bit before hanging up with a, "Thanks, Stan." Then she turned back to Rios.

"I suggest you call your ADA before meeting me and my attorney at the station, Officer."

"It's Detective."

"I wouldn't know the difference." She flipped her wrist dismissively. God, I loved her. Of course she knew the difference, and she would have enjoyed toying with Rios if the matter weren't so serious. "Go ahead, make the call."

Rios got on his phone and turned his back to us from across the room, his shoulders squared, ready for an argument. He spoke softly so that we couldn't hear what he said, but his shoulders fell before ending the call. He turned back to us, squaring his shoulders again.

"We'll expect you at the station within the hour. If you do not arrive by"—he looked at his watch—"one fifteen, we'll be back and will place you in custody for questioning."

"Right," Carmen said. She opened the door for the detectives. Chan gave a curt nod, but Rios avoided our eyes as he walked out.

"That was lovely." Sydney gave us a huge smile after Carmen closed the door.

"Oh, my god," Carmen exclaimed. "What an asshole!"

I nodded. "And, just so you know, he was one of the assholes at Langer's the day I was shot. I still think he's the one who left the love notes on my locker."

"Damn. I'm glad I didn't know that, or I might've said something I shouldn't."

"How'd you get him to back off?" Sydney asked.

"One of my partners called the DA and suggested a public thrashing claiming prosecutorial misconduct, abuse, and harassment. It's an election year." Carmen shrugged. "Not a hard call to make, but because this involves a possible murder, that's all Stan could get. That and a good defense attorney to meet me at the station. But first, do you guys know anything about this?"

"Andy called to let us know that Luis's been taken in for questioning too," Sydney said. "He said he tried calling you."

"He called while I was on the phone with you guys, but I didn't want to call back with the cops here."

"There's a blurb online about a dog walker finding Tony's body near the pony ride in Griffith Park," I said. "But let me call Clara to see if her friend at the morgue can tell us anything." I dialed Clara, who said she'd put in a call from Mel's.

"Just ask if he knows anything about Tony and listen," I said. "He may assume we're related. We're both Gonzalezes."

"That's right. And don't mention Carmen and Luis. Thanks, *mujer*."

She called right back before the three of us reached Joey's room.

"No dice," Clara said. "My friend said they're swamped and haven't gotten to the body yet. And they probably won't until the DA or LAPD gets there because it's Sunday." I reported her update to Carmen and Sydney.

"Doesn't that sound odd?" Sydney asked. "No cause of death yet, and they're already taking two people in for questioning?"

"Overly aggressive policing," I suggested. "Or the condition of the body pointed to homicide. Hope the autopsy results don't take too long."

"The morgue is always swamped," Sydney said. "The paramedics probably responded. Maybe I can ask around." Sydney had several paramedic friends from her time as an EMT between the Navy and med school. She'd made new ones as an ER doctor as well.

"No worries," Carmen said before opening Joey's bedroom door. "Sometimes it's best not to know too much when being interrogated. I'll be fine." I saw a familiar resolve on her face and hoped she was right. Joey greeted us with a smile and hugs.

"*Mijo.*" Carmen dropped to one knee to face her son. "I gotta go talk to the police again. Your *nina* and Sydney will take you to their place and I'll come get you later, okay?"

Joey frowned when Carmen embraced him, but he hugged her back tightly before saying, "Okay." My heart ached for both of them.

I drove us back to our house, Sydney distracting Joey with talk of his birthday party. I dropped them off and checked my neighborhood crime app for a more specific location of the crime scene before heading to Griffith Park. When I got there, some lab techs I didn't recognize were packing up. I figured the uniformed officers near the yellow tape would shoo me away, so I tried to look like a curious neighbor on a walk, a little perturbed that my routine had been disrupted.

"Can I go up around this?" I asked, glad for my sunglasses again.

"Sorry, ma'am, the park's closed." The officer with a buzz cut stood ramrod straight, his thumbs in his belt at a nearly nonexistent belly. *Good. A rookie.*

"What happened?" I asked, standing a few feet to his side looking at the scene. I was careful not to engage him face-to-face in case his training officer looked up from his phone about ten yards away.

"A dog walker found a dead body, ma'am."

"Oh, no! A murder?"

"Unclear, ma'am. Could've been a heart attack." He sounded like he was trying to put me at ease—good cop material if the department didn't beat the compassion out of him. His training officer spotted us and walked over.

"A heart attack?" I asked. But the rookie clammed up. I didn't think I'd get more from him. I considered approaching the lab techs but wasn't sure they'd share anything. Then I saw a small group of joggers and a dog walker approaching the police tape. I walked over.

"What gives?" a jogger in shocking pink spandex asked, not a hair on his head out of place.

"My wife found a body this morning while walking Larry, Mo, and Curly here." The dog walker looked down at three adorable pugs straining at their leashes to sniff his audience for attention. Several exclamations came from the handful of joggers.

"Who was it?" Pink Spandex asked.

"Dunno. She just freaked out and called 911. Didn't finish her walk. Hurried home instead. I wanted to check it out, so I came back with the pugs, but the cops got here first, and they're not talking." We all followed his eyes glancing at the officers.

"What did your wife see?" I asked, turning back to him.

"She said he looked middle-aged. Hispanic. Wearing jeans and a gray T-shirt. Said he was in a fetal position, kinda grabbing his chest. But what really weirded her out was that his eyes were open, like he was surprised. Guess I'd be surprised by a heart attack too, but now she says she can't unsee it." He shook his head.

"Well, at least it wasn't a shooting," a second jogger, this one in less-fashionable black shorts and a faded blue T-shirt, said to nods all around. Gang-related shootings were always a concern in LA because they often gave rise to escalated violence in retaliation. But I wondered why the cops were interested in Carmen and Luis if this had been a heart attack. And how had a reporter learned his identity so quickly? Someone must've leaked information or been carefully monitoring a police radio scanner. But on a Sunday with all the cutbacks in the journalism sector? My bet was on a leak. But who? Probably Rios. I wouldn't put it past him to muscle in on a high-profile case. I walked over to the lab techs, who were loading their van. Thinking they wouldn't be up for small talk, I took the direct approach.

"Hey, was that the body of Tony Gonzalez, like the news said?" I asked. "Was he killed, or was it a heart attack, like the lady who found him said?"

The two eyed me warily and did not respond. *Damn. Too direct.*

"Come on, guys. I just want to confirm for my neighbors that we don't need to worry about a murder here."

"You'll have to talk to the Public Information Officer, ma'am," the tech nearest me replied.

Ma'am. Again. I suddenly felt the age he probably thought I was—my age.

"I heard they already took someone in for questioning. Why would they do that if it was a heart attack? And why so fast?"

"No telling what the eager beavers at Homicide will do." The look on his face told me he didn't care for the detectives on this case. "But the ID seems to be accurate." That meant they'd found a wallet, so it wasn't a robbery. Depending on the condition of the body, murder would be my next guess too.

The lab techs wouldn't say more, so I thanked them and left.

On the way home, I welcomed having some facts to chew on without any of the juju interference. It bugged me that Jesse seemed to be right about coincidences in hindsight. But how reliable was that? It might make us feel better about what we'd speculated, but I was duty bound to follow facts, wasn't I?

My phone rang before I philosophized too long. It was Clara again.

"Hey, *mujer*. My buddy at the morgue says the body had an orange-sized contusion in the middle of the chest, but some senior detectives showed up so he couldn't talk anymore."

"Orange-sized? Sounds like Wanda Sykes," I said, referring to the comedian's old bit in *I'ma Be Me*. We watched her HBO special at least once a year with our friends. "Thanks. Invite your buddy to Mel's next time and I'll buy him a drink." I was glad the senior detectives were on the case. That meant that Carmen and Luis wouldn't be held for long, but it also meant that they'd face another round of questions from a second set of detectives.

I stopped at the store for some groceries. We hadn't eaten at Mel's and I was hungry. I figured we'd eat with Joey and Carmen, assuming she was done at the station soon. She hadn't been arrested, only taken in for questioning, so I hoped I was right.

When I got home, Joey was napping on the sofa. All the excitement had finally caught up with him. Sydney had examined him while they'd chatted.

"Kids are so resilient," she said. "He's gotten past the worst of the initial shock. His body temperature is normal, and he says he hasn't even had any nightmares. But he didn't want to go to the guest room, wanted to nap near me. That's normal. We'll need to keep him close, help him feel safe."

I agreed. I filled Sydney in on what I had learned at Griffith Park and from Clara, especially the bruise on Tony's chest.

"Could a heart attack cause that?" I asked, putting away the groceries.

"Hmm. Not likely a heart attack." She leaned back against the kitchen counter, thinking. "But any number of things could cause a chest contusion. The most obvious one would be blunt force trauma, which may explain why the cops are questioning Carmen and Luis. Pericardial tamponade, maybe?"

"English, please." I peeled a cheese stick and popped strings of mozzarella into my mouth. *Damn*. I was starving.

"Blood in the heart sac, but that wouldn't necessarily present as a contusion." She continued to think aloud in her

Doctor Garrett voice. "Aortic dissection is a possibility—a ruptured aorta," she added in response to the question on my face. "The autopsy would determine that. It would usually mean a weakened aortic wall. A rupture can be triggered by anything from a cough to a blow in the area, depending on the person's condition."

"Like the Five Point Palm Exploding Heart Technique from *Kill Bill*?" I asked.

"Hardly."

"Well, that would've been my guess."

"I just can't believe Carmen or Luis would go after him." She shook her head.

"Neither can I," I agreed, "but think about what the cops see. Couldn't a former boxer or a black belt have done it?"

"Probably both. But not any more than a fall." Then she crossed her arms, going back to her doctor voice. "An experienced boxer could deliver a direct jab or uppercut to the spot. A Taekwondo black belt could deliver a more powerful blow. In Carmen's case, given her height in relation to Tony's, I'd say maybe an elbow strike or a side kick, based on what I've seen her do at the *dojang*." Then she shook her head out of doctor mode. "I still don't see either of them doing it."

"I agree, but all of that just means that both of them are definitely suspects in the cops' eyes. If they didn't do it, who did?"

"Maybe sleep on it, love?"

I gave her a side-eye.

She winked at me. "Just a thought." Then, reaching for the last of my string cheese, she added, "Jesse called while you were gone. He's really feeling the 'messages from Mom' thing. I think he's looking for validation and feels a bit frustrated that he can't get that from you."

"That's why I tried to go easy on him."

Sydney gave me a sad smile. "How about doing the same for yourself, hmm?" She raised her hands before I could protest against another speech on how my guilt was keeping me from grieving.

"Can we talk about this some other time?" I asked. Joey thankfully joined us in the kitchen with a yawn, wiping the sleep from his eyes.

"I'd really like you to think about it, then," she said. That was new. Sydney had never asked me to just think about the connection between guilt and grief, but this time I thought she meant the juju too.

"Okay," I said, mostly to stop the conversation. It worked. Sydney turned to Joey.

"Joe! My man! How about dinner? Want to help with the salad?"

Joey smiled and wiped his eyes again, then climbed up on his usual barstool at the kitchen island. Sydney pulled out vegetables, goat cheese, and balsamic vinegar for a salad, and I grabbed some rib eyes from the refrigerator for grilling.

Out on the deck, I salted the meat and waited for the propane grill to heat up. I wondered whether Sydney could be right. I didn't want to believe the "messages from Mom" thing, but did that mean I was avoiding grieving? I didn't think so. We all grieve in our own way. I didn't make it a practice to talk to Mom like Jesse did, but that wasn't because I didn't miss her. I thought about her all the time, avoiding it only when the shadow of guilt loomed large. It was too painful. But that only meant that I felt guilt and regret. Those were the feelings I had trouble with, not grief. I hadn't gone through grief counseling like Jesse and Dad had because all they talked about at the one session I attended was grief, not what I was feeling.

I knew Sydney worried that my guilt wasn't letting me grieve fully, but I was lucky she didn't push her views. She let me deal with it in my own way, on my own time. I loved her for that, but I could tell she was going to start pushing now that the juju had surfaced with Joey's kidnapping. As I mulled this, Sydney came out to the deck with another steak, saying Carmen had called and was on her way over from the station. I pulled Sydney close and held my arms around her waist.

"I'm okay, love. And I love you for loving me." I kissed her softly, slowly. She returned my kiss, and I tightened my embrace.

"I love you too, *all* of you," she said and gave me a quick peck on the lips before releasing my hold and turning to go back inside. I wasn't sure if she meant a psychic me or a guilt-free me, but the guilt-free part of me had died with my mom. As I thought that, a heavy weight settled in the pit of my stomach. I tried to shake it off with a deep breath, but it continued to sit there. *What was that? My guilt calcifying?* I'd just have to deal with it. I turned to the sizzling steaks searing on the cast iron griddle and transferred them to the grill rack. I finished grilling and tried to take on a breezy attitude when I walked back into the kitchen. Carmen had just come in the door.

"Hey, Shawshank!" I teased. "How'd it go?" I'd expected her to smile at the line from *Pitch Perfect*, one of our favorite movies, but she didn't.

"Well, those guys weren't exactly LAPD's finest."

"No kidding," I agreed. The image of Rios on her sofa made my blood boil again.

She kissed Joey on the cheek. "*Mijo*, just this once, you can watch TV with dinner, okay?" She looked from me to Sydney and back for agreement.

"Sure," Sydney said, a little sheepishly. "Go ahead and get the tray table, Joe."

"All right!" Joey jumped off his stool and headed straight for one of the folding tables wedged beside the refrigerator. Sydney helped him set it up, and turned on the TV, already tuned to cartoons.

"Hmm, I guess it's not just this once, eh?" Carmen cocked an eyebrow.

"Afraid so." I shrugged an apology. "Well?" She waited for Sydney to return before answering.

"Well, the junior dicks were overruled by the senior dicks from, let's see…also Robbery-Homicide." She read from two business cards before handing them to me. I didn't recognize either of the names. "But both sets of dicks were just that."

"What was their line of questioning?" I asked, digging into my steak and savoring it while Sydney poured our favorite red blend.

CHAPTER FIFTEEN

Sunday, 9:00 p.m.

After Carmen and Joey left, the knot in my gut tightened again, this time accompanied by a rapid pulse and clammy, cold sweat. Then I started taking quick, short breaths. *What's happening to me?* I tried deep breaths as Sydney washed and I dried. It didn't work.

"Syd, I don't know what's going on, but all of a sudden I'm feeling really antsy. Sweaty too. What is that?"

"You've had a rough couple of days, babe." She turned to me from the sink. "It's probably a bit of anxiety catching up with you. That's normal. Try some deep breaths." She glanced at the clock on the microwave. "Let's see how long it lasts."

I placed the last of the flatware in the utensil drawer, but when I turned my back to her, I thought I might hyperventilate.

"Damn, love. Looking at you right now, I feel like I've had five cappuccinos." I looked away, but when I turned back I felt another rush of adrenaline. I couldn't deny it. Every time I looked at Sydney, my anxiety spiked. "Shit, I know I keep arguing against this stuff, but I kinda feel like there's something up that has to do with you." I walked over, looked her in the eye, then held her in my arms, resting my head on her shoulder. "You're okay, right?"

She hugged me back, then pulled away and held my shoulders at arm's length, squinting eyes examining me. I rocked on the balls of my feet but stopped as she ran her thumb over my cheek below my black eye.

"This time it's not a dream," I said. Dreams were one thing, but having this happen while wide awake scared the hell out of me. "Tell me I'm not cracking up." I bit my lower lip, worried.

Sydney pulled me close. "You're definitely not cracking up."

I closed my eyes, welcoming the warmth and security of her embrace.

"I've never felt like this before," I said into her shoulder.

"You've never had to rescue Joey from a kidnapper either." She rubbed my back.

But I've been shot at, and I've chased suspects before. I closed my eyes, letting myself sink into the soothing calm of her caress, the low hum from deep in her throat, and the gentle rise and fall of her chest. She held me like that for I don't know how long. When I opened my eyes, I looked out the open window into the dark. My palpitations had settled into a regular rhythm, my breathing normal again.

"Feel better?" she asked.

"Yep." I inhaled the sweet fragrance of our neighbor's night-blooming jasmine. I'd loved the scent of those small, white flowers since I was a kid. Carmen hated it because she thought the strong odor triggered her asthma—which made me wonder.

"Could this be latent asthma?" I asked.

"Don't know." Sydney released me as I stared into midspace. "Let's see if it comes back when you're not chasing bad guys."

She placed a finger under my chin, lifting my gaze to her eyes.

"You'll be fine. You'll see. Let's go to bed and I'll show you." Sydney smiled and placed a light kiss on my lips.

We checked doors and windows, and I let her take me upstairs by the hand. In our bedroom, the only smell was of clean linens, Sydney's favorite. But as we embraced, I welcomed the vanilla-almond musk of the light pomade in her hair. I took in the familiar touch of her hands swirling slowly against my back, and the featherlight warmth of her breath on my neck. I needed this and was glad that Sydney knew it. She'd always been the better lover, knowing what I wanted—what I needed—and routine was fine tonight. It was normal, comforting, safe.

My lips grazed her ear and neck. Hers did the same to mine before tracing a line along my collarbone. We continued like that as we shimmied and twisted out of our clothes. Sydney stopped and held my breasts in her hands, stroking my nipples with soft thumbs before kissing and tongue-flicking just enough to get their attention. I closed my eyes, taking in the gentle, loving touch. She rested her hand securely on my bare hip and leaned over to pull back the covers, never letting go while guiding me into bed. I welcomed her lead.

The only sound was the rustling of sheets and contented moans as we continued to explore each other's contours. My earlier anxiety was gone, replaced by increasing tension as Sydney reached down, teasing the curve above my hip, the inside of my thigh. God, I loved how this woman knew me. She stopped for a moment, our eyes meeting—hers making sure I was okay, mine pleading for more. Her lips grazed mine, then lingered when I reached up for a longer, deeper kiss. She pulled away, leaving me wanting more as her lips and tongue continued to roam, following fingertips that barely skimmed my breasts and midsection, sending tingling ripples in all directions. Her fingers slowed and drew concentric circles lower and lower, her lips and tongue following only when my moans and my hands on her shoulders insisted.

I lost myself in the increasing rush of sensations. Whatever I'd felt earlier was long gone in the warmth of our intimacy. This was what I needed, all I wanted. And I wanted more. My heart quickened with increasing desire, craving her. I gasped when she finally stroked the throbbing between my legs and I gulped between heavy breaths when she continued there, alternating between slow, soft whirls and a more vigorous rhythm in response to my moans and the rise of my hips, reaching for her. Then, a perfect stillness before my back arched with shuddering waves of gratifying release.

"Damn, I love you." I tried to regain my breath. I was so grateful for the love washing over me, something only Sydney could provide. I lay exhausted, smiling at the sudden weight of her body on mine.

"Come 'ere," I whispered between short, shallow exhalations, my body covered in a moist sheen. She gave me a self-satisfied smile before entering my embrace.

"How you feeling now?"

"Mmm." I closed my eyes; my chest continued to rise and fall in rapid spurts.

"Wow." I finally said, still recovering. I removed the sheet she had pulled over us.

"Wow?"

"Oh, yes." I smiled, and when Sydney bent in for a light kiss, I added, "You smell like sex."

"I smell like you, love." She chuckled and pulled the sheet again, snuggling up to me. I returned the gesture and was about to return more, my fingers lazily circling her breast and starting to meander down her side, when she stopped me.

"Shh." Her lips met mine then pulled away. "Relax. You can use some sleep now."

"Mmm. I love you."

"I love you."

Her words coated me in comfort, her arm holding me until I fell into a delicious, deep sleep.

* * *

I was looking for Sydney. She was in danger and needed me, but I couldn't get to her.

"Syd, where are you?" I called out. I couldn't see through a thick fog. "Sydney!" I cried out again. I heard a faint response, but she seemed to be moving farther away. "Sydney!" I shouted as loud as I could.

"It's okay. I'm right here. I'm right here." Sydney held me tight. "You're having a nightmare."

"What?" My eyelids fluttered. I couldn't see much, but there was no fog, only darkness as Sydney held me. My eyes slowly adjusted in the dull red glow emanating from the alarm clock.

"You screamed my name," she explained. Now I was awake.

"Please don't tell me it's three twenty-three." My heart raced.

"Well, it's three twenty-four now."

I looked for her eyes, barely seeing them in the dark and I clung onto her as if to keep her from getting away.

"Oh, god. I felt like I was losing you. Damn, that was scary shit." And knowing the time now made it even scarier. If my other dreams were any indication, there was no way to deny what this meant. Something was going to happen to Sydney.

"I'm not going anywhere. I'm right here."

"Fuck." I gave her a tight squeeze before loosening my grip, and tried to slow my breath.

"Anything else?" She rubbed my arm at my scar. My fear felt similar to when I got shot, but then I realized I'd felt more anger back then, could see the shooter. This was different. The threat was invisible.

"Just heart-pounding fear." I released her, flopping on my back, drained, but reached to hold her hand.

"Want to talk about it?"

"Uh-uh." I shook my head. I needed to process it first. This was scarier than my dream about Joey. I wasn't about to dismiss it, but I needed to think about what to do, how to protect Sydney.

"Okay, let's get some sleep and talk about it in the morning," she said with a yawn, nudging me to turn on my side so we could spoon.

I relented, but as much as I loved the press of her body against my back, I didn't think I'd be able to sleep, my mind churning over how to keep her safe. When Sydney's breathing signaled a deep slumber, I lifted her arm carefully and got up to retrieve my Glock from the gun safe, placing it under my nightstand within easy reach. I slipped on the shorts and T-shirt I used as pajamas and eased back into bed, gently placing Sydney's arm back on me. She barely stirred, and I finally slept.

We must've knocked out, because we woke up in the same position, her arm still around me when the alarm clock began its rising trill. Sydney exhaled a sleepy groan. I yawned in response.

"The magic arm works every time," she said. "But what was that nightmare?"

"Damn. I don't know, but I don't want another one." I turned my body to face her, holding her close. "It felt like a warning about you. Maybe you should stay home today."

"Can't." She brushed my lips with hers and inspected me with her eyes.

"I'm okay," I lied a little, still worried about her. "Let me drive you. I can get a Lyft from the hospital to the car rental place for my loaner."

"Sounds good to me," she said, still eyeing me.

"I'm fine, love. Really. Just worried about you."

"Okay." But she didn't sound convinced.

We showered and dressed. Sydney frowned when she saw me put on my shoulder holster over a black tank. "Is that really necessary?"

"Wouldn't want to find out without it." I holstered the Glock and slipped on an oversized, blue button-down. It hung open and loose just for the occasion. She raised a corner of her mouth, not liking the gun but handing me one of the protein shakes she'd prepared.

"Let's both be careful today, okay?"

I gave her a peck on the lips in affirmation before downing my shake.

On the way to her hospital, Sydney interrogated me about my dream, but there really wasn't much to it other than feeling she was in danger somehow. I was alert to the cars around us and kept checking the mirrors.

"You're making me nervous," Sydney said.

"Can't help it. I know it was only a dream, but that and the anxiety attack have me spooked."

"Does it feel better to act on it, instead of ignoring it?"

"I know, I know. Not my usual reaction to these dreams, but this time it's about you." I glanced at her before turning back to the road. "I can't explain it, but what can I do? I don't want you to get hurt." *Not this time.* I'd screwed up when Mom died. I was not going to screw up again.

Sydney placed her hand on my knee and squeezed. "I'll be okay, love. I'm just glad you're thinking that the dream may mean something—even though the thought of it is a bit unnerving."

"You *want* me to believe in this dream?"

"Well, I don't want it to come true, but your concern kind of feels like a breakthrough, don't you think?"

"Because I'm taking it seriously?"

"Yeah, like maybe it'll be easier to do that from now on."

I shook my head. Here we were, taking steps to ensure her safety, and all she could think was that I was making progress with the juju.

"Right now, my only concern is for you."

"Okay." She sounded more optimistic than I felt. "Tell you what. I'll even let you walk me to the door."

"You don't have a choice about that." I pulled into the employee parking and picked a spot that would be well-lit after dark. I didn't want to take any chances. I walked her to the door of the ER, with its full-time security staff, kissed her goodbye, and set up a Lyft pickup to get to the car rental place.

Waiting for my loaner, a serviceable, black, midsize sedan, I mentally thanked Sheila for convincing me to get good car insurance. I needed to talk to her, to get my bearings. It hadn't been just a dream this time—it was a dream coupled with an anxiety attack, which had never happened before, and this time it was about Sydney—but I still needed to stay objective. I had to talk with someone who understood my work, someone who could help me remain focused. At times like this, working alone was a disadvantage, but I was glad Sheila was a good friend.

"Sure, honey," she said when I called and asked if we could meet to talk about some of the business inquiries we'd discussed at Joey's birthday party. "Actually, I was going to call you about some office space in the Bradbury Building."

"What? You won the lottery?"

"No, but Harold Winston, a board member at the Fair Housing Coalition, is a private investigator. He's retiring. His partner, Jane Stern, is looking to sublease his office. After Sydney's comment this weekend, I thought you might be interested in going legit and—okay, I'll fess up—letting me land there whenever I'm in your neck of the woods. If those calls over the weekend drum up more business, you may need the space anyway."

I worked from home and usually met my clients, mostly law firms and insurance companies, in their offices. The historic Bradbury Building was a beauty, with its classic wrought iron railings around a skylit atrium, but the LAPD Internal Affairs Division took up two of the upper floors, muting much of its charm for me. If not for the LAPD presence, I would've loved an office in the building. But I couldn't deny that this was a great opportunity. And if I took on more clients, I'd need someplace other than Starbucks to meet with them. Still, I was wary as we arranged to meet for an early lunch at Grand Central Market, another historic site across the street.

"Nice shades," Sheila said when we hugged in greeting later that morning.

"Do they work?" I asked, hoping the Ray-Bans did. I felt butterflies in my stomach, but I wasn't sure if they were due to my apprehension about Sydney or the thought of entering the building for the first time since the less-than-satisfying Internal Affairs hearing on my complaint five years ago.

"Hmm, a little discoloration by your temple." She inspected my right eye. "If you wore makeup, no one would be the wiser."

I gave her a side-eye.

"Didn't think so." She chuckled softly. Then, sniffing at the open-air market, she added, "Sure smells good. What's for lunch?"

"Don't know about you, but I'm going for tacos." I walked toward a market stall, and Sheila followed.

"Check it out." Sheila pointed with a smile. "Chitterlings!"

"*Tripas*," I translated.

"Gotta have me some of those, see how your people fix 'em."

I chuckled and ordered for both of us, sticking to *tacos al pastor* for myself.

The tacos settled my stomach before we jaywalked to the Bradbury Building. As we waited for the security guard to find our names on the guest list, I took a sheet on the history of the building from his desk.

"Did you know that the guy who designed this building consulted his brother about it in a séance?" I asked Sheila.

"It's a great story, isn't it?" a voice said from behind me. It was Jane Stern, back from lunch herself. She was younger than I'd imagined, late thirties at most, with the deep copper, shoulder-length hair of a classic ginger. Matching freckles on a round, almost pudgy face accentuated girlish looks. After Sheila introduced us, I couldn't help but ask, tapping the paper in my hand.

"You don't think it's kind of creepy?" The last thing I needed was more juju in my life.

"Not at all," Jane said with a smile. "I kinda like the quirky stuff about the building."

I wasn't so sure I did myself. That and the LAPD presence might nix the idea of leasing space here. I must have telegraphed my doubt because Sheila tried to find some common ground.

"I thought you two knew each other."

I wasn't sure if she meant that we were both detectives or both gay. Jane certainly gave off the vibe with her thick-soled Fluevogs.

"We don't all know each other, you know," I said.

"I trend to the older set," Jane said with a disarming smile behind rimless glasses that confirmed her statement. Her khaki slacks and tweed blazer did the same—only the beige, amply filled camisole gave a nod to a less conservative look. "Comes with the territory when you take over your dad's business at thirty-five." She motioned us toward the old-fashioned elevator in a wrought iron cage.

"So, it's been just you and Harold Winston since?" I asked as we walked.

"Yup. Mr. Winston carried most of our water after Dad passed. Solid, shoe-leather detective work. He's really the one who taught me the ropes, but now he says he can't keep up with the Title IX and cybersecurity work coming in—I'm kind of a nerd and love it. He wants to retire to Jamaica. He's definitely earned it."

"How'd your dad and Mr. Winston get in this building?" Sheila asked, craning her neck to take in the atrium as we waited for the elevator. I wondered the same.

"Stern and Winston." Jane smiled. "We're at the edge of the jewelry district. Pretty sure the building manager at the time thought he was leasing to jewelers. My dad's name was Hirschel, but he went by H. Stern for business, same as the jeweler. And Harry Winston was an even bigger name in diamonds back then. Still is. I bet the owners never met Mr. Winston. Probably figured the Black man they saw worked for my dad."

I liked that Jane called the elder Black man "Mister." She obviously respected him and honored the nomenclature of the Black community.

"I'd love to meet him," I said as the elevator clanked to a stop on the third floor, two below the LAPD hearing room I'd rather avoid. I wanted to hear from Harold Winston himself the story Sheila had told me about the Jewish man and the Black man who couldn't get into law enforcement and instead formed a bond helping the Black Panthers and some of the lesser-known victims of McCarthyism. "The more things change, the more they stay the same," I'd said over tacos. "They couldn't get into the LAPD and I couldn't stay in it."

Jane turned to me when we exited the elevator.

"Well, if you're interested in his office, you might run into him." She unlocked an oak door with a frosted glass window that let in light from the atrium. On the glass, simple gold lettering read *Stern & Winston*. "He's taking his time moving his stuff out. Doesn't come in too often anymore, but he'll be here, eventually." As Jane closed the door, I wondered if I'd want *Ávila* added to the names on it, but one look at the space and it seemed to fit just fine.

The reception room had a big desk, brown leather guest chairs, and a matching sofa sitting on polished red oak parquet. A small fireplace with a wood-and-tile mantel added a perfect vintage touch. Jane led us through a door on the left and into Mr. Winston's wood-paneled office. It had the same furniture as the reception area, plus a green banker's lamp on the desk and gray steel file cabinets lining the wall opposite the windows. Dark rectangles stood out above the couch and another fireplace where frames had been removed. It was straight out of a Hollywood set. All my misgivings washed away. I couldn't believe my luck. I mean, I'd known the Bradbury Building would be impressive, but the office—and its history—was perfect. If Jane had handed me a lease right then and there, I would've signed—no questions asked. Instead, she invited us to sit on the sofa, taking one of the guest chairs herself. She followed my eyes.

"We can't use the fireplaces anymore, but we like the ambiance."

"I can see why." We talked a bit about each other's work, but it was Sheila's connection and my union ties, once removed, that sealed the deal.

"Mr. Winston said your recommendation was all he needed," Jane said to Sheila. "He's retaining an interest in the agency, so I'm good with his judgment." Turning to me, she said, "Sheila tells me your mother-in-law is a labor leader."

"And my best friend represents her union," I added.

"Cool. My dad would've liked that. He worked with some of the lawyers representing UE when McCarthy went after them. Nearly wiped them out."

"I'm not familiar with them." I wasn't up on my union history.

"United Electrical, Radio and Machine Workers of America. Ask your union friends. They'll know. They still show up to support picketers—wear those 'Kicking Ass for the Working Class' T-shirts."

"Those guys? Yeah, I've seen them." I recalled seeing some at a Justice for Janitors picket that Sydney and I had attended to support her mom. We'd delivered food to the picketers on one of our early dates. I smiled at the memory of the double takes I got from the cops who recognized me. I was so into Sydney at the time, they were easy to ignore. I smiled more when Jane said she'd draw up a lease and I could move in anytime I wanted. She even offered to help with online sleuthing if Sheila or I ever needed any help in that area. We both thanked her.

"Just so you know," Sheila said. "I'll be using the office from time to time too."

Jane smiled. "Mr. Winston will be happy about that. Now, if you'll excuse me for a few minutes, I need to check on a security scan I'm running. You're welcome to stay and explore some more." Sheila and I stood to shake hands with her before she headed to her office on the other side of the reception area. I turned to Sheila when we sat again.

"Oh, my god! Pinch me. Thank you so much!"

"Right?" Sheila grinned. "You are quite welcome. Thought of you right away when Mr. Winston called this morning."

"Thank you. I wasn't so sure I wanted to be in this building with Internal Affairs upstairs, but damn, this office?" I looked around again. "Wow."

"Thought you'd like it." Sheila was still grinning. "So, you want to go over the calls from this weekend?"

"Sure," I said, coming back to earth. I'd printed the messages from my answering service and we split up the calls. The reports I owed to a couple of reliable clients weren't going to write themselves, and I didn't know how much I'd be tied up helping Carmen and Luis, so Sheila took the calls that likely needed immediate attention and those we couldn't figure out so that she could triage them. She also took the calls with Inland Empire area codes, figuring those would be more geographically convenient for her. We both agreed to refer the calls involving marital disputes. Neither of us had the stomach for the drama those entailed. Most of the calls were about missing persons, cold cases, or new cases having trouble getting police attention—a far cry from the discrimination and fraud cases we each handled, but exciting to contemplate.

Once we'd finished, I leaned back into the soft, worn leather, exhaling a breath I hadn't known I'd been holding. Sheila put down her notes and looked me in the eye.

"So, what did you really want to talk about?"

I sighed again.

"Come on. Out with it."

"Okay." I took another deep breath and leaned forward, resting my elbows on my knees and joining the fingertips of both hands. "I just need a gut check with someone in our business. And"—I glanced at Sheila—"this stays between us, okay?"

"Of course." A vertical line deepened between her brows.

"I want to make sure I'm not losing it." I looked back at my hands. "At Joey's party, you heard some of Jesse's theory about messages from Mom and my weird dreams, but what really freaks me out is that now I kinda feel like I felt right before my mom died." I paused, not quite sure how to put it. "See…" Sheila waited. "I'd had a dream about this guy I was tracking. I had a lead on a license plate, but I fell for the dream instead. Got cocky. Thought I'd catch him in Vegas. He turned out to be the same guy who ran my mom's van off the road." I rubbed my face with my hands at the memory and leaned back again. "Since then, every once in a while, I've had dreams that—*after the fact*—seemed to foretell something about what I was facing that day. Nothing really helpful, mind you," I added quickly, looking at her to make sure she didn't think I was crazy.

Sheila nodded, letting me continue.

"I can dismiss all of that. But last night I had what I think was a bit of an anxiety attack—out of nowhere. It got worse when I looked at Sydney. She calmed me down, but I can't shake the feeling that it had something to do with her. Then, to make matters worse, I had a nightmare that she was in danger. I was looking for her, but I couldn't find her. I woke up shouting her name. Scared the shit out of me, probably her too."

Sheila placed a comforting hand on my knee. She seemed about to say something but stopped and removed her hand when I continued. I'd come this far sharing with her what I'd shared only with family and Carmen until then. It felt good to finally tell someone in my line of work, and now I needed to get it all out. I turned to face Sheila.

"That dream, and the strong feeling I got about Sydney, while wide awake…They hit too close to home. I need to stay objective, but I want her safe too. I can't let this juju stuff get in the way, like it did when Mom died." I looked back down at my hands, willing away the guilt and regret. Sheila paused a few beats before speaking.

"You know, Yolanda, there's nothing wrong with what you call 'the juju.'" She paused, waiting for me to look her in the eye before continuing, "And there's nothing wrong with developing strong intuition. Yes, you need to remain objective and focused, but how many of us can get anywhere in our business without following our gut too? Even Miss Cybersecurity over there." She motioned with her thumb toward Jane's office. "I bet she has to rely on her gut from time to time. We all do. I'll tell you this. It sounds to me like you're developing a gift that you won't be able to ignore for long. The more you resist it, the more it'll get in the way."

I stifled a groan. It wasn't exactly what I wanted to hear, but somehow, I wasn't surprised.

"You sound like Sydney. She thinks that blocking out the juju keeps me from grieving for Mom. But grief isn't the issue. My cross to bear is all this guilt." My throat ached with the tears I held back. It felt good to share with Sheila, but I still didn't expect it to change how I dealt with the guilt, my penance for not looking out for Mom. "What I'm really concerned about is not repeating my mistake with Sydney. I can't shake the feeling that whoever killed Tony may come after her—that my work is exposing her to danger. I know that doesn't make sense—not even to me." I wrung my hands.

"You'll both be fine. You're watching out for Sydney as best you can. If I know you, you'll be there when she gets out of work to make sure." Sheila was right. I would be there. "And as for finding the killer, if there is one, I'm sure this Rudy guy'll show up soon enough. If he didn't do it, he'll provide leads on who did. But the only advice I have for you in the meantime is to go back to the beginning."

"You're quoting *The Princess Bride*?" I smiled, feeling better.

"Am I? Well, it's still good advice. It all started with the kidnapping, right? No, with that Tony guy wanting to distract Luis. Maybe sit down with Luis again and see if he has any more insight now that he's beyond the stress of the kidnapping. Or check with someone who knows those union and developer folks." That jolted a memory—I'd meant to call Sydney's mom to ask her for her insider intel on the unions, but in the aftermath of finding Joey, I'd completely forgotten.

"You're right. I should talk to Sydney's mom. And I gotta call Luis too. He was pretty pissed that he didn't get to finish his proposal. Carmen said he was probably more angry about that than being accused of murder. But maybe now he'll remember more about Rudy and the other people around Tony. Thank you, Sheila. Really."

"No problem. Just let me know if there's anything I can do to help. You don't have to work this alone, you know."

I hugged her, grateful for the talk and the friendship. She returned the hug and gave me a motherly kiss on the cheek. I welcomed the affection and the solidarity it invoked.

"Now, I gotta get going before traffic gets worse," Sheila said. We both stood. It was close to two o'clock. If she hurried, she might catch the first wave of traffic back to the Inland Empire, the increasingly populated, sprawling desert with the dissonant name.

We walked over to Jane's office to say our goodbyes. Her office couldn't be more different that my soon-to-be one. It had the same wood paneling, fireplace, and parquet floor, but two long banquet tables formed a V shape and held what looked like a control room's worth of screens and gingerbread lights. Jane stopped tapping away on a keyboard when we knocked on the doorframe. She responded to Sheila's open-mouthed stare, much like my own.

"I told you I was a nerd. This is my Zen Zone."

She showed us her setup and explained some of it—most of it going over my head—before promising to be in touch.

"And one more thing, Yolanda," Sheila said before we parted ways near our cars.

CHAPTER SIXTEEN

Monday, 2:00 p.m.

On the way home from the Bradbury Building, my cell phone rang on the passenger seat. The loaner didn't have a Bluetooth connection, but I saw from the caller ID that it was Sydney's work phone. She never called from work. I pulled over before getting on the freeway.

"Are you okay?" I said without a greeting.

"Yes, didn't mean to scare you."

"What's up, then?"

"Well, I went to lunch with Sylvia," she said, referring to one of the supervising ER nurses. "To talk about some new reports we have to submit."

"You left the hospital?"

"Really. I wasn't alone. And we went right nearby, but I'm glad we did."

"Why?" I was about to get angry that she hadn't heeded my advice, but then I couldn't remember if I'd told her not to leave the hospital. My curiosity got the better of me in any case.

"Well, on our way back, we walked by the employee parking and I noticed a note on my windshield."

Shit.

"It says 'Better get your *ruka*,' r-u-k-a," she spelled out, "'to back off.' Let me send you a picture of it."

"Holy shit. How much did you handle the note?"

"Mostly the back of it. It was facedown. I touched it in the front when I turned it over, but I folded it from the back without creasing it once I read it."

"Good girl! Now, will you please stay inside the hospital until I get there?"

"Definitely. Gotta get back to work. Just sent you the picture. Love you."

I thought she was trying to sound unconcerned so as not to alarm me, but she wouldn't have called if the note hadn't scared her. I opened her text after we hung up. The note was on white paper and written in what looked like old *cholo*—gang member—script in black marker.

No one writes like that anymore. Ruca, slang for wife, was misspelled, but the meaning got across. The *cholo* script, a combination of block letters with upper and lower peaks, wasn't sloppy, but I couldn't tell if it was from a practiced hand or someone trying hard to copy it. I forwarded the text to Detective Lan—the only LAPD friendly on this case so far—telling her I'd bag it for her as soon as I got to the hospital. I provided a description and the location of Sydney's car, and I looked up her license plate number in one of my phone apps before giving her that as well.

But, damn. Is this what the dream and the anxiety attack were about? I rushed to the hospital, hoping that was all, but I couldn't relax now. Someone wanted me off this case, but who? Tony's killer, most likely—meaning there probably was a killer, and he hadn't died of a heart attack. And it was someone who knew about Sydney. Someone who knew they could get to me through her. That could be anyone who knew we were married. I didn't think anyone had followed us when I'd driven her to the hospital. Did that mean it was someone who knew her car? Or someone who saw us leave home and didn't bother to follow because they knew where she worked? Anyone could find that on the Internet.

I sped up the winding Pasadena Freeway, confident that the CHP rarely patrolled LA's oldest freeway because it was too narrow to pull over drivers.

At the hospital, I ran through the waiting area, attracting the attention of a security guard at the reception desk. He started toward me but stopped when he saw a nurse wave a greeting and hold open the emergency room door. I mumbled a "Thanks" and rushed to the open horseshoe where doctors and nurses shared desk space. Sydney was between patients, looking over the shoulder of a resident entering data at a computer terminal.

"Got here as fast as I could."

"Hey," she said, looking up. "Here you go." She handed me the note in a file folder.

"Hey, Yolie," Sylvia greeted me, coming around the corner. "Nice shiner. Great job rescuing your godson." She patted me on the back. "You come for that creepy note?" She said it with the casualness of an ER nurse who'd seen everything and wasn't phased by a written threat, but she frowned, a bit worried when I held up the file folder in response. I asked for a clear bag.

"Like this?" Sylvia pulled a specimen bag from a box under the counter and handed it to me. I thanked her and turned to Sydney.

"Someplace we can talk?"

"Sure," she said, leading me to an empty exam room. I noted Sydney's demeanor, much calmer than my own. On the way, she stopped to give some instructions to another resident. When he scurried off, she turned to a nearby copy machine.

"Here, you'll want to make a copy." How I appreciated this woman. I slid the note into the mostly clear bag without touching it and copied both sides. When we were in the exam room, we exchanged a quick peck on the lips in greeting.

"I'll have to report it to hospital security, babe," she said. "But I was waiting for you first."

"Thanks. I forwarded your text to Detective Lan. We should let your security know about that too. We need to check out security camera footage."

"Maybe we should've talked to them this morning."

"And said what? 'I had a nightmare; can you look after my wife for me?' No, love. We have something solid now, let's go tell them." Sydney frowned, unable to come up with a better way to explain our concern after my anxiety attack and dream. On the way to the security office, I examined the note again.

"So, what do you think?" she asked.

"Can't tell if this is authentic or someone trying to imitate a *cholo*. The note's almost too neat. And who writes like this anymore? I think the last time I saw it was as a doodle in junior high—on one of those retro Pee-Chee folders. Could've been my own. Maybe an old *cholo*?" It was all I had. That and a dream that I didn't want to come true. I hoped the note had prints.

When we arrived at the security office, we found a very cooperative, twenty-something Duc Ng, one of two security guards on camera duty.

"That's Duc, D-U-C," he said, standing to shake my hand. Seemed a bit formal for a young guy, but I liked it. He turned to Sydney to explain. "The guys think it's a John Wayne thing, but my mom wouldn't know who he is." Then he paused awkwardly, his eyes still on Sydney.

I coughed to get his attention and showed him the note, explaining where Sydney's car was parked. He didn't skip a beat, going into professional mode.

"Chuck, can you get the chief?" Duc addressed his partner, pointing his chin at the door on the far side of the room. "This is serious." It wasn't every day these guys got to do something other than act as muscle with belligerent patients. Then he turned to Sydney with a huge smile. "Please have a seat, Dr. Garrett. You're welcome to review footage with us." More absently to me, he added, "You too, ma'am. Just give us a minute to set up the video."

Ma'am? I smiled, but we remained standing. He clearly had a crush on Sydney. She was oblivious.

My phone rang when Duc turned and busied himself with a bank of monitors.

"It's Jesse," I said to Sydney. We both stepped into the hallway and I put the phone on speaker.

"Oh, good," Jesse said when I told him I was with Sydney. "Can you guys come to *Doña* Mercedes's tonight after Sydney's shift?"

"Yes," Sydney said quickly. And in response to my raised eyebrow, "This is personal now. We can use all the help we can get." I had to agree that it was personal, but I didn't know how *Nina* Mercedes could help. We didn't need a spiritual healing, we needed to identify a stalker.

"Help with what?" Jesse asked. I filled him in on the note.

"Oh, shit! Bring it over tonight. And be careful."

"You're there now?" I asked.

"Yeah, doing some research you'll find interesting." Before I could ask what could be so interesting, he said, "See you later," and hung up.

I stared at my phone. It wasn't like Jesse to hold things back.

"What was that about?" I asked. Sydney shook her head, and then I added, "He's right about being careful, though. Will you make sure you don't leave the ER without an escort? I'm sure Duc would be more than happy to guard his crush."

"Oh, stop it," she said. But her smile told me she wasn't oblivious to him after all.

Back in the security office, Sydney introduced me to Chief Johnson, the head of security. He was a stocky African American man with a perfectly round, shiny, bald head—the kind that, after Sydney's OB-GYN rotation, we sometimes joked meant a cesarean birth. Chief Johnson was a retired captain from the Pasadena Police Department and was all business in a tailored blue suit. No one was going to mess with one of his doctors. I could see why Sydney felt safe at work, despite the shooting victims and assailants who sometimes arrived at the trauma center together.

I recounted Joey's kidnapping and what I knew of Tony Gonzalez's death, and the possible connection here. Chief Johnson had seen news reports of the kidnapping and rescue but had not heard about Tony's death. Out of the corner of my eye I saw Duc raise his eyebrows, impressed. The chief was glad I'd alerted the LAPD but said he'd put in his own call to the

Pasadena PD as well. He then explained that the video monitors had views from all the cameras near Sydney's car. Unfortunately, none of the cameras captured the car itself. I made a mental note of the parking spaces where Sydney should park in the future.

Chief Johnson instructed Ng to call up two additional cameras to capture vehicular access to the complex. The chief offered me a chair, but before sitting I asked him about an escort for Sydney whenever she left the ER. Sydney rolled her eyes, but Johnson agreed without hesitation.

That settled, Sydney returned to work and the rest of us moved slowly through early-morning footage. We tracked a lot of activity during the shift change; and more visitors than I'd expected arrived around midmorning. Several people moved in the direction of Sydney's car. None looked suspicious, but we noted their appearance. Finally, at the 11:03 a.m. mark, a guy in a black, oversized hoodie came onto the screen. His face was in shadow under the hood and below the brim of a black baseball cap low on his forehead. He held his chin to his chest. It wasn't cold out, so he definitely didn't want to be recognized. He walked fast but with a slight limp toward Sydney's car. *Rudy walked with a limp.*

"The dead guy's friend walks with a limp. He's still missing," I said, turning to Chief Johnson.

"This guy could be affecting that limp," the chief said. I wasn't sure I agreed, but it was a good reminder to remain objective. The man appeared about average height, but he could have been any age. With his hands in his pockets, we couldn't make out skin color either.

"Heck, it could be a woman for all we know," Ng observed. He had a point. He rewound the video and stopped it at the best view he could get.

"Looks like baggy pants, but waist-high, not sagging," I said. That might put the person on the older side, not a kid. "Can you print that out for me?"

"The LAPD and Pasadena PD will want copies too," Chief Johnson added. "And we'll need some for each of our stations."

"Got it." Ng clicked away. The printer behind us sputtered to life and spewed out several printouts. I reached over for one and stared at it. *Who the hell is this guy? He's threatening Sydney to get at me, but I'll be damned if he's going to get to her before I get to him.* I folded the picture into my back pocket, along with my copy of the note.

"Let's see where this person came from," Johnson said. Ng entered some commands and brought up camera views to a minute before the man in black appeared.

"Right there." Ng pointed at a screen. "Looks like he came from the public parking structure."

"We'll have to zoom in on drivers and get plates," Johnson said. This was going to take a while.

"He could've put on the baseball cap and hoodie in the car. So, let's look at facial expressions too, in case anyone looks nervous," I said to nods all around. We were in the middle of that round, zeroing in on several drivers who appeared more lost than nervous, when Detectives Lan and Conroy arrived. I stood and introduced them to the chief and his staff, and we filled them in on what we'd found so far. When we were done with the update, Lan and Conroy took me aside, but they didn't appear too concerned about being overheard in the small room.

"Just so you know," Lan said. "Lieutenant Peak took Rios and Chan off the Gonzalez case. I'm not sure that we'll get it, because our victim's parents are among the suspects, but he told us to check this out and to ask you to let us take care of it."

"He said to tell you to stand down," Conroy said more pointedly.

"Of course he did. But this is my wife we're talking about. What would you do?" I asked, looking from one to the other. Lan gave me a sympathetic eye, but Conroy left no room for argument.

"Look, the kidnapping's over. We don't need you getting in the way and having us worry about another homicide, okay?" He almost sounded concerned. I was almost touched. I rolled my eyes, but that only prompted him to step up to the console and take my chair without so much as an "excuse me."

"We got it from here," he said. Not the best bedside manner, but I'd resolved to ignore the admonition. I handed Lan the plastic bag with the note and stayed back to let them sit in front of the monitors. No need to press my point when I knew neither of us would budge. Ng gave me a sympathetic glance before resuming his scan of the video footage. Nothing else came up.

"He could have entered the parking structure from a pedestrian entry," Chief Johnson suggested. "Two sidewalk doors don't have cameras yet." He shook his head, seemingly frustrated with hospital bureaucracy. I'd bet he'd get his cameras now.

"Thanks for all your help, guys," I said to the hospital security staff. And, turning to Lan and Conroy, "Can you at least let me know if any prints turn up?" I hoped I sounded cooperative so that I could get cooperation in return.

"The lab techs are printing the car now," Lan said. "But you know they'll need to take the note back to the lab." I'd given her the information on Sydney's car, but I hadn't expected this quick a response. I was grateful for it and thanked her, wondering how upset Sydney would be when she saw her car covered in black dust.

After the detectives finished viewing the video, Duc walked me back to the ER entrance, where we settled in at the reception desk to wait for Sydney to be done with the residents. He asked more about the kidnapping and the people involved, genuinely concerned for Sydney. He wanted a detailed description of Rudy so that he could be on the lookout. I appreciated his concern. We also discussed tips on joining the LAPD, and I gave him advice on getting into, and through, the Academy. I couldn't help throwing in a speech on the need for more good cops. Sydney came out of the ER a little after three o'clock and we all walked into the parking garage. If she noticed the dust on her car, she didn't comment on it. She was distracted by the condition of a six-year-old boy who'd come in with severe injuries from a chainsaw accident.

"He's no older than Joe," she said. "We stabilized him, but I hope the surgeons can save his arm." She shook her head, getting into her car.

Duc offered to walk me to mine, but I declined and asked Sydney to drive me to it so that we could leave together. On the way, I updated her on the LAPD's visit. There wasn't much to add other than my suspicion that it was Rudy who'd left the note. I asked her to lead the way home so that I could keep an eye on her car.

Alone in my loaner, I considered my dream and my anxiety attack. Neither offered anything other than triggering a nervous stomach. Was there something to them after all? Even if they were a warning of some kind, what was I supposed to look for? And what did it mean that I seemed to get a warning while wide awake? That frightened me more than the dream. How was I supposed to function with that going on? How could I do my job? And how was I supposed to protect Sydney if I needed *her* to calm *me* down? Antsy all over again, my left leg bobbed up and down as I drove. I had to figure this out before I went nuts. I scanned the area around Sydney's car for anything suspicious, concerned about the space between us.

A car tried to cut in between us without signaling.

Oh, hell no. No way was I going to let that happen. I leaned on the horn and almost rammed it. The car swerved back so fast it fishtailed to keep from going into oncoming traffic. As I passed it, I saw a startled elderly lady staring at me, one hand on her chest. *Damn.* I'd nearly given both of us a heart attack.

I didn't even signal an apology as I rushed up to tailgate Sydney. I caught her look in her rearview mirror, more concerned than frightened. I tried to relax my face—*everything's under control.* If I kept thinking that, it just might be.

I tried focusing back on the road but caught a glimpse of someone familiar pulling up slowly into the almost-hidden drive of The Raymond restaurant. *Was that Leon James?* I couldn't be sure, wishing I'd gotten a better look. I was torn between following him and trailing Sydney, but decided to stay with my wife. I'd have to check with Carmen on whether Leon drove a newish, black, Ford F-10. What was he doing there, so close to Sydney? I'd only been to the restaurant in the old craftsman house once on a date night with Sydney, but knew the place as a secluded, upscale restaurant good for romantic or private dinners. It was a bit early for dinner, but he might be there to meet someone in the dark, wood-paneled bar for one of their boozy cocktails. Still, his presence unnerved me. I couldn't tell if he was wearing dark clothing, but he didn't seem to be avoiding detection, driving slowly. Or did he mean to be seen? *Shit.*

I dialed Carmen at the stoplight before turning onto the Pasadena Freeway but got her voice mail. I considered leaving a message, but remembered she had an appointment with a trauma counselor Rox had recommended from her work with students. I'd check with her later.

At home, Sydney and I switched to my car for the drive to *Nina* Mercedes's house.

"You okay back there?"

"What?"

"You almost took out that little old lady."

"I know. Shit. Scared us both."

Sydney studied me, a frown matching the worried look in her eyes.

"We're good. We're okay." I tried to reassure her. She said nothing but didn't seem to mind me checking mirrors this time. "I need to tell you something," I added, then didn't wait for her response before describing my sighting of Leon James.

"Are you sure it was him?" Her concern seemed to equal mine.

"Don't know. Tried calling Carmen to ask what kind of car he drives but got her voice mail."

"Do you want to go back and check?"

I did, but I didn't want to be late getting to *Nina* Mercedes's.

To get our minds off the threat, I told Sydney about the opportunity to share an office in the Bradbury Building. She was all for it.

"And I think you'll like Jane. Pretty sure she's on our team," I said, using the lesbian reference. "She's cool in an offbeat kind of way. It'll be nice to bounce ideas off someone close at hand."

"Good. And I agree with Sheila about going legit. More for you than for your clients. They already know you're good."

"It does feel like I have a chance to step things up and be taken more seriously."

"By the cops?"

"Yeah. I'd like to think I don't need any affirmation from them, but Conroy's comments back there reminded me that most cops hate PIs. I know I didn't care for them when I was in uniform—thought they interfered more than helped."

"Even former cops with a full-fledged agency?"

"Especially former cops. They tend to think they still have the authority of a badge. Sheila once told me that a good PI has to have the mindset of a social worker—be a good listener. I've never forgotten that. I met only one ex-cop like that when I was on the force, and I guess I did give him the benefit of the doubt because he had all the trappings of a serious business. So far, the former cop thing alone isn't enough to cut it with Peak and Conroy. And," I added, still feeling uneasy. "I wouldn't blame them if any of this juju stuff gets out." I turned to Sydney at a stoplight. "It worries me. Scares the shit out of me and worries me. As much as I'm concerned about your safety right now. How the hell am I going to get it under control?"

"Maybe your godmother can help," she said as we arrived at *Nina* Mercedes's house.

CHAPTER SEVENTEEN

Monday, 7:30 p.m.

Nina Mercedes's short, round figure stood at the open back door of her corner duplex. She was wearing her signature black Keds and a pale green apron over a dark blue smock. Her age had finally caught up to the shock of white hair I'd always known her to have.

"*Pasen, mijas.*" She waved us into her kitchen. No one ever used the front door. Stepping inside was like stepping into the seventies. Sydney, who'd visited only a few times, smiled at the avocado-green refrigerator and matching, rotary dial telephone mounted on the wall next to it. It no longer worked, long ago replaced by a wireless phone, but *Nina* saw no need to part with it. The O'Keefe & Merritt stove, where she'd taught me to bake *bizcochos*, was even older. HGTV designers would call it a vintage kitchen, but to *Nina* Mercedes, it was home, warm and inviting. I felt hugged even before she embraced me. Jesse would say her home had good energy. *Where is he, anyway?*

"*Buenas tardes.*" I hugged my *nina* before Sydney did the same.

"*Ay, mija. ¿Tu también?*" *Nina* said, taking in my black eye. "Here, I have a *pomada* for you too." She went to her bedroom to get it.

"A pomade?" Sydney asked.

"Ointment," I translated. "She probably gave some to Jesse too." I thanked my *nina* when she returned with an unmarked, repurposed, spice jar. I didn't know what it was, but I was sure it would speed up the healing and agreed to apply some before bed.

"Where's Jesse?" I asked.

"He went for *carnitas*," she said. "He said he did not want me to cook." She shrugged as if to say, "What can you do?" I hoped he'd show up soon. I wanted to know what his "research" was all about and was starting to feel antsy again, this time as if surrounded by the buzz of an electrical charge. *What the heck was that?* I looked to Sydney, but she just smiled again as we passed under the swinging tail of a Felix the Cat wall clock and into the dining room.

Nina Mercedes offered us a seat at the dining room table, so I knew this was going to be a serious meeting. Otherwise, we'd be sitting on the other side of the beaded curtain in the living room. In addition to being the site of delightful meals, the dining room was where *Nina* Mercedes did all her business and healing work. *Is that why Jesse wanted us here? Some connection to her* curanderìa? I looked around to see if anything triggered a thought related to the last three days. Against the near wall was the familiar, three-tiered altar covered in a simple, red cloth. A daybed sat next to it. We sat opposite the daybed, and I took in the altar, my left knee bouncing up and down again with nervous energy. The altar held ceramic saints of various sizes, most of them wearing condensed milk necklaces—home repairs from long-ago earthquakes. On the tiers below the saints were an assortment of unlit candles, bottles of holy water and anointing oils. But pictures of loved ones and others who had passed stood out the most.

My knee stopped bouncing when my eyes dropped to a picture I knew well, one I hadn't even realized I was looking for—

my mother, just to the left of center, next to John F. Kennedy.
I loved that it wasn't a formal picture like the president's but a
snapshot I took of Mom in open-mouthed laughter at a party. It
was my contribution to the altar and made me smile every time
I saw it. The shadow of guilt did not intrude here. Never had.
I figured it had something to do with the positive, protective
energy of *Nina's* healing space.

Next to Mom's picture, an old Polaroid captured my uncle
Bobby strutting down what was then called Brooklyn Avenue,
with youthful vigor. "Forever young when you die young,"
Mom used to say.

On the daybed next to the altar lay a blue-and-white,
imitation San Marcos blanket imprinted with an image of the
Virgen de Guadalupe. As a girl, I'd loved watching through the
beaded curtain while my *nina* worked on "patients" lying on
the bed. I especially liked when she prayed over them while
scanning their body with an egg. She had used that on me once,
when I was having nightmares as a kid. She'd broken the egg
into a glass of water and had told my mom to put it on my
nightstand. In the morning, we'd know what to do by the shape
of the egg. I remembered that it looked like Sleeping Beauty's
Castle at Disneyland, but my mom said it was a church and that
we had to go to the *Santuaurio de la Virgen de Guadalupe* to light
a candle and pray. I told her it looked more like we needed to
go to Disneyland, but she didn't find that as funny as I did. We
went to the ornate church in the nearby City Terrace hills, lit
a candle, and prayed. Sure enough, the nightmares went away.

I chuckled to myself, thinking that a *limpia* might be just
what I needed to get rid of my dreams. It had worked before;
it might work again. I was trying to recall the details of those
childhood nightmares, beyond the terror they evoked, when
Nina Mercedes brought in some of her refreshing cucumber
limeade. A moment later, Jesse arrived with dinner. He took a
deep breath after greeting each of us with an embrace—huggers,
all of us.

"Thanks for coming, Yolie, Sydney." He looked at each of
us. "I asked you to come here because I learned something from

Doña Mercedes." He got to the point with odd formality— probably what he sounded like as a Philosophy TA in the classroom.

"You learned something about the case?" I asked, glancing from him to my *nina* and back.

"Not exactly," he said. "But it could help."

Great. He's going in for the kill on the juju stuff. I should've known, but now I had to sit through it. Getting up and leaving would be an insult to my *nina*.

"It's about Bobby," he said, to my surprise. I'd thought for sure he was going bring up how his visions and my dreams meshed with what we'd experienced in our search for Joey. "*Tío* Bobby," he added when I cocked my head with a confused frown.

"Yeah, what about him?"

"Did you know that *Doña* Mercedes has his personal effects from when he died?"

"*¿Como?*" I looked to my *nina* for an explanation.

"It is a long story," she said in accented English for Sydney's benefit. She sat on the daybed and patted the space next to her, signaling Jesse to join her. He relaxed and appeared relieved to sit and let *Nina* do the talking.

"Your *mamá* came to me to talk about *el don* when you were little, but what she had was not the gift of healing, it was the gift of seeing." She pointed between her eyebrows to the spot Jesse and Sydney called the Third Eye. "She was scared of it. Scared of it like you are, but for different reason."

I frowned. *What did she mean my mom had the gift of seeing?*

Mom had never once said anything about having a gift of her own. And how did my *nina* know how scared of it I was myself? Until getting spooked last night, I hadn't been afraid of my dreams. And we hadn't mentioned last night's dream to Jesse when he'd called. Did she assume I resisted my dreams because I was afraid of them?

"This gift?" She looked me in the eye. "Many people have it, some more strong than others. Some more open to it, some not too much. Your *mamá*, she was afraid of it, so she tried to fight it." She shook her head sadly. "She said she saw things she did not want to see, should not see. Sometimes she saw the bad inside people. So, she came to my church," *Nina* said, referring to the storefront Pentecostal sect she attended on Boyle Avenue, "to see if we can help her to stop it. But this is not something to stop. We prayed over her to help her to control it, but the *visiones* still scared her. Until they stopped."

Nina paused, looking me directly in the eye again. "They stopped coming to her after Bobby died. He had a little bit of the gift too, not so much like your *mamá*. When he died, she blamed herself for not helping him more. She tried so hard to block her *don*, that she could not help him with his."

Nina gave me a hard look, but I couldn't meet her gaze. I turned to stare at Mom's picture on the altar, my mind reeling. I'd never heard this before, had never known my mom had a psychic gift. Why had she never told me? If Mom was psychic, did that mean that I should be too? That Jesse was too? Is that why he wanted me to come? And if Mom was able to reject it, why couldn't I?

"How did she block it?" I asked, a stab of grief piercing my heart. Here was yet one more thing I'd never get a chance to ask Mom. I so wished I could, especially if she could help me prevent more anxiety attacks. The thought of having another one of those scared me more than any nightmare, no matter how helpful the warning. Or was it just a matter of controlling it? Not letting it get in the way? And if so, how?

"She blocked it *con pena*, *mija*." *Nina* shook her head again. Then she looked to Jesse for help translating for Sydney. They seemed to be on the same page.

"With guilt?" Jesse suggested for the term meaning "aggrieved." I knew what she meant. My own grief surfaced with a dull sadness.

"*Sí*, she blocked it with guilt," *Nina* said. "After Bobby died, she used her guilt to build a wall between her and the other side. But she never had peace. She had to keep her guilt alive, you see? To keep up the wall. I could not convince her to let it go." The pain in her eyes telegraphed her disappointment with what must have been a long effort.

Guilt.

Mom blamed herself for Bobby's death? Like I blamed myself for her own? Tears welled. If Mom ever felt what I was feeling now, she'd never shown it. I could only imagine her torment. It must have been worse than mine if she'd kept it bottled up. I wondered if that was why she was so judgmental about psychic stuff. At least I talked to Sydney and Jesse and Carmen about it. Maybe not as much as Sydney thought I should, but still... I hoped Mom had not suppressed it all and had shared her concerns with *Nina* or Dad. I'd have to ask Dad. And why didn't she tell me about it when I got older? Did she feel like she was protecting me from it? I had so many questions, things I'd never have a chance to ask her now, but mostly I was reminded of my own guilt. I opened and closed my mouth, not sure where to start.

"*Mija,*" *Nina* said in response to my confusion. "What you have is not the same thing as your *mamá*. She saw things people did before, things she could not control. From what Jesse tells me, you get messages about things that will happen, things you *think* you can control."

She raised her index finger at me. My pursed lips must have betrayed my resistance, because she continued, "It is no good to reject the gift. But it is different for everyone. Sometimes it can make you not a very nice person," she said carefully. "Your *mamá* was a good person, but she did not treat Bobby so good when he wanted more learning about his gift and when he started drinking because it gave him problems."

I remembered how angry Mom had been when that couple had come to exploit Bobby's gift and rob him, nearly hurting me and Jesse when they'd knocked us down running from his apartment. My mom had said some ugly things to him then, and again later when he'd tried to apologize. But why would she blame herself for Bobby's death? Why would *Nina*?

"You're saying it was her fault Bobby died?" I raised my voice, feeling the electrical buzz again. "Mom was probably just trying to help him—to protect him from himself. His fortune-telling was kinda goofy." I turned to Jesse. "How many times did we hear 'Bet he didn't see that bus coming' when we were kids?" I shook my head at the memory of merciless teasing by our classmates and glanced at Bobby's picture.

"I did not say that his death was her fault, *mija*," Nina Mercedes said softly. "Your *mamá* said that. She blamed herself. She thought if she helped him instead of *criticando* him for his gift, he would not drink so much, maybe not fall in front of that bus. He would still be alive. I could not get her to stop blaming herself, but I do not think she would want you to blame yourself." I didn't understand what she was getting at.

"I don't get it. This is why we're here?" I turned to Jesse. "To tell me Mom was psychic? That we should be too?" My voice rose again. I thought of last night's anxiety attack and nightmare. They'd felt like legitimate warnings. They made me worry about Sydney but, now, more than ever, I didn't want them to come true. I shivered at the recollection and the image of the anonymous note.

"Yolie," Jesse said in a level voice, interrupting my thoughts. "There are some things you should know." He continued through my eye roll. "Mom felt so bad about Bobby that she didn't want his things in our house. She asked *Doña* Mercedes to take them."

"So?" I asked as *Nina* got up and shuffled to the hutch at the other end of the dining room table. I could be rude to Jesse, but not to my *nina*, so we all waited. I looked back at Mom's picture and tried to remember her saying anything about psychic matters other than berating Bobby for his attempts at it. Maybe she'd said something I hadn't caught at the time. But nothing came to mind. *Nina* picked up a file folder from the hutch. I hadn't noticed it earlier. She placed it in front of me, and Jesse got up and came near.

"Among Bobby's things is his death certificate," he said as *Nina* opened the folder.

"I know how Bobby died." I raised a corner of my mouth in annoyance, but I glanced at the certified copy of the death certificate.

"Look at the time of death." Jesse pointed.

Sydney and I gasped. 3:23 a.m. We looked at each other, then up at Jesse and my *nina*. My jaw dropped; the low-level electric buzz I'd felt earlier became a surge emanating from my gut to my extremities and remained there like the faint vibration of a tuning fork. But I couldn't think about it right then. I was too busy staring at the death certificate.

"Holy shit," I exclaimed. I leaned back in my chair, stunned. "Sorry, *Nina*." This was too much to take in. I didn't want to believe that Bobby's time of death and my morning wake-up calls were connected. I didn't want to believe that my mother had blamed herself for Bobby's death. I looked a question at *Nina*, wanting to ask about it, but not knowing what to ask.

"It is okay, *mija*." She placed her hand on my shoulder. "You understand what this means?"

"That Bobby's the one waking me up at three twenty-three?"

"Could be. I think he watches over you a long time, *mija*. And I think your *mamá* watches over you too. You believe me, no?"

The buzz turned into goose bumps and a rush of adrenaline. I was trained to put credence in facts and evidence—not intuition, not dreams. It felt like something I wanted to run from. But the death certificate was evidence, the time of Bobby's death was a fact. My palpitations increased, but this time I recognized the feeling. I knew what I was afraid of. I didn't want any harm to come to Sydney, and harm to her was exactly what the dream and the anxiety attack foretold. I shook my head and willed away the thought. But then something else intruded.

"How can any client, any cop, or any judge or jury, for that matter, take me seriously if they find out I get these so-called messages from the other side? My business is on the verge of taking off, but this could tank it. It could set me back indefinitely!" My voice rose with each word. "I can't risk it. Not now." The new office, all those new cases, came to mind. I might lose all of that if word got out. But even as I said it, I knew I was voicing this to avoid acknowledging the thought of Sydney facing harm.

But *Nina* Mercedes's words nagged at me.

Could I play off the "messages" as gut feelings like Sheila had suggested? Could I separate the juju from fact? Could I control it?

I didn't know. Maybe there was something to the messages, but how could I keep them from interfering with the basic tenet of detective work—follow the facts? Then something else came to me. Maybe this was all just a great big coincidence.

"But Bobby died when I was ten. I've been waking up at three twenty-three only since Mom died."

"Try to think, *mija*," *Nina* suggested. "Remember the nightmares after Bobby died? The ones that went away after the *limpia*?" I nodded at the memory. "I think maybe he came to you back then, but you were not ready. You were too little. I did not know it at that time, but now it makes sense, no?"

"I don't know," I said, mostly because I didn't want to say yes. "I don't know what to think."

"At important times in your life, when things go wrong, do you wake up at that time, *con ansiedad*?"

"I don't think…" I stopped myself. "The day I was shot." I shook my head at the death certificate. "I don't remember what time it was, but I know that I woke up in the middle of the night feeling anxious and tossed and turned until morning. When I told Mom about it later in the hospital, she said it had been a premonition." And still she hadn't told me about her own gift? Even then, when she knew I might have some semblance of it too? Why? God, we could have worked through it together.

Nina Mercedes sat back on the daybed and patted the space next to her, this time signaling me to sit where Jesse had been. We exchanged places. When I sat next to her, *Nina* held my right hand in both of hers.

"*Mija*, I am an old woman and I am used to people not believing me, but I am going to ask you to believe me when I tell you that Bobby watches over you, *y ahora, tu mamá también*. Maybe that is why their messages are stronger now. They are doing it together."

I listened in silence. I didn't want to believe her, but something told me I'd have to. *What else could explain last night? What else would explain the dreams after Mom died?*

"I do not know if that makes you a psychic, like you say, but I do know one thing," *Nina* said. "You maybe do not feel it now, but listening to your *mamá* and your *tío* Bobby will help you grieve."

I stiffened and glanced at Sydney. Had she put her words in *Nina's* mouth? Was that why she had agreed so readily with Jesse to come tonight? Sydney shook her head innocently.

"I had nothing to do with this, but I agree with *Doña* Mercedes a hundred percent. Think about it. The facts are what they are. Bobby died at three twenty-three a.m. You wake up sometimes at three twenty-three, like he's warning you about something. You get these warnings more frequently, or maybe just more strongly, after your mom dies. These are all facts you can't ignore." Of course, she would bring it back to facts. Facts I couldn't deny. And I couldn't shake the feeling that Mom and Bobby were somehow present—especially Mom.

I glanced at her photo again. *Why didn't you tell me, Mom? Were you trying to protect me from it like you tried to protect yourself?* I shook my head with a bittersweet smile. *Are you trying to tell me something now, Mom? Is that why I had the anxiety attack on top of the nightmare?* I didn't make it a practice to talk to Mom like Jesse did, but as I did now, the weight in the pit of my stomach got a little lighter, somehow.

"It makes sense, Yolie," Jesse said. "Don't you think?" he added quickly, as if interpreting my silence for denial.

But I'd barely heard him. I couldn't deny it anymore. The mere thought of accepting this as my gift—it was so much to process. And suddenly, all the weight of my guilt and more came crashing back down. If I had not fought my dreams so much, maybe I would've had a clearer warning about Mom dying instead of just dreaming about the identity thief I was chasing. I doubled over, hugging the knot in my middle, Sydney suddenly at my side, her arm over my shoulders, holding me close.

"Did I block a warning from Bobby about Mom?" My stomach tied itself into all sorts of knots, and the tears that had been welling up spilled. I asked my *nina*, "If I had paid more attention before Mom died, would she be alive today?"

"*Ay, mija,*" *Nina* Mercedes said in a soothing voice, placing her arm around me as well. "Do not torture yourself. Like I say, Bobby's messages are not so strong like your *mamá's.* They are maybe more strong now because they watch over you together." I stared at the pictures on the altar again. "You must honor them now by listening, Yolie. You dishonor them when you shut them out. *¿Me entiendes?*"

"*Sí.*" I understood, sniffling. She was right. Everyone was right. Maybe it wasn't a matter of being psychic so much as just being open to these messages. Maybe Sheila was right too. Maybe this sixth sense could just be another version of that gut, that instinct most detectives have—the good ones, anyway.

"We should tell them about last night too," Sydney said. I blinked, a little dazed as Sydney described my anxiety attack and nightmare, and told them about the anonymous note. Jesse's jaw dropped, his turn to be surprised.

"Wow. It has to be Mom and Bobby warning you."

"I don't know what it was." I shook my head, coming out of my reverie. "The nightmare I could handle, but this new thing—it really freaked me out."

"You're taking it seriously, though, right?" Jesse asked.

"Of course. I drove Sydney to work, and we talked to the cops and reported the note."

"She even got our hospital security to escort me whenever I leave the ER," Sydney said. She sounded relieved at the notion now.

"I talked to Sheila about it today too. She's a private investigator I work with sometimes," I explained to my *nina.* "It was good to talk to her."

"What did she say?" *Nina* asked.

"She said that I should think about it like a gut feeling that most detectives have."

"Maybe she is right, *mija.*"

"Maybe," I said.

"The weird thing is the anxiety attack," Sydney said, addressing my *nina.* "That's never happened before. Do you think it's something that Yolie's mom could have done? It scared her. Would Yolie's mom scare her?"

"Oh, never on purpose, *mija*. It is how we receive the messages that can be a problem." Then, turning to me, *Nina* said, "This is new for you. But if you stop fighting it, you will learn to receive the messages."

"How?" I asked, really wanting to know.

"Pay attention to what you feel. First, listen to your body. Then, if it makes sense to you…How do you say?" She turned to Jesse again. "*¿Si te resuena?*"

"If it resonates with you," he translated.

"*Si, eso*. If it resonates with you, you can trust it. We are all different, but that is how *el don* comes to me. Maybe you will know it when you feel calm. If you feel calm, it maybe means you understand the message that comes. If you do not understand it, or if you try to fight it," she added, shaking her finger, "you will not feel calm. But, like I say, we are all different. I do not know if it is the same for you. You will have to see. See if there is a pattern. And if you cannot see it, I am always here to talk about it."

It was so much to take in. *Okay, maybe I'll listen. It won't hurt this time, and it might even help.*

"*Y mija…*" My *nina* paused for a couple of beats and waited for me to look her in the eye. "If you pay attention to them"— she pointed her chin at the photos of Mom and Bobby—"you will honor this gift in you too."

"I'll try, *Nina*. Thank you. And," I added, looking from Jesse to Sydney, "thank you guys too. It still freaks me out, but I'll just have to figure out how to deal with it."

"Do not force it, *mija*," *Nina* Mercedes offered. "It will come to you or it will not. But do not be afraid when it does."

"Meditation and dream logs may be a start," Sydney said. I looked at her with a raised eyebrow at the familiar suggestion.

"Just saying," she said and smiled.

"Right," Jesse agreed, beaming. "Best to do whatever feels comfortable to you."

"I will," I said, mostly to myself. I stood and turned to the altar, touching my fingers to my lips and then to Mom's picture. I did the same to Bobby's image. To both, I silently apologized for ignoring them, I thanked them for watching over me, and I asked them to help me handle this so-called gift.

The moment I thought that, the vibrating energy around me dissipated like a dimming light, replaced by fresh, clean air with a scent of cucumber from *Nina's* limeade. I took a deep breath to soak it in and sensed a calmness I had not felt in a long time. I still had lingering guilt, or something closer to regret, but it was somehow easier to breathe. It felt right. Yes, this was the right thing to do. I took it in for a moment, and then managed a smile at the three of them before my *nina* folded me into another embrace that the others joined.

Later, as we sat to eat the cold *carnitas*, I ate mostly in silence, glancing frequently at the pictures of Mom and Bobby, welcoming the crisp, light air around me. But a nagging feeling remained. I still needed to keep Sydney safe.

CHAPTER EIGHTEEN

Tuesday, 6:00 a.m.

I hadn't shared with Sydney the odd energy I'd felt, and how a refreshing lightness had replaced it before we'd left my *nina's* place. I wasn't sure what to make of it and wanted to process it some more. Instead, we recapped the rest of the evening. When I yawned deeply, Sydney suggested going to bed.

"But first, how about trying that ointment your *nina* gave you?"

I looked at her, unsure of her endorsement of the homeopathic tincture.

"I'm sure it can't hurt," she said with a shrug.

I applied the ointment to the bruise around my eye and went to bed, where I fell asleep almost immediately. A deep sleep. In the morning, I recalled only one dream. I was at my favorite *birria* place on First Street, enjoying a bowl of goat stew and a beer. I wasn't anxious, and I was so sleepy I didn't look at the clock when I stirred. Instead, I fell right back into a steady slumber.

"If it means that I'm gonna have some *birria* today, I'm all for it," I said to Sydney when she quizzed me about any dreams.

I was upbeat and ready to start the day. *Nina* had said that if I felt calm about my interpretation of the "message," I had it right. I had no idea what the message was, but I figured something would come to me. Eventually. I was a little surprised that I wasn't worried about it, didn't feel anxious. The talk the night before had definitely helped.

"I'm seeing your mom today, but I'm going to her office in mid-city, so no chance of *birria* there."

"Well, let's both still be careful, okay?" Sydney advised.

"Always." We exchanged a quick kiss. "Now, let's get ready so I can get you to work." I was glad she'd agreed not to drive. I didn't want to risk her car being booby-trapped at the hospital. It may have been overkill. I mean, when was the last time a car blew up in Pasadena? But I wanted to be careful. I drove my loaner, again checking that no one followed us. This time, Sydney didn't seem to mind.

"Will you tell Mom about the note?" she asked. "She should hear about it in person."

"Of course. She won't blame me for putting you in danger, will she?"

"Oh, she will." Sydney smiled. "But she won't give you any grief."

"You sure?"

"She'll want to help. May even know what kind of car Leon James drives."

"Okay." I hoped she was right. Sydney was her mom's treasure. Those closest to her—namely me—knew they'd be blamed if anything happened to her.

When we got to the hospital, I told Sydney to call if I should pick her up any time other than 7:00 p.m. We kissed goodbye at the curb, and I watched her go into the ER before driving away.

Back home, I called Carmen to ask about Leon James and his car. She was already in meetings, so I'd missed her, but left a message this time. I took care of other business by checking in with Sheila on the cases we'd split up. I spent the rest of the morning completing an overdue insurance fraud report and compiling my tax documents, all the while thinking about Rudy and the questions I wanted to ask Sydney's mom about him. Her union connections were bound to help.

Before heading to Mrs. Garrett's office, I got an email with a lease agreement from Jane Stern. I signed it, scanned it, and sent it right back before she could change her mind. I pumped a fist in the air, celebrating my luck at having snagged an office in the Bradbury Building.

Then I called Luis to ask if we could meet so I could pick his brain about Rudy. He sounded rushed, saying he was tied up working on revisions to his proposal, still hoping for an extension, and planned to meet with Manny Martinez for an early dinner to discuss it with him.

"Why don't you join us at La Serenata?" he offered. "I was just going to text Manny to confirm." The restaurant was a discreet, Eastside watering hole frequented by Latino politicos. Manny was from the Valley, but this was closer to City Hall. I agreed to join them, figuring I'd still have time to get Sydney.

After we hung up, it hit me. The *birria* place from my dream was up the block from La Serenata. Could the dream mean that I was supposed to meet with Luis? I felt no anxiety, so maybe the dream was a helpful hint instead of a warning. But a helpful hint about what? This was the problem with giving dreams any credence—I still didn't know what they meant. I dismissed it, unconcerned. Or maybe I was just feeling optimistic from my visit with *Nina* Mercedes and my new office lease. I might be having trouble identifying Sydney's stalker, but other things were starting to fall into place. And these psychic messages might only be "gut feelings," like Sheila had said. Maybe they could help more than get in the way. I'd still have to figure out how, but as I headed to my mother-in-law's office on Wilshire, I somehow knew that I'd get a break soon.

"Oh, honey," Mrs. Garrett said, taking in my black eye in the lobby of the union building. I'd noticed it had started turning yellow-green, healing advanced by *Nina* Mercedes's mystery ointment. I lowered the sunglasses I'd lifted onto my head to adjust to the indoor light, glad that my arm bandage had been replaced by a simple, albeit large, Band-Aid.

"I'm sorry I couldn't meet earlier," Mrs. Garrett said, "but how about I take you for some coffee to make it up to you? You look like you could use some."

"Sure." I greeted her with a hug and disappeared into her flowery, turquoise-and-yellow Mumu that smelled of gardenias. I really liked Sydney's mom. She was a self-assured, fifty-nine-year-old Black woman whose husband had also been a union organizer. They'd met in the early days of the union's efforts to diversify its membership and leadership. Mr. Garrett had died of a heart attack when Sydney was ten and her brothers were seven and eight. Sydney, ever "Daddy's girl," said it was what made her want to go into emergency medicine. After his death, Mrs. Garrett had risen through the ranks to the number two spot at the union. She'd raised her children on her own and was rightfully proud of them: a doctor, an engineer, and a pilot. Not bad for a single mom. She often lamented that only Tony, the pilot, was a union member.

We walked two blocks to a hotel diner because it was the closest union shop around. It wouldn't do to have a union official patronizing a non-union establishment. On the way, she asked about Joey, and I filled her in on the counseling the school and Carmen had arranged for him. I also mentioned the Bradbury Building and how my connection to her had helped.

"Ooh, those UE brothers are definitely badass," she said. "Wish more of the movement was as committed to the struggle as they are. Nowadays, too many career staffers get lazy. Don't want to organize. Sign 'no strike' agreements instead. May as well get on the employer payroll if you're gonna do that." She shook her head.

Once we sat and ordered, Mrs. Garrett got down to business.

"Okay, so what would you like to know about Rudy?"

"Well, before we start on Rudy, I should tell you about the latest developments."

She cocked her head to the side, curious, and leaned forward, resting her elbows on the table, ready to listen. I took a deep breath. "Someone is trying to warn me off the case, through Sydney," I said, as calmly as I could.

"Through Sydney?"

"I'm afraid so. Someone left an anonymous note on her car at work."

"Someone threatening my girl?" Mrs. Garrett raised her eyebrows and sat up straight. *Here it comes. This is where she'll blame me.* I tried to reassure her before she could say more.

"Now, the LAPD and the Pasadena PD are both on it. And the chief of security at the hospital has been especially helpful. He's offered to provide Sydney with an escort whenever she leaves the ER." I watched her face go from growing concern to relief to concern again. "Let me show you a copy of the note." I took it out of my pocket and unfolded it on the table between us. She pressed the creases on the paper, understanding dawning on her face. Sydney was right. I didn't get any grief, and now I saw determination to protect her daughter.

"Why, that good for nothing…You think Rudy did this?" she asked.

"That's just it," I said. "We don't know. But he disappeared along with Tony after the kidnapping and hasn't been seen since. No telling where he's gone now that Tony's dead. Do you think this could be him?" I handed her the printout of the security camera image. I spied it to see if it could be Leon James too, hiding his long hair under the hoodie.

"Hard to say." She examined the image closely. "Could be anybody, but this guy sure doesn't want to be identified." She pursed her lips at the printout. "Covered up like that on such a beautiful day? Uh-uh…But I will say this. I don't know Rudy very well. I've run into him mostly at union events—conferences and marches and such. Never worked directly with him. But he has a reputation for hitting the bottle pretty hard. Did this guy look drunk?"

"I didn't know that. He did walk with a slight limp like Rudy does, but Chief Johnson at the hospital suggested the guy could be faking it. And from what I recall, he seemed pretty intent on getting to his destination. Didn't seem to weave or stumble."

"I've seen plenty of drunk people walk with hyper focus when they're trying to get to the restroom at a bar. May not look drunk, but a simple distraction or bump sends them to the floor."

"Hmm." I might've done that on occasion in my youth. Of course, she didn't need to know that. I stayed on topic. "Do you know anything else about Rudy's background?"

"He's been Tony's sidekick long as I can remember. I heard once that Tony helped him get out of jail and helped him sober up. But he was always falling off the wagon. I think Rudy was pretty loyal to him."

I made a mental note to check online court records for any convictions against Rudy, especially anything that might involve stalking.

"Do you know if he has a *cholo* past?"

"Don't know for sure, but he does have lots of tattoos," she said. I didn't remember any tattoos, but he had worn long sleeves when I saw him at Carmen's the day Joey was kidnapped. "Come to think of it," Mrs. Garrett continued, "he was part of a clique at conferences that some of us called 'The Eses.'" She paused when I furrowed my brows, not understanding. "As a joke."

"Eses?" I still didn't get it, thought she meant the letter S.

"Yeah, you know, 'Hey, *ese!*'" she said, imitating a deep-voiced Latino and lifting her chin in a mock greeting. I had to laugh at the clever name and her imitation. "You know how it goes. Some of them were wannabes, but you can tell the more authentic ones by their swagger. I think Rudy was one of the ones with the swagger when he was sober, and I do recall him wearing khakis and a Pendleton when he was younger. Not to profile or anything, but…" She arched her eyebrows and tilted her head to the side as if to say, "You know."

Mrs. Garrett may have been from Talladega, Alabama, but she'd been an organizer in LA long enough to immerse herself in the culture.

"So, authentic *cholo* or wannabe, he could have written it," I concluded, but that didn't prove anything. I looked at the note again. "There's something else."

Mrs. Garrett's frown returned.

"On the way home from the hospital yesterday, I think I spotted Leon James in a black Ford F-10. Do you know if he drives one?"

"He drives a truck. Don't remember, but I do think it's a dark color. You think this could be him?" She took back the image of the stalker. "Hard to say. Could be Leon, but could be anyone." But I noted that she didn't dismiss my suspicion of him this time.

"Wish we could find Rudy."

"Sorry I can't tell you more, but my best contact at his Local passed away last year. Only a few of us old-timers left nowadays." She sighed, then went back into help mode. "You may want to poke around his Local. I can go with you if you'd like."

"That would be great. Can we go today?"

"Let's go." She gathered her purse and glasses. "I'll call the office from the road to let them know I'll be out. You can drop me off at the Gold Line downtown when we're done so you don't have to drive all the way back out here at rush hour." I stopped her.

"Thank you," I said, placing my hand on hers and looking her in the eye with gratitude. "Really." We both looked away, me before I telegraphed more concern than I'd meant to, she with an embarrassed smile at the intimacy of the gesture.

"Ain't no one messing with my Sydney," she said, going into Momma Bear mode. She stood and placed cash, including a generous tip, on the table.

I was getting up myself when my phone rang.

"It's Sydney," I said, walking ahead of Mrs. Garrett to the door.

"Hi, Syd. I'm with your mom. Told her about the note. Let us walk outside and I'll put you on speaker."

"Hey, Mom," Sydney said when we were outside, and addressing me, she added, "Babe, I got another note. Same warning. Texting it to you now. Chief Johnson sent it to Detective Lan."

Mrs. Garrett and I both leaned into my phone.

"Are you okay?" Mrs. Garrett asked.

"I'm good, Mom, no worries," Sydney said. I could tell she was trying to sound unconcerned, but she came off a bit weary.

"I'm sorry, Syd," I said. "How was it delivered?"

"Well, that's what kinda freaked me out. He put it in my purse."

"What?" Mrs. Garrett and I said simultaneously, eyes wide, looking to each other then back at my phone.

"I was with Duc. We went across the street to grab some takeout. I needed a break, but the ER's pretty busy today, so had to come right back."

I was about to scold her for leaving the hospital but held back with her mom next to me.

"And we weren't alone," Sydney said, likely reading my mind. "Another security guard joined us. On our way out of the deli, I put my change in my bag and saw the note sticking out."

My heart raced at the thought of the guy watching her, getting that close.

"He put it in your bag between the cashier and the door?" I asked. My voice rose despite my effort to sound calm in front of Mrs. Garrett. She frowned with renewed concern.

"Could have been earlier. I took out my money when we walked in, and we were in line for a bit. The place was kinda crowded with other hospital folks and visitors, but they move through orders pretty fast. I didn't look at my bag again until we were walking out, when I reached in with my change."

"And you didn't see anyone?" Mrs. Garrett asked.

"No. We looked around right away, and Duc and the other security guard did a quick circuit of the shopping center and sidewalk, but we didn't see anyone who looked like the guy in the garage video—at least no one trying to hide their appearance." She paused before adding, "Love, this is getting scary. I'm glad Duc was with me, but I'm taking your advice and not leaving the hospital while at work until you or the cops catch this guy. Chief Johnson offered to have someone watch our place too."

"Good, take him up on that, Syd," Mrs. Garrett said before I could respond. "Yolie and I are heading out to Rudy's Local to see if anyone's heard from him."

"We'll get 'em, love," I said, feeling more pressure than ever to find the guy, and soon. "I'm meeting Luis for dinner to see if he has any ideas where to find him, but I'll be by to pick you up after. Don't leave the ER before then."

"Okay," Sydney agreed. "Love you."

"Love you," her mom and I responded as one. We looked at each other and nodded, acknowledging the mutual sentiment, and ended the call.

I brought up Sydney's text and shared the picture of the note with Mrs. Garrett. It was the same *cholo* script, but this note was longer than the first. "Yes, I can get this close. I'm not telling you again. Call off the bitch or she'll never see you again." I couldn't pinpoint it, but something about the note was off.

"Does this sound like a *cholo* to you?" I asked Mrs. Garrett as we bent our heads over the image.

"I don't know. You mean the full sentences and contractions?"

"Yeah. Almost too neat, don't you think?"

"Maybe. But where does that leave us?"

"I don't know, but I'm having dinner with Luis and Manny Martinez before I pick up Sydney tonight. Maybe they can add to whatever we learn about Rudy at the Local."

"Now, Martinez, I can give you some dirt on." She punctuated her statement with a knowing glance over the top of her wire-rimmed glasses.

"Oh?"

She explained as we walked back to my car. "He's in tight with some of the building trades, but his expensive tastes tell me he'll either leave public office and go corporate, or start looking to his *friends* to fund his lifestyle."

"What do you mean?"

"You know what happens to these guys once they taste a little power and get used to being wined and dined." Mrs. Garrett shook her head.

"Their oversized egos get bigger and they start representing themselves more than the people they purport to represent?" I quoted Jesse.

"Not only that. They start getting used to the good life. Don't want to lose it. I've seen it happen too often, with men especially. And it's more noticeable with men of color because so many of them come from poor backgrounds." She raised a finger. "Not all of them, mind you, but some. They start out wearing cheap suits, then move on to Brooks Brothers, then Armani. You can see the envy among those who haven't reached the Armani stage when they get together."

Her description reminded me of the media's portrayal of the Eastside political machine—"The Boys." There were no women among them, and they tended to look alike with their short-cropped hair, Brooks Brothers suits, and silk ties. The more successful among them did, indeed, wear Armani. Their staffers, the next generation of The Boys, tended to look like them as well, but they sported the hipster uniform of skinny pants and skinny ties. The Boys backed each other and supported each other's acolytes. Manny was a beneficiary of his own mentor's largesse, winning his council seat after Ben Chavez, Mr. Armani himself, had termed out and made a successful run for the state senate.

"And Manny Martinez is at what stage, would you say?" I asked, getting the picture as we crossed the street.

"I'd say he's about to enter the Armani stage. But you can tell he's struggling with what to do next."

"How so?"

"He's a political boss now. Can make or break political careers with his endorsements and his campaign coffers, but from what I can tell, he's trying to stay clean." She leaned in close and lowered her voice even though we were alone on the sidewalk. "He's no dummy. When they bring out the cocaine, he's always the one to walk away." And in response to my cocked eyebrow, "Mmm-hmm. He's no Boy Scout, but he's image-conscious."

"And the media hasn't picked up on it?"

"Oh, they know. They just don't report on it. They don't want to burn their sources. They're probably saving the information for when one of them steps into a real scandal. It's a very symbiotic relationship."

I shook my head as Mrs. Garrett continued.

"They don't even notice the erosion of their principles. They call their deal-making 'political pragmatism.'" She used air quotes, sounding like Jesse.

"My brother would agree with you. He says they aren't even aware, or don't care, that activists like him think of them as mere ribbon-cutters. Says they keep the old-school, 'poverty pimp' nonprofits in business with government contracts." She nodded at my own use of air quotes for the term Jesse and Carmen often used.

"Yup, politicians aren't the only ones enriching themselves while pretending to serve the community. They all start out with good intentions. Some of them can't help but go bad. It's so sad." She shook her head. "And they make it harder for the good nonprofits and the clean electeds."

I thought of Jesse's political activism and how it might be more legitimate than idealistic, if Carmen and Mrs. Garrett both agreed with him.

"But now, about my Sydney," she said when we reached my car and got in. "You'll look out for her, right?"

"Of course!"

"Good, cuz she's told me about your dreams and I agree with her that it won't hurt to pay attention to them."

I should have known Sydney would discuss my dreams with her mom. They were close. A part of me felt good that Mrs. Garrett didn't think I was crazy—that she wasn't afraid of the juju like my mom had been. My heart ached a bit at the thought. But the feeling was quickly replaced by concern at how easily word could spread about these weird episodes.

"You too?" I turned to her before starting the car.

"Honey, my grandmother in Talladega had the eye," she said. "She didn't talk about it much, but when she did, she said that it was to be used only for good, and failure to do so was a waste of God's gift."

What? I vaguely recalled Sydney mentioning her great-grandmother, but she had died before Sydney was born, and I didn't think she'd ever mentioned anything about her being psychic. But I welcomed Mrs. Garrett's casual way of talking about it, so different from my own mother's rejection of psychic matters. The only exception she ever made was my *nina's* healing work.

"Why am I feeling like everyone I know is within six degrees of the juju? It's like a psychic Kevin Bacon connection." I turned to her then back to the road.

"You'd be surprised, my dear. It's not as rare as you might think, but most people don't talk about it." My peripheral vision caught her peering at me over her glasses. "Promise me you won't ignore signs that can help you protect my Sydney."

"I promise." *Was psychic ability really that prevalent? And if it was, how on earth do people harness it so that it doesn't get in the way of their daily life? And why wasn't it helpful when you need it most?* I hoped my *nina* would be able to shed some light on that when we talked again. We rode the rest of the way in silence, my thoughts swirling.

Why had Sydney received another note so quickly? I hadn't taken any action since the first note, other than meeting with her mom and arranging to meet with Luis for dinner. And he was so rushed, I hadn't even mentioned the first note to him. But something must have set off whoever was leaving the notes. Did Luis tell Manny Martinez that I'd be coming to dinner? Did Martinez know that I was working on this case? Was he somehow involved? Maybe tipped off Rudy? But Manny was helping Luis, so that didn't make sense. Then again, Tony had been helping Luis too—or so we'd all thought. I needed to be on alert with the councilman at dinner. He was no longer just a source of information, he was a potential suspect.

"I think I'm not going to mention the notes at dinner," I said when I reached the union building. "And we shouldn't mention them in there either. You never know who could be helping Rudy, or whoever the stalker is. Let's just see if anything comes up when we ask about him."

"Okay, but you may want to let me take the lead." I looked at her. "No offense, but if they think you're a cop they'll clam up. They might want to protect their brother." I smiled as we got out of the car, appreciating her savvy. Mrs. Garrett entered the building like the union pro she was, greeting everyone with such familiarity that you'd think she'd known these strangers forever. *How did she do that?*

She made small talk with a couple of union members in jeans, work shirts, and construction boots. They were hanging out waiting for calls to a job. I couldn't help but wonder how similar they were to the undocumented laborers who stood on corners around the city, waiting for homeowners to pick them up and hoping they wouldn't be cheated. At least these men would be paid a union wage on a jobsite with decent working conditions. After the small talk, Mrs. Garrett worked in a mention of Rudy.

"Where is he nowadays?" she asked. The men looked at each other, shaking heads.

"Well, good luck getting called to a gig," she said. Then we moved on to the office. We were greeted by a Latino man dressed much the same as his members.

"Sorry about Tony," Mrs. Garrett said. She'd switched to a more somber tone with the union official. She introduced herself with a handshake and a hand on his shoulder—greater intimacy than I would have with a stranger—before introducing me as her daughter-in-law. I enjoyed watching her operate.

"How's Rudy doing with Tony gone?" she asked. *Damn, she's good.* You'd think she did this every day.

"Dunno." The man shook his head. "Haven't heard from him. And he's not answering his phone. Hope he's okay and not on a binge, you know?"

Mrs. Garrett patted his shoulder sympathetically.

"The cops came around yesterday asking about him. Got us thinking we should find him first. To support him, you know?"

"And no luck?" Mrs. Garrett asked. It was a nice prompt to get him talking some more. And it worked.

"Naw." He shook his head. "A couple of the guys checked out some of his usual dives, but nothing. Hope he turns up soon." He looked genuinely concerned.

"Me too," Mrs. Garrett said. They talked a bit about the change in union leadership occasioned by Tony's death before ending the visit. "Well, please give the other officers our condolences from our Local."

Back on the sidewalk, she nudged me with her elbow. "How'd I do?"

I had to smile. "Mrs. Garrett, I'd take you on as a partner any time. Let me know when you'd like to switch careers."

"Oh, honey." She chuckled as we got in my car. "That was all in a day's work. But you let me know any time I can help."

"I may take you up on that," I said, starting the car. "I don't know that I would've gotten such genuine responses. I'd probably still be wondering whether I was getting the truth. Thanks."

"No need to thank me. We gotta help Sydney." When we reached the Seventh Street Metro station, she said, "Well, keep me posted. And keep my daughter safe."

"I will." At least, I hoped I would. I watched her head to the station entrance on the busy corner and I mentally checked the union Local off my list of places to search for Rudy. A car honked at me to get going, and I pulled into traffic, my thoughts returning to dinner with Luis and Manny Martinez. I needed to know more about the councilman. *Could he have warned Rudy that I was still poking around? Could he be working with him?*

I thought Carmen might be able to help, and she hadn't called back, so I called her on my way to the restaurant, cursing the downtown construction traffic on the one-way streets. It was going to make me late.

"*¡Chingado!*" Carmen said when I'd filled her in on the anonymous notes and my Leon James sighting. She said she wasn't sure what he drove, but offered to find out. She was more concerned about security for Sydney. "Why didn't you call me earlier? We use security for our union activations." I knew she referred to pickets and protests. "I can get you guys a bodyguard."

"*Gracias, mujer,* but the hospital security chief is being great. He offered to have one of his guys watch our place."

"No, Yolanda, really." She used that tone she did when she was about to go pit bull on something and wouldn't let go. "There's one dead man out there already. This is no time to go all superhero. I can get you someone better than a rent-a-cop, no offense to the hospital security guards." The more she talked, the more I had to agree with her, and the more concerned I became. Her alarm heightened my own fears. "I'll make some calls, get a couple of guys. They'll contact you before heading to your place tonight. You can put them in touch with the hospital security guard."

"Damn, Carmen, you're right."

"Of course, I am," she said, and then we both chuckled despite ourselves. Carmen had become a bit of a know-it-all after law school. I'd figured that was typical, but at least she'd learned not to take herself too seriously since.

"I don't know what I was thinking, trying to handle this on my own." I thought about Carmen's lack of hesitation to call me for help the instant she'd realized Joey was missing. "Thank you. I'll let Sydney know when I pick her up tonight. Now about Eleanor's assessment of Rudy and Martinez…" I referred to Mrs. Garrett by her first name as I did with friends out of her presence, especially with Carmen, who was on a first-name basis with her. After all, she wasn't her mother-in-law. "She says Rudy is likely a former *cholo* and a heavy drinker. She also said Martinez is in tight with his Local."

"Eleanor may be right, but I don't see Manny being involved. Rudy is definitely an alcoholic, but he's not smart enough to stalk Sydney, unless someone like Tony gave him very specific instructions."

"And now that Tony's dead? Could that someone be Manny Martinez?"

"I don't think so, he's too cautious. Wouldn't trust a guy like Rudy."

"Then who?" Even cautious criminals make the mistake of associating with the wrong people. It's often what gets them caught.

"Don't know anyone else who'd take Tony's place, but those guys do stick together. If anyone else is involved, Rudy would go to them. Don't know who that would be. Never cared for his drinking much, so mostly keep my distance. Luis would know more, but you'll need to get him past his denial that his friends aren't necessarily his friends. He's as loyal to them as they are to each other. Wish I could say the same about us."

I knew from the dip in her voice that she was referring to herself and Joey. But not one to wallow in self-pity, she quickly added, "Yolanda, you and Sydney be careful, okay? And let me know if there's anything else I can do. I can come over with Joey and stay at your place, or you guys can come stay with us."

"*Gracias, comadre.*" We were each other's Ride-or-Die, and I appreciated that she'd always be there for me, but I didn't want to put her and Joey at risk. "You're doing more than enough by getting the bodyguards. Thank you. And, it's probably best for Joey to stay close to home and close to you. How's he doing?"

"Struttin' around like a little hero." I could hear the smile in her voice. "The counselor the school brought in is pretty good. He's loving all the attention. He's still clingy with me at home, but I certainly don't mind. And I'm glad Rox recommended getting him his own counselor too. She seems pretty good."

"Good. Let us know if there's anything we can do. Give him a hug for me. And, Carmen, I'm not bringing up Sydney's stalker at dinner with Martinez there, so keep it to yourself for now, okay?"

"You got it. Let me know how it goes. *¿Cuidate, eh?*"

"I'll be careful. *Gracias, mujer.*"

CHAPTER NINETEEN

Tuesday, 5:30 p.m.

I arrived at La Serenata, across from Mariachi Plaza, only a few minutes late. A black Escalade with E plates took up most of the red zone in front of the restaurant. Perks of our public servant Manny Martinez, I assumed. I passed the restaurant and turned into the alley behind it. There was no parking in the small lot, but mostly because two cars had taken up two spots each. *Assholes.* I backed up to a space behind the *birria* restaurant two doors up the alley. *Is that what my dream was about? Parking karma? Unbelievable.*

I shook my head, something in the pit of my stomach nagging at me. *Was that from my dream, or was it anticipation of confronting Martinez?* A scruffy, gray alley cat followed my movements from its perch on a dumpster. Hopefully he was keeping the rodent population in check, but the thought added to my queasiness.

Then I recognized Luis's car as one of those taking up two spaces. *Really, dude?*

Inside, Luis sat by himself at a corner table looking over at another table a few feet away where Manny Martinez leaned over in deep conversation with someone. Leon James sat at that table, a grave look on his face. *What the hell? Him again?* I stopped in my tracks. I hadn't seen a black truck outside, but he could have arrived with the other man at the table. What was Manny discussing with Carmen's opposition? Manny turned and headed toward Luis's table, rousing me from my stupor. He got to Luis's table first and sat down. The councilman had his back to me, but he turned around with a smile when Luis waved. Recognition wiped the smile from his eyes if not his lips. The men stood, and since he was the closest to me, I shook Manny's hand first.

"I'm not going to be deposed about this, am I?" he asked, referring to the deposition that had blown my case open against the LAPD. From what Carmen had told me, he'd never regretted triggering that episode, nor the rushed settlement to avoid trial publicity about the city council's influence on LAPD enforcement tactics.

"Only if you have something to do with kidnapping and murder," I said, moving to hug Luis. Five years, and my wounds were still fresh. Being civil to the man took so much energy. Getting shot will do that.

"Now, now." Luis tried to stop an argument before it started. Martinez couldn't help but stare at my black eye.

"Occupational hazard," I said by way of explanation. I'd have to keep trying *Nina's* ointment to speed up the healing.

"What gives with Leon James?" I pointed my thumb over my shoulder. I'd tried to sound nonchalant, but Luis's frown told me I sounded a bit eager.

"Nothing," Martinez said, similarly surprised. "Just saying hi."

I decided to drop it, still feeling uneasy about the coincidence. We all sat, and Luis called over a waiter to take my order of *enchiladas Suizas*, the best in town. They both had already ordered the *carne asada. Lack of imagination.*

"Well, Manny and I are done with our business," Luis said. "So, what's this about Rudy? The cops are looking at him as a suspect in Tony's murder, right?"

"At least a person of interest," I said. I was glad we could get right down to business. I didn't have a lot of time before I needed to pick up Sydney. "No one's heard from him. I know he was tight with Tony, and I figure he's involved somehow, but he likely panicked once the kidnapping plan failed. The question is whether he went into hiding with Tony. Or maybe they argued or something, and Rudy did him in." At least, that was the best theory I had. "But, with Tony dead, he could have gone for help from someone else too." I looked at Martinez, trying to gauge his reaction, but all I got was attentive concentration. "That's what I wanted to ask about. That and anything about his past that may help locate him."

"Well, you're right about him and Tony, but I don't know who else he runs with." Luis glanced up, his eyes drifting to the right, thinking. Looking back at me, he added, "As for his past, he and Tony used to talk about *Primera* Flats." One of the oldest gangs in Boyle Heights was still around, as far as I knew. "I think that's how they knew each other from back in the day. Tony never got jumped in, but they were close because his mom used to babysit Rudy. They kinda grew up together. Tony called him 'a real OG *veterano.*'"

"How about other *veterano* friends?"

"Dunno. I only know him through Tony."

"Is Rudy a drinker?"

"Yeah, I'll say. Reeks of it, most times. Why?"

"Just something I heard. Could explain his losing control and hitting Tony, maybe killing him accidentally."

"Sounds like a good theory to me. But I don't know him to be violent. He's more of a 'cry-in-my-beer' type of drunk."

"Hmm." I didn't think that would rule out an outburst. "I assume the cops are staking out his place, but do you know any of his hangouts?"

"You might try the union hall," Martinez said, breaking his silence. "He probably won't be there if he's hiding out, but his union brothers might know something."

I was surprised at the helpful suggestion, same as Mrs. Garrett's.

"Just came from there. No one there has seen him either."

Other than confirmation that Rudy was an old *cholo*, the men had nothing else to offer. He seemed like a shadow in union politics, always in the background, often unnoticed. We talked a bit about the trade unions. Martinez sounded like he was giving a stump speech, expounding on the partnership between unions and developers, and all the good that was coming to the local economy from the construction boom around the city—the nasty turn in national politics notwithstanding. It came off practiced, with a tired delivery. I wondered what was behind that tailored suit and whether he could be involved somehow, maybe not dirtying his hands but using his labor buddies for that, whether Tony or Leon. Sydney's mom had said he was tight with Tony's Local. Maybe he was closer to Tony and Rudy than he'd let on. Then I had an idea after Luis picked up the tab.

I took the pen that had come with our check and started tracing a Y in *cholo* script on the back of one of my cards, just to see if Manny noticed. I started with the vertical lines and then formed the peaks at the ends of the letter.

"What's that?" It was Luis who noticed.

"The talk of *Primera* Flats reminded me of the *cholo* writing we all practiced in our notebooks in junior high," I said. I looked from Martinez to Luis and back.

"You did that?" Martinez said with brows raised.

"I'm from Boyle Heights. We all did. Didn't mean we were in a gang or anything. Didn't you?"

"Not me," he said. "Straight arrow." He held up three fingers in the Boy Scout salute. "Nothing to mess up the permanent record." He laughed—a little self-consciously, I thought.

The rest of the conversation turned to childhood shenanigans between Luis and Martinez that belied the Boy Scout image, some of them at the boxing gym. I took note of that as I listened, remembering the line of questioning the detectives had pursued with Carmen and Luis.

I excused myself to go pick up Sydney, and Martinez mentioned that he had some business to wrap up with Leon James, who had just dug into his dessert of chocolate-drizzled churros. *If I didn't need to go get Sydney…* We said our goodbyes, and Luis and I walked to our cars in the alley.

"What kind of business does he have with Leon James?" I asked.

"Who knows. Probably just city stuff."

"Really, dude?" I said to Luis when we reached his car. "You couldn't take up more than two spaces?"

"Sorry," he muttered sheepishly. We said good night and I walked to my car as he got into his.

The sky glowed with the early rays of another beautiful sunset. I checked my text messages and caught a glimpse of the gray alley cat bolting from behind the dumpster to my left. I couldn't tell if I'd startled him or if he was after prey. But then the hair on my arms stood. Could've been static electricity from the dry air, but I looked around to confirm that the cat and I were the only ones around.

I clicked the keyless remote and the locks chirped. Something scampered from under the car toward the dumpster.

Agh, gross.

Reaching for the car door, I sensed a sudden movement behind me. I started to turn to see what it was, only to be met by the hot sting of a blow behind my right ear. My vision blurred, and I staggered, trying to stay on my feet while reaching for my gun, but the ground rushed up to meet me first. I blacked out.

CHAPTER TWENTY

Tuesday, 9:00 p.m.

I woke up confused. *Is this a hospital bed?* Everything looked hazy, especially when I glanced to the left. I made out some dark shapes there, heard voices, then someone in a white lab coat. I blinked a few times, and my vision cleared enough to see that Sydney, Jesse, and my dad were at my side. Sydney, in her doctor's lab coat, moved closer, holding my hand, I realized now. She stared intently into my eyes.

"Wha' happen'?" I managed to sputter with a tongue dry as gauze.

"Here, drink this." Dad handed me a cup of water, his forehead etched with concern.

"I'm so sorry, Yolie," Jesse said.

I swallowed. "'Bout what?"

Sydney shushed him. Going into Dr. Garrett mode, she asked me to count her fingers. Then she asked me to follow one of them as she moved it around in front of my face. She took out a penlight and looked into my eyes. I winced in pain from the brightness.

"Ow, oww! Is that really necessary?"

"Sorry, love. Looks like you have a concussion. We're waiting for a CT scan." I had to concentrate hard to follow what she was saying.

"What happened?" I asked again. The right side of my head was pounding, and I was super thirsty. I struggled to remember if I'd had anything to drink.

"First, how do you feel?" Sydney asked.

"Like I have a major hangover—the worst ever."

"Here, *mija*, have more water." Dad poured another cup from a plastic pitcher and handed it to me. I downed it gratefully.

"Let me see you move your fingers and toes," Sydney instructed. I did as I was told. "Okay, let's see you walk a bit." I swung my legs off the bed and walked to her, steadier than I felt. She walked backward then turned me around and walked me back to the bed. I was awake enough now to yank at the flimsy hospital gown. Hate those things.

"Is anyone going to tell me what happened?" I tried for the third time.

"What's the last thing you remember?" Sydney asked, helping me get back in bed. I sat back on the bed and tried to focus. *What did I remember?*

"I was going to my car to go get you. The car locks chirped and…and that's it."

"Okay. Someone hit your head with something hard—maybe a metal pipe. The cops found one on the ground. A cook from the restaurant came out to the dumpster near your car and saw you coming to, trying to get up. He made a pillow for you with his apron and called 911. You've been in and out of consciousness since you got here."

"Here? Huntington?"

"No, this is White Memorial," Sydney said.

Sydney doesn't work at White Memorial. But I let it pass, trying hard to understand what she was saying.

"It's probably a good thing that the pipe broke skin, or the swelling would be worse."

I touched the bandage on my head, noticing it for the first time. Nice accessory to go with my black eye.

"You probably moved just as you were struck, because the X-ray doesn't show any fracture in that hard head of yours. But I still want to rule out any other damage. You'll get a CT scan in a bit."

We weren't in an emergency room bay, but in a private room. Probably a professional courtesy to Sydney.

"Damn, I was supposed to pick you up." My memory was a little slow.

"You told me you were having dinner with Luis, but you didn't say where. When you didn't show or respond to my texts or calls, I called him. He told me you'd both left La Serenata at the same time. Then I called Jesse. He hadn't heard from you either, so I figured something was wrong. Jesse was concerned too." She glanced at him before continuing, "He drove over to the restaurant and Duc gave me a ride home, but on the way, the staff here called me. They found your emergency contact info in your wallet. You must've been out there a good half hour before the cook found you." Her eyes squinted in deep concern. She held my hand again, squeezing it.

"Your wallet was in your pocket," Jesse said, "and your phone and keys had fallen next to you, your gun was still in your holster. The cook took you for a cop. Nothing was taken, so it wasn't a robbery. I'm so sorry, Yolie."

"Why?" I was still trying to take it all in.

"Well…" He looked to Sydney and my dad before continuing. Both nodded. "I should've warned you, but I got distracted with some news you'll want to hear."

I blinked at him, willing my mind to clear.

"I got this uneasy feeling about you in a dark place, but I didn't know where, and I didn't know you'd be in an alley tonight."

My mind was clear enough to think that one is almost always near an alley in the inner city, but I didn't say it. I wasn't sure I was following everything he was saying. I squinted in concentration. After the talk with my *nina*, I figured I'd better listen. Jesse seemed to take my confusion as encouragement to continue.

"Well, I was distracted cuz I heard something from one of the undergrads who volunteers on political campaigns. He said Manny Martinez's wife just took a cushy *consultant* job with Barrio Homes."

He paused as though he was expecting a big reaction from me, but all I could manage was a frown. He went on.

"Isn't that one of Luis's competitors on the Boyle Heights project?"

I nodded, slow to catch on.

"Apparently, it's all hush-hush cuz she doesn't have a contract. He heard she's getting big fees, and some of the staff aren't too happy about it."

My mind focused through the fog. "Martinez? I just had dinner with him. His wife? Holy shit."

"I thought you had dinner with Luis," Sydney said, her turn to be confused.

"Both." Then I recalled a movement behind me before I was struck. "Was it Martinez who hit me? He stayed behind to talk to Leon James when Luis and I left." *Damn, could it have been James instead of Martinez? Could it have been both?*

"I found Detective Lan's card in your wallet and called her," Sydney said. "She asked me to call when you were able to talk. I'll call her after your CT scan."

I barely heard her. "So, it was Martinez all along?" I remarked, mostly to myself. "Or was it James?"

"Leon James?" Jesse asked. "Why him?"

"He's the guy Carmen's battling on that union certification."

"But Carmen represents unions, why would she be fighting him?"

"Because he doesn't want my mom's union to get the certification," Sydney said. "Wants to keep expanding his own empire."

I nodded, grateful to Sydney for verbalizing what would have taken greater concentration than I was capable of at that moment. Jesse and Dad gave each other a concerned look but said nothing. While we waited to be called for the scan, Sydney explained the concussion protocol.

"Your pupils aren't dilated, and your balance seems to be okay, so the best thing for you is rest."

"Don't we have to make sure to wake her up every hour or so?" my dad asked. My heart ached at his concern.

"That used to be the protocol, Mr. Ávila," Sydney explained. As I did with her mom, she never called my dad by his first name either—claimed her mom would call her out for lack of manners. "That's why I checked her eyes and her balance." She tried to reassure my dad. "When that checks out, the new protocol is plenty of rest."

My dad nodded, a little more at ease. An orderly came in to take me for the scan, Sydney at my side. She hung back to go over the results with the ER doctor while I was wheeled back to my room. When she returned, we all turned to her expectantly.

"The concussion could have been worse," she said. "But you'll still need to be careful. The discharge papers will take a while, so I'll call the detectives. Why don't you try to sleep a little before they arrive? Then I'll take you home."

"She doesn't need to stay overnight?" Dad asked.

"No, sir. She's able to walk, and I'll be there to look after her." Then she turned to me.

"You really need to rest, love." Sydney looked up at my dad and Jesse. They took her cue and moved quietly to the two chairs by the window.

I didn't think I'd be able to sleep with all the information I had to process swirling around in my brain. So much for my *birria* dream and how calm I'd felt about it. The dream was not a helpful hint after all.

Had I missed a warning? How was I supposed to interpret the damned thing?

I squeezed my eyes shut, frustrated. But I must've dozed off because I was shocked awake when Lan and Conroy entered the room.

"How's she doing?" Lan asked Sydney, taking the lead this time.

"Better. She lost consciousness, but her equilibrium and memory seem to be okay. She'll need some rest." Sydney stepped back so that Lan could approach.

"Rough night, huh?" Lan gave me a smile I hadn't seen before.

"I've had better." I tried to sit up. My dad came up on my right side and pressed the remote to raise the bed and helped prop me up with a pillow. "Thanks, Dad." I squeezed his arm, willing away his worry.

"We'll try to make this quick," Lan said, glancing at Sydney before turning back to me. "Tell us what happened. Start with what you were doing before the attack."

"I was having dinner at La Serenata with Luis Ochoa and Councilman Martinez."

"What was the purpose of the dinner?"

"Luis invited me at the last minute. I wanted to ask him about Rudy."

Conroy pressed his lips and shook his head, but kept taking notes.

"Anything come of that?" Lan asked.

"Just confirmation that he's a former gang member, and an alcoholic, and was really tight with Tony."

"Anything else?"

I shook my head. It didn't trigger any dizziness. That had to be a good sign.

"Dinner was pretty uneventful. We all got up to leave at the same time, but Martinez hung back. Wait. Leon James was there too. Martinez stayed to go talk to him. What was he doing there?"

"He was having dinner with you too?"

"No. He was at another table with a guy I didn't recognize. Martinez was talking to Leon when I got there and went back to talk to him when Luis and I left. We said our goodbyes, went out the back, and I went to my car. I felt some motion behind me, but before I could see who it was, BAM." I instantly regretted raising my voice, the pounding in my head returning.

"Any idea who it could have been?"

"Well, Martinez for one," I suggested. "But, shit, could it have been James? The second note came after Luis and I arranged to meet. He invited me to a dinner he'd already scheduled with Martinez. Any prints on the notes, by the way?" Lan shook her head.

"Well, Luis probably told Manny I'd be joining them. That communication would've been the only indication since the first note that I was still looking for the stalker. But could James be involved too?"

Conroy sighed. "Why do you suspect Leon James?"

Sydney was about to step in again, but Lan raised a finger to let me tell her. I did with some effort.

"Leon James wants the workers Carmen's helping for his own union. If she can't help them, they fall into his lap." Lan glanced at Conroy, who continued writing in his notepad. "Plus, I think I saw him near Sydney's hospital when we drove home." I looked at Sydney. "When was that?"

"After the first note, on the way home," she said, new concern on her face.

"Yes," I said. "In a black Ford truck, I think." My recollection was still faint.

"Where?" Lan asked.

"Going into Raymond's on Fair Oaks."

"Okay. And why do you suspect Martinez?" Lan continued.

Jesse was about to jump in to tell her about Martinez's wife, but this time I raised a finger to stop him, thinking the information would be better coming from me. Given Manny's position and ties to the department, the cops weren't going to believe he'd be a suspect, but maybe I could get them to listen to the evidence.

"We just learned that the councilman's wife got an undefined consultant gig with one of Luis Ochoa's competitors, Barrio Homes. Martinez didn't mention it at dinner, but a cushy deal like that could present a potential financial interest in the bid outcome. The kidnapper said he'd taken Joey to distract someone and give someone else a leg up. That someone could be Luis, and the someone else could be Barrio. That would provide Martinez with plenty of motive for the kidnapping, possibly for Tony's murder after it failed, maybe for stalking Sydney or getting someone to stalk her, and he certainly had the opportunity to attack me from behind tonight." But so did James.

The detectives listened but had stopped taking notes. They looked at each other at the mention of Martinez and his wife. Maybe the scenario I'd painted was a bit too much for them to believe.

Lan confirmed my suspicion. "That's a pretty heavy accusation."

"It's all I've got," I said. The more I thought about it, the more my theory made sense. He had a messier—but closer—connection than James.

"Motive and opportunity," I repeated. "They're both there." So much for the Boy Scout. "Martinez might not be able to be everywhere, but he was definitely near me tonight."

"So was Mr. Ochoa," Conroy said. We all turned to him. "Wasn't he?"

What? Luis couldn't be involved, could he? My head hurt some more at the thought.

"Has anyone talked to him?" Conroy asked.

"I did," Sydney answered. She frowned and fidgeted with her stethoscope, likely at the thought of Luis hurting me. Jesse and Dad looked at each other with similar concern.

"When was that?" Conroy asked.

"When I was looking for Yolanda," Sydney said, her voice steadier now. "But he just said they'd left the restaurant at the same time, and I haven't called him back."

"Leave that to us," Conroy told her. And to the rest of us, he added, "Got that? No contact until after we speak with him."

We all nodded, but I couldn't let it go.

"How about Martinez or Leon James?" I asked. *Were they really going to pin this on Luis?* I wasn't sure what to believe anymore but didn't want to believe it was him. It had to be Martinez or Leon.

"We'll have to check the councilman's whereabouts before questioning him about Sonia Martinez's job," Conroy said, much to my relief. "You understand that. We'll see about Leon James too."

"Of course," I agreed. He knew Martinez's wife's name. That's why they'd stopped taking notes. They'd already made the connection Jesse had.

"And, now, will you leave this alone and let us work it?" Lan said. She looked at me closely. The ER doctor came in and Sydney pulled him aside. "Well?" Lan tried again.

I must have been tired, because I nodded sleepily. The ER doctor chimed in.

"Are you done here, detectives?" His voice made it clear they should be. "We need to get my patient home to rest." The police left, and I wondered if Sydney had prompted him to say that. Then he came to my bedside.

"You really should rest and leave the police work to the cops," he said. The sting of his words surprised me. I was about to protest but stopped when I caught Sydney's eyes, half-apologizing, half-pleading with me not to argue. She'd probably told him to tell me to rest, but I was sure he'd added the cop reference on his own. Fine, I let it pass.

"Can I go home now?" I looked past him and at Sydney.

"Yes, as soon as they finish the paperwork," Sydney said. "I'll check with Chief Johnson again, see if he received authorization to have someone watch our place." That further explained her concern. She was worried that someone would come after me—us—at home. Then I remembered my conversation with Carmen.

"Wait, Carmen was going to get us bodyguards. They were supposed to call before coming over." I reached for my phone to check for messages. Sure enough, there were two calls from a number I didn't recognize. I was about to dial the number when my phone buzzed in my hand. It was Carmen. I showed Sydney the caller ID.

"*Comadre*, the security guy I got you is trying to get ahold of you," she said without a greeting. "Where are you?"

"I'm at White Memorial." Another wave of exhaustion hit me. Sydney must have noticed, because she reached for my phone, which I gratefully handed to her.

"Carmen, I'll fill you in, but right now, your *comadre* needs to rest," she said. She waved to the ER doctor on her way out of the room. Before following her, Dad and Jesse hugged me gently. Jesse said he'd stay with us tonight.

"Me too," Dad said. He kissed me on the forehead through my bandage before he and Jesse stepped out. The ER doctor took my vitals before leaving himself. I was about to doze off again when Sydney returned.

"Hey," she said, kissing me where my dad had.

"What did Carmen say?"

"She has a couple of guards lined up, but one is on another assignment until Friday. Fortunately, Chief Johnson got authority for Duc. The bodyguard can tag-team with him for now. Carmen's having him come over now. He'll escort us home." She lifted the thin hospital blanket and placed it over me before turning off the light. "I'll get more blankets. Try to sleep while we wait."

I did just that, grateful to Sydney and Carmen for taking charge of things, and confident that this was almost over.

My discharge paperwork took forever. Before it was ready, the bodyguard arrived—a beefy thirty-something who looked like a bouncer: tight black T-shirt, colorful tattoos, and all. His T-shirt was emblazoned with white lettering—"KICKING ASS FOR THE WORKING CLASS." I shook a hand attached to a red-and-green dragon wrapped around the biggest forearm I'd seen this side of Popeye. Kyle McCormick introduced himself and didn't seem to mind my taking in his appearance. He had the longish, sun-bleached blond hair of a surfer and an easy, toothy smile under reflective-orange sunglasses. I wondered about the indoor sunglasses, likely an affectation of some kind. Maybe one I should adopt with my black eye—not that it would disguise the mummy bandage around my head, but maybe I'd look cool just the same. He listened to Sydney's description of the arrangement with her hospital's security. Kyle said he'd take first watch and work out a schedule with Duc until his partner was available.

"Nice T-shirt," I said. "Just learned about the UE recently." He gave me that toothy smile again.

"Gramps was big in the UE back in the day. Gave me this T-shirt a long time ago, but I found it the other day. Glad I did before it doesn't fit anymore."

I doubted it wouldn't fit anytime soon. He obviously worked out.

With that, we headed home in a three-car caravan. I rode with Kyle, Sydney taking the lead in her car and Jesse and Dad following us in Jesse's car. Sydney had vetoed getting my car from the restaurant, saying it could wait because I wasn't going anywhere anyway. When we got home, Sydney took Kyle to introduce him to Duc, who was already parked across the street.

Dad and Jesse bickered over who'd get the couch. I was glad Dad finally agreed to let Jesse take first watch while he took the guest room. He looked more tired than he'd admit. Sydney returned with Kyle and said Duc had insisted on standing watch overnight.

"He said he slept most of the afternoon to prepare," Sydney said. "He's probably too hyped up to sleep tonight anyway, with all that soda and candy in his car." She shook her head. I imagined the young security guard excited about his new assignment, recalling my own first overnight stakeout. Mine hadn't been as exciting as I'd expected. I hoped the same for him.

CHAPTER TWENTY-ONE

Wednesday, 3:23 a.m.

I woke from another nightmare, sitting up and looking around in a panic.

"Who's there?" I said to a billowing curtain. Sydney reached out to hold me, saying something and repeating herself until I looked at her.

"It's just a nightmare."

It took me a moment to steady my breathing, my heart pounding.

"It was warm, so I cracked the window open," she said, getting up. "No one can get up here. It's just the curtain moving. Look." And with that she closed the window.

"Damn. When is this shit gonna stop? Maybe I do need a *limpia*." A spiritual cleansing couldn't hurt.

"You took a blow to the head and have a concussion." That explained the headache. She returned to bed and eyed me closely in the red glow of the alarm clock.

"That's what the nightmare was about. Someone attacked me. But who?"

"You had a suspicion last night, but right now I think it may be best to relax. You really need your rest to recover. Two blows to the head in less than a week are not good for anyone, not even someone as hard-headed as you. Promise me you'll try to go back to sleep?" She held my face with one hand, stroking my cheek with her thumb. "I mean it, love. I've seen enough head injuries to know that this is a critical time for you. Promise me," she said again.

"Okay, I promise." I took my time easing back against the pillow to avoid increasing the throbbing in my head. But I promised mostly because I was still trying to remember what had happened. I didn't want to worry her with my lack of recollection. Then it came to me. Slowly. I'd been at dinner with Luis Ochoa and Manny Martinez. Leon James was at the restaurant too. After dinner, I was hit from behind as I approached my car. Everything went black. Seeing stars is a myth.

And there was something else about Martinez and James. What was it? I suspected them, but why? I went back to sleep thinking I'd figure it out in the morning.

When I woke up again, groggy from sleep, or drugs—I wasn't sure which—Sydney was texting in a chair she'd brought in and positioned next to our bed. This time I remembered where I was but had no idea how long I'd slept.

"What time is it?" I asked with a dry mouth.

"Just before noon." She handed me a bottle of water. "You may be a little slow to move for a bit. The sedative will take a while to get out of your system. The water will help." I drank almost half of it in one gulp, her words registering.

"Noon? You gave me a sedative?"

"You needed to rest." She got up and looked into my eyes.

"Stop looking at me like they're changing color or something."

She ignored me and took my pulse. "How's the headache?"

"Just a mild throbbing now. Not painful, much. And I'm starving." My stomach growled as if on cue. "Has to be a good sign, right?"

"Sure. Drink more water first."

"That smells good," I said, sniffing the air after swallowing some water. "You cooked?"

"No, Jesse did."

"Jesse's here?" I brightened, more at the thought of breakfast than my brother.

"Spent the night. So did your dad, but he went to work a while ago. Told him not to worry with Kyle here, but you should call him to let him know you're okay." Then, to the question on my face, she added, "The bodyguard Carmen got for us?"

"Got it," I said, remembering.

"Do you remember what happened?"

"Someone hit me on the head," I said, touching my bandage.

Sydney recounted our conversations of the night before and after my nightmare.

"I didn't want to ask you about your nightmare last night because you really needed to rest."

"There wouldn't be much to say. I was attacked in a dark place, but I couldn't see my attacker. I think I was reliving last night," I said, as much to calm her fears as to check my recollection. It did feel familiar, but no new information came from it. No new information came from the previous dream either, and I'd been attacked, so I tried harder. "I do get the feeling that I need to talk to Luis...and Carmen, about Martinez and James maybe." But I wasn't sure whether the feeling came from my dream or my recollection that Martinez's wife's consultant arrangement gave him a stronger motive than James.

"Detective Conroy said to leave any contact with Luis to him. I told Carmen about it last night. She was a bit concerned, but said she'd call Luis this afternoon to give the cops time to talk to him."

"What? She thinks Luis could have attacked me? Damn, if she does, I should too."

"No, it's not that. She just doesn't want to interfere with the police investigation since they're both still suspects in Tony's murder—according to the cops, anyway. Wanted him to be able to say truthfully that they hadn't spoken."

"Right." I stared into midspace. "It has to be Martinez." I knew it. But I had to find a way to prove it. I needed to find out more about him, but Sydney wouldn't leave my side if she thought I was rushing my recovery.

"I'll ask Jesse to put together a plate for you and we'll go downstairs," Sydney said.

When she stepped out, I called Sheila.

"Oh, honey," she said when I'd recounted what had happened. "I'm glad Sydney is there to keep an eye on you or you'd be running around to everyone's aggravation. Let me do that for you. How can I help?"

"I knew I could count on you. How about some research on Martinez and his wife? I know he has to be involved, but it would be great to find a paper trail connecting him to Tony and Rudy, or the developers."

"How about that Leon James guy?"

"I don't know, but any connection to him would be good to know about too."

"Well, you know Jane Stern offered to help with online research," she said, reminding me of our conversation at the Bradbury Building—at my new office. Now I wondered when I'd ever move in. "I'll poke around online, but I'll call her. She'll know more about that than I do." I'd forgotten about Jane's offer but was grateful for it now.

When Sydney returned, she frowned at my phone.

"It's Sheila. I'm not working, just asking her to do some research."

"Hi, Sheila," Sydney said, taking my phone. "Thanks for your help, but let's let her rest some more." Then, looking at me, she added, "Or I'll put her back in the hospital." She laughed softly, listening to Sheila's response. My heart warmed at her smile. I knew she must be tired.

"Really?" I said when she hung up without letting me say goodbye to Sheila.

She gave me her "Doctor knows best" look to stop any argument. I knew she was only trying to take care of me, so I let it go.

"No worries. I'm not running around on this today. Maybe tomorrow I can check in with Luis and Carmen. I do want to follow up on that feeling about talking to them. I figure it'll confirm our suspicions and maybe help the detectives."

"Maybe tomorrow. Let Sheila do the running around today. Let's go downstairs so you can eat."

I gave her no argument on that. Sydney walked down the stairs ahead of me, making sure I didn't rush. At the kitchen island, I dug into my *huevos con chorizo*. The scrambled egg with spicy Mexican sausage was the only thing in Jesse's culinary repertoire besides ramen. A good thing, because it was also my favorite breakfast. I held out a fork, offering some to Sydney, but she shook her head.

"I grabbed a bite while you slept. Now, if you're good and get some rest"—here she eyed my phone—"and eat, I might risk leaving you alone while I check in on the new resident." A twinge of guilt nagged at me. Sydney was a newly minted attending doctor, and while that gave her more flexibility, I knew she'd been on call and had to get one of her partners to cover for her while she took care of me.

"I'm sorry, love."

She waved a hand in dismissal.

"How's she doing?" Jesse asked Sydney.

"Hey, I'm right here," I said.

"Yeah, but I want the doctor's opinion. I know you'd say anything to get back out there."

He was right, so I let him and Sydney share thoughts on my condition.

"She looks better," Jesse continued.

"I feel better too," I said. I gave them an I'm-still-here wave that they both ignored.

"She'll be okay," Sydney said. "But only if she takes it easy." She eyed me again and looked around. "Where's Kyle?"

"Said he was going outside to do a circuit of the place. He liked my cooking." Jesse smiled.

The fog in my head started clearing, and I remembered Duc.

"Is Duc still out there too?" I asked.

"No. Kyle and I convinced him to go home and nap," Sydney said, rinsing what must have been Jesse and Kyle's dishes before putting them in the dishwasher.

"Didn't take much convincing," Jesse said. "Dude looked tired. Said he'd be back around three o'clock in case Syd wanted to make her rounds."

"I'll take him up on that only if you stay put," Sydney said to me. Then, to Jesse, she added, "She did have a nightmare last night at that time again."

"Yup," I said in response to Jesse's glance. Sydney's shoulders relaxed when I didn't discount the dream outright. We were still trying to figure out how to work with the juju. I repeated what I'd told Sydney about reliving the attack and feeling the need to talk to Luis and Carmen.

"I'd go with that, then," Jesse said, and I had to admit it felt good to have his confirmation, to be able to talk about this stuff without the walls I'd always thrown up before. Sydney then provided a litany of concussion side effects. I half listened as I ate. By the time I had used the last of my *tortilla* to wipe my plate clean, I'd resolved to get Martinez or James. I wasn't sure which or how, but I would.

Sydney went upstairs to shower, saying she hadn't wanted to wake me earlier. Then my phone buzzed with Sheila's name on the caller ID.

"Is it okay to talk, honey?" she asked. "I told Sydney I'd call back only if I had something important. You doing okay?"

"Sure. Dr. Ratched just went upstairs."

"Oh, she's only looking out for you."

"I know." I felt bad making Sydney out to be overbearing when she really wasn't. "She's been great. I just need to get back to work."

"Well, I have some interesting news for you to mull over while you wait."

"Oh? Let me put you on speaker so Jesse can hear." They greeted each other before Sheila got down to business.

"You guys know the *Boyle Heights Beat*?"

"Sure," I said. "The news site run by high school kids?" Jesse gave a thumbs-up, acknowledging his familiarity with it as well.

"That's the one. The USC School of Journalism sponsors them. Looks like a good program. Anyway, they have a story on Boyle Heights gentrification. The reporter asks about rumors of two developers merging—something about rebranding and going into big box retail and pedestrian malls. And guess who they're talking about."

"Barrio Homes?" Jesse and I said in unison.

"And Las Casas Builders."

I was all ears. Barrio Homes was the outfit that had hired Martinez's wife as a consultant, and Luis had mentioned both developers as competitors when we'd worked through kidnapping scenarios on Friday. *Was that only a few days ago?*

"Any confirmation from either organization?"

"Now, it wouldn't be just a rumor then, would it? But you never know. I'm sending you a link to the article now. We'll see if Jane finds anything else."

I opened the link. The merger was a question posed in the article. A simple "What if?" But Sheila was smart to catch it. I hoped Jane would get lucky too.

"Seems like a pretty big leap to rebrand and go from low-income housing to commercial development, don't you think?" I asked, looking to Jesse.

"You tell me," Sheila said while Jesse's eyes explored the ceiling, thinking.

"I wish we could ask Luis, but he's off-limits right now. It could mean that Martinez's prospects would improve significantly if the merger happened. I wonder if that's why his wife took the position she did." I remembered Luis and Jesse agreeing, during a late-night bull session, that Las Casas Builders had the better know-how but Barrio Homes had the stronger political connections. They called them "Barrio Homies," a tongue-in-cheek reference to their founders.

"I don't know who benefits, but we'd better let the cops know about the rumor," Jesse suggested.

"Good idea," Sydney said from the stairs, freshly showered. I thanked Sheila for the information, and she promised to call back with anything else she or Jane dug up.

"What rumor?" Sydney asked.

We filled her in on the merger rumor Sheila had uncovered. Jesse squinted, thinking again before speaking.

"I hadn't heard about it, but I don't know. It would be an interesting marriage, that's for sure. Can't imagine Casas wanting to dirty their hands with the Homies, unless the OGs at Casas are reverting to their old ways."

"Would Martinez's involvement help smooth things for a merger?" I asked. "Would he benefit?"

"Well, now that his wife is with Barrio Homes, I'd say yes," Jesse said. "But maybe they brought her in to get Martinez to help make the merger happen, to apply pressure on Casas. Maybe they're struggling and looking for a bailout with a merger, with Martinez's help. That would be their MO, dipping into every funding source possible."

"We need to talk to Luis." In my eagerness, I'd forgotten that Sydney was listening. But maybe if I got Jesse on my side, and the two of us went together, she could be convinced. "He'll know more about Martinez's connections to the developers."

Jesse agreed, but Sydney shook her head.

"No. You're going to stay home and rest," she said, vetoing the idea. This wasn't her doctor voice, but her I'm-your-wife-and-I'm-putting-my-foot-down voice. Then she turned to Jesse. "You can stay as long as you want, but I can tell I'll have to be here to make sure she doesn't run off somewhere."

"Okay, tomorrow, then," he said. "And I'll stay overnight again, in case anyone comes around."

I called my dad at work to let him know I was okay. Sydney was right that he'd worry otherwise.

"How's your head, *mija*?" he asked.

"Not bad, Dad. Not much of a headache anymore. I slept until noon today, so I'm sure that helped. And we have that bodyguard Carmen got us until they catch the stalker and whoever hit me." I wanted to put his mind at ease. "Jesse's staying with us again tonight too."

"*Que bueno.*" He sounded relieved, more about the bodyguard than Jesse, I was sure. "But you still be careful. And let me know if you need anything."

"I will, Dad. Love you." It was our normal sign-off, but I choked up a little hearing his response before hanging up. I knew he'd been worried and feeling a bit powerless. I hoped the news about the bodyguard would lessen his worry.

But my own anxiety crept up again, wondering why Kyle hadn't returned from his review of the property. *Where was he?* I got up and looked out the living room window, trying not to show too much concern, but Sydney picked up on it.

"Any sign of Kyle?" She came up next to me and put a hand on my hip.

"Nope." I welcomed the calming touch, but it didn't seem to have its usual effect.

"I'll go out and take a look," Jesse said, heading toward the door.

"Hold on." Sydney stopped him. "Let's go together. And maybe we should go out the garage instead." Turning to me she added, "We'll come back around to the front door. Don't go anywhere." I could tell she was trying not to sound nervous, but I knew that full-alert look from her Taekwondo competitions.

"I'll just go get my gun," I said, pointing upstairs. *Why hadn't I done that earlier?* Normally, Sydney would have stopped me. She had a healthy respect for firearms from her military days, but she saw enough results of their misuse in the ER and didn't want one of her own in the house. She said she could always use one of mine, a Glock or Beretta, like the ones I'd used on the force.

I'd put on my shoulder holster and had just picked up the Glock, checking the magazine, when a sudden chill slithered up my neck. I shivered involuntarily, the hairs on my arms at attention. Looking out the bedroom window, I saw nothing amiss, but every muscle in my body jumped when I heard the front door slam. I went into full alert myself, slowly descending the stairs, ready to fire. Before I had a full view of the downstairs, I heard Sydney's voice.

"He's gone!"

"What do you mean, he's gone?" I said, holstering my gun and holding down a bit of bile.

"No sign of..." My phone buzzed in my pocket and I answered it before Sydney could finish. My stomach almost lurched at the sight of Jesse running around checking the locks on all the windows, but I was able to hold down my food when I heard Kyle's voice on my phone.

"Don't let anyone in," he said in a hushed tone.

"Where are you?" I put the phone on speaker.

"Up the street, following some muddy footprints, but the mud ran out. I'm going to do a wider circuit. Hold tight and stay inside. Back in a bit." He hung up.

"We saw them too," Jesse said. "Just outside the kitchen window."

It hadn't rained recently, but the HOA's sprinklers had run the night before. We'd convinced the property manager to let them run an extra few minutes for a good soak to keep the skunks away. It worked. Sometimes. But the overflow made a muddy mess outside our kitchen. We tolerated it because we never walked there, and the skunks seemed to avoid the area— at least until water restriction days, when they'd come rooting around for bugs in the grass. Now I preferred them to a stalker.

"Shit." No wonder Jesse had checked the window locks. I took a deep breath to help me think straight. "The sprinklers run at eight thirty. Could have been any time after that if it's still muddy out there."

"It is," Sydney said, "but some of the footprints on the lawn still looked wet."

"How about the sidewalk?"

"Didn't get a good enough look. We ran back around to make sure you were okay first. Kyle said to stay inside. Best we do that and wait for him."

I agreed silently and was about to run my hands through my hair but stopped at the bandage on my forehead. Instead, I held the back of my neck, my eyes on the ceiling, frustration replacing the anxiety I'd felt upstairs.

"And I'm sure as hell not going anywhere today," she said.

"Me neither," Jesse added.

We all looked at each other, not having much else to say.

Sydney broke the spell, directing us to the sofa and armchair in the living room to sit.

"You wanna get the Beretta from the safe?" I asked Sydney. She hesitated a couple of seconds. Normally, she would have dismissed the suggestion outright, but she didn't leave my side on the sofa.

"Let's see what Kyle finds out."

We all returned to our own thoughts. *When was this going to stop? How could we have not detected him this morning?* Sydney must have been thinking the same thing.

"Maybe we shouldn't have told Duc to go home," she said.

"Naw," Jesse said. "He would've fallen asleep in his car if he'd stayed much longer."

"What time did he leave?" I asked. Jesse turned to Sydney, who responded.

"About eight. I'm sure he would have seen anyone last night. Must have happened this morning."

My phone buzzed again. Kyle wanted to let me know he was outside so as not to startle us. Jesse got up to open the door for him.

"I'm sorry," he said when he came in. "I should've done a circuit when we came out to talk to Duc. Won't make that mistake again." He went on to explain that the mud prints were dry on the sidewalk, and some of them had been stepped on by dogs or dog walkers, meaning that they had been left there earlier in the morning, perhaps soon after Duc left.

"I talked to a lady from the next complex over. She said she saw a jogger in a black hoodie around eight thirty."

"Did she get a good look at him?" I asked hopefully.

"Said she didn't. Or maybe didn't want to get involved. She did say he didn't look familiar, and that he was wearing a black baseball cap."

We all looked at each other. The guy in the hospital video wore that outfit.

"But he didn't leave a calling card this time?" I asked.

"None that I could see, but I was focused on the footprints. Let me check again in case there are any markings outside the window." Sydney and I watched Jesse go with Kyle, then she turned to me.

"Maybe whoever it was saw Kyle in here and ran away."

"Maybe. I'm more concerned that no calling card means he really meant to do harm this time. I actually hope they find something." I hesitated before continuing, "You know, when I was getting my gun, I got a little creeped out, goose bumps and all—not a good sign."

"How do you feel now?"

"Pissed. This fucker is disrupting our lives. I want to get him!"

Sydney placed her arm around my shoulders but wouldn't offer any false reassurance. We sat silently until Sydney got up to open the door when Kyle and Jesse returned.

"Nothing," my brother said.

"Looks like maybe he got spooked," Kyle said, holding up his phone with a picture he'd taken. "The footprints come directly to the window, and it appears one foot slipped back toward the wall as he rushed away."

I glanced at my wife.

"Sydney thinks he may have seen you in here and cut his losses."

Kyle shrugged before suggesting we inform the cops. I wasn't sure we needed to, but Sydney convinced me to at least text Detective Lan with the photos Kyle had taken.

Jesse and I settled in the living room. We were both antsy, feeling confined, unable to leave or do much work as long as Sydney was around. I shared with Jesse the feeling I'd had upstairs, but he didn't have anything more to offer than Sydney had.

Duc arrived at three o'clock as promised. He was sorry he'd missed the morning's excitement and said there was no way he'd missed someone approaching the side of our townhouse while he was there. He walked the perimeter with Kyle and took his position across the street when Sydney told him she wouldn't be going into work.

"The new resident will be fine," she said, stalling. Guilt gripped my chest again when she avoided eye contact. She did that when she didn't want to reveal what she was thinking, but it only confirmed what I believed. A part of me loved her lack of guile, but the rest of me struggled to control my guilt. I tried to let it go, my knee bobbing up and down uselessly, mostly because I didn't know what to say.

Jesse ordered pizza, then turned on HGTV—good, mindless therapy. Plus, neither Sydney nor I could stand watching the news nowadays with all the coverage of hateful national politics.

"Is it okay if Carmen comes over?" Jesse asked as Kyle's phone rang. The bodyguard moved to the front door, and Jesse continued, "I almost forgot she called earlier to see how you were doing. Didn't want to bother you two, but I told her—"

He hadn't finished when, sure enough, Kyle opened the door, recognizing Carmen. The call must've been Duc announcing her arrival.

"Thanks for being here, Kyle," Carmen said when she walked in with Joey. Then she came to me with open arms. "*¡Comadre!*"

"Are you okay, *Nina*?" Joey asked. He stopped himself from hugging me, staring at my bandaged head.

"I'm good, *mijo*." I brought him into my arms. "We ordered pizza. Wanna help Sydney with plates?" He skipped into the kitchen and chatted with Sydney as they set the table and a TV tray in front of cartoons for him.

"I can't believe the *cabrón* didn't walk you to your car," Carmen said in a lower voice, following me to the dining room table. "I called him and let him have it. But he said he didn't know you'd been hurt until the detectives showed up to question him. He's coming over to apologize."

"I'll order more pizza." Jesse got back on the phone. Kyle took a chair near the door, trying to be unobtrusive.

"Well, we did want to talk to Luis about a theory." I filled her in on what we'd learned about Martinez's wife and the two rival developers.

Carmen let out a low whistle. "*Chingado*. How do those *vendidos* sleep at night? They'd sell out their own mother to make a buck."

"Thing is," I said. "Leon James was at the restaurant too. Martinez spoke with him before I got there and after I left. Wanted to ask for your take on that too."

"And that's not all," Jesse said. "We had a prowler early this morning." In response to Carmen's raised eyebrows, he added, "Muddy footprints outside the kitchen window and up the sidewalk."

Kyle's phone rang again. This time he was on full alert and got up quickly to peek out the window. Sydney was at his side in an instant. I was glad for the extra security, but he was making me nervous—everyone else too, from what I could tell, all eyes turning to the door.

"Two men approaching. Pizza guy too," he said.

"Luis and Andy," Sydney said to sighs of relief. She opened the door and greeted them with hugs before paying the pizza man. They helped her carry the boxes to the dining room table, and Sydney took a couple of slices to Joey, who ate with gusto after hugging his dad and his *nino*. Jesse took a plate out to Duc. The rest of us sat at the dining room table, but Kyle hung back, declining any food. His muscled body told me he never ate pizza.

Luis and Andy glanced at him, curious, while Carmen made the introductions and explained, "No one will mess with Yolanda and Sydney with bodyguards around." The men nodded appreciatively before turning back to me. Jesse returned and Kyle locked the door behind him.

"I'm so sorry, Yolanda," Luis said. He looked genuinely chagrined. "Carmen's right. I should've walked you to your car."

"And be a second casualty?" I asked. "Thanks, but none of us had any idea."

"But we do have an idea about who might be behind it all," Jesse offered. He looked at me to continue. After we all sat and Sydney had distributed slices on paper plates, I repeated what we'd learned about Martinez's wife and the merger rumors.

"No way," Luis said. He and Andy shook their head in unison. "Manny would never do something so stupid."

"You give him too much credit," Carmen chimed in, voicing my own thoughts.

"How about Sonia's job?" Jesse asked.

"Naw. It's just a job," Luis said, but he furrowed his brows and glanced at Andy as if wondering why he hadn't known about the connection. Andy shrugged, arching his eyebrows, admitting he didn't know either.

"What else don't you know about your buddy?" Carmen asked.

"I don't know." Luis looked pensive. "It has to be Rudy behind the stalking and the attack. He's still out there somewhere. But now I know why the cops were asking me about Manny."

Good. Lan and Conroy had not dismissed my theory about the councilman after all.

"I'm glad they're onto him," I said. "Could Manny have been prowling around here this morning?"

"What?" Luis objected. "No way! I don't see it. Manny's a good guy, really."

"Why do you defend him?" Carmen said. "He's just another ribbon-cutter." She looked from Luis to Jesse for support, but Jesse wasn't about to get between them. He stuck a chunk of pizza crust into his mouth, chewing and cocking his head to the side in a noncommittal gesture.

"You know, Luis," I suggested. "Politicians sometimes have more to lose than the rest of us—power, prestige…"

"They're not all stereotypes," Luis said. "I've known Manny since we were kids."

"People change," Carmen said, a twinge of bitterness in her voice.

"What I don't get," Andy interjected, playing peacemaker, "is how Martinez would be involved with Tony. The kidnapping was so heavy-handed."

"People have done worse for less," I said. "Greed is a powerful motivator."

Luis still shook his head, so I turned to him.

"I know you said Tony stood to win no matter who won the Metro bid. But what if he was in it for himself *and* Martinez?"

The more we talked, the more convinced I became that Martinez was our man. And the more defensive Luis became about his friend. I could see why. He'd been betrayed by Tony, and now Manny was keeping information from him about his wife's job with a competitor. It had to be hard for him to accept that his friends were not as close as he'd thought.

"Maybe we should all step back from existing relationships to remain objective," Sydney tried.

"I appreciate that, but it still doesn't change who he is," Luis maintained. Andy had returned to sitting quietly, thinking before he spoke.

"Doesn't it make more sense that Rudy's behind the attack?" he suggested. He leaned forward. "Don't they say the simplest theory is usually the best?"

"Occam's Razor," Jesse said. He brightened at the scientific theory that the simplest possible explanation was usually the most accurate.

"Fine," I said before Jesse launched into a lecture. "Then we have two suspects. Three if we count Leon James. For all we know, they could all be working together." I wasn't letting go of the Martinez angle. Andy sat back, thinking again. And to my surprise, Jesse didn't expound on the theory. Instead he turned pensive, holding his chin and staring with knitted brows at his remaining pizza crust.

"Well, I hate to break up this party," Sydney said, intending to do just that. "But our patient here needs to get some rest." I hadn't thought about it, but as much as I felt like we were making headway, I welcomed the time-out. It was still early, but I was feeling a bit tired. We all said our goodbyes and I gave Joey an extra-long hug. I smiled when he held me a bit tighter than usual. After they left, Jesse helped us clean up.

"You know, guys," he said, putting the last of the paper plates in the trash. "I got this weird feeling tonight." Sydney and I both stopped to listen. "You know how I got the heebie-jeebies about Tony?"

"Yeah," we said in unison.

"Well, I just got the same feeling about Andy right after you mentioned the prowler. Isn't that weird? I mean, he's a friend and I like the guy, but there was something about him tonight." That explained why Jesse had stopped talking after Andy had brought us back to Rudy. But I didn't know about Luis's best friend and *compadre* as a suspect.

"Andy? He's such a mensch. I don't see it, but…Hold on."

I went upstairs to get the picture of the stalker. I couldn't see Andy in it, but I couldn't rule him out either. When I showed it to Sydney and Jesse, they thought the same.

"You know," Jesse said, "the guy in the picture has his chin almost to his chest. Could be hiding a beard, not just his face."

"I don't know," I said. "But I don't know who to trust anymore."

"And damn." Jesse looked from me to Sydney and back. "That would mean strike three for Luis's friends: Tony, Manny, and Andy." He jerked his thumb, mimicking a baseball umpire calling an out.

"If that's the case," Sydney suggested, "Luis's going to have to do some serious soul searching. It'll definitely make it harder to rebuild his relationship with Carmen. I'd have a tough time trusting anyone after that much betrayal."

"And Carmen will have trouble with his incredibly bad judgment." I agreed with Sydney's assessment but knew Carmen was going to have more trouble than Luis. "I don't want to jump to conclusions, but it may be worth looking into Andy's whereabouts last night. He's Luis's best friend and sidekick, but he wasn't with him at the restaurant."

"Do you think Luis could be involved too?" Jesse asked. "I mean, not with the kidnapping, but with Tony and Rudy somehow? The cops did question him again."

"The cops are focused on a motive for a murder. A kidnap victim's parents would be obvious suspects. But what about a motive for the kidnapping itself? They'd all have to be in on the same, or related, conspiracies. I just don't see it. Tony was trying to distract Luis, and I don't see Luis being involved with his rival developers. Doesn't make sense."

"Could Andy be involved with them?" Sydney asked.

"I don't know." I tried to wrap my mind around the possibility when my phone buzzed, still in vibrate mode. It was Detective Lan. I turned on the speaker and sat on a stool at the kitchen island.

"Thought you'd want to know, Rudy Fuentes was apprehended in an alley behind a bar in Lincoln Heights. From the looks of it, he'd been on a multiday bender."

"Does that mean he was too drunk to stalk Sydney?" I asked. "Or attack me? Or prowl around this morning?"

"You know we can't say for sure. But he was in pretty bad shape from what I hear. He could've left the first note, but I doubt he would've been unnoticed at the crowded deli where your wife got the second one. And you probably would've smelled him long before he got to you in that alley last night. No telling if he was at your place this morning, but he was in pretty bad shape, so I kinda doubt it."

"Hey, thanks." I appreciated the detail. She didn't have to provide it, and Conroy probably wouldn't have.

"No problem. Thought you and your wife would want to know. There's probably someone still out there gunning for you, so you'll want to keep your guard up." I glanced at Kyle, glad Carmen had gotten him for us, but I still didn't feel safe. Sure, Rudy remained a suspect, but now two others, Martinez and Andy, loomed larger. And I still couldn't rule out Leon James.

"I have some info for you too," I offered. "You know that developer Sonia Martinez started working for? Barrio Homes?"

"Yeah."

"There's a rumor that they may be merging with Las Casas Builders. I'll forward the article that mentions it. Means Manny Martinez may be more vested in their success than we'd originally thought. Do you have anything else on him yet?"

"That I can't tell you," Lan said. "I probably shouldn't tell you this much, but know that we're working on whatever we can find on him."

Thank god.

"And, Ávila?"

"Yeah?"

"You may want to stay away from this for a while." I sensed her hesitating. "Focus on your recovery." There was something she wasn't saying.

"Come on, Lan. What is it? I can take it."

"Well…the guys don't like you getting in the way. You kinda showed us up on the kidnapping."

"And they think I'll do it again?"

"It's not that simple. They're concerned that if something happens to you, the department will take a hit in the press."

"What?" I raised my voice and retriggered more head pounding. "They're more worried about their image than catching this guy?"

Sydney placed her hand on my thigh, our universal sign for *lower your voice*. I knew she didn't want me getting excited.

"They're worried about both," Lan said. "You know that."

"No, I don't." I strained to keep my voice down. "Shit, I can't believe it."

"I wasn't supposed to tell you any of this. Please don't make things worse. We'll take any leads from you, but let us work them. That's what this call was supposed to be about. Trying to get you to pass on any leads and limit your activity on this case—for your own good. And the department's."

"Listen, I appreciate the call. I do. But I'm not gonna stand down. I'll share whatever I have, but you have to promise me one thing."

"What's that?"

"Don't ask how I get some of this information."

"Okay…" Lan sounded unsure of what she was committing to.

"I have one more item for you," I said.

"Shoot."

"Andy Stewart. I think he may be involved." I looked from Jesse to Sydney and back.

"Luis Ochoa's partner?"

"Yes. Don't ask me how, but you may want to look into any ties he may have with the developers or Tony. Maybe look for muddy shoes too."

"You know I'll need a helluva lot more than that for a warrant."

"If I come up with anything myself, I'll let you know."

"Okay. I can't commit, but we'll keep that in mind."

"Thanks," I said. "And, Lan?"

"Yes?"

"You're a gem."

"Thanks. Take care of yourself."

We hung up and I looked from Jesse to Sydney.

"I don't know what triggered it, but I'm sure glad she's on our side," I said.

"I sense the beginning of a beautiful friendship." Sydney paraphrased *Casablanca* with a smile. "And you acted on the Andy thing." Her smile grew wider. Jesse wore a similar grin.

"I know. I can't believe I did that without any facts. An unsubstantiated allegation." I brought my hand to my mouth. A part of me felt bad for making it, but another part of me felt good for acting on the juju. "This is some weird shit. I should feel guiltier, but it just feels right. Is this the calm that *Nina* Mercedes mentioned?"

Jesse and Sydney looked at each other wordlessly, not knowing any more than I did.

Then I dialed Sheila, still on speaker, to see if Andy's name had come up in the research she and Jane were doing on Martinez. I described the call with Detective Lan.

"Uh-oh. Now we'd better find something on him. If it's there, rest assured we will, honey. You just follow Sydney's orders and get some rest. Right, Sydney?"

"Right. Maybe she'll listen more to you." Sydney glanced at me. I cringed a little, knowing she'd stayed home from work because of me and had to call in another chit with one of her partners, never a good thing for a new attending doctor. She stood after we'd hung up. "Okay, that's enough. You need to take a sleeping pill and get to bed."

"Don't think I'll need one, love. I'm pretty tired." Plus, I knew a sleeping pill would cloud my mind. I wanted to wake up fresh and able to work out how Martinez or Andy might be involved. I went to bed as ordered, without protesting that it was only eight o'clock. We offered Jesse the guest room, but he insisted on the sofa again so that he could be alert to the front door "in case Kyle needs help." I didn't know what he'd do if we had an intruder, but I was too tired to contemplate it. And I knew I'd sleep well with the extra security. Sydney asked if she should take Duc some coffee. I suggested something sweet like grapes or some of the leftover pizza. Sugar and carbs are better than liquid on a stakeout. As she put me to bed, Sydney seemed pensive.

"I'm glad you're considering Jesse's feelings about Andy," she said. "I think your mom would be happy to know you two are working together on this."

"Thanks, love. Don't think she'd be too happy about the juju, but I think my *nina* was right. Sheila too. Good detective work includes using your gut too."

"Good." She kissed me when I got in bed. "Baby steps." With that, she left the room.

I figured she meant I was accepting the juju more. I still wasn't sure how useful it would be, but my last thought before closing my eyes was that my *nina* was right. Maybe I had missed something by not listening more to my gut, psychic or not.

CHAPTER TWENTY-TWO

Thursday, 2:30 a.m.

I was wide awake. Sydney slept soundly next to me, but I had gone to bed too early. I got up and put on my gray flannel robe, looking out the window at a full moon. It shined brightly in the cloudless sky, casting charcoal shadows on the deck. The community pool in the distance shimmered like silver mercury in the light breeze. But the clear night didn't mirror my brain, where jumbled thoughts, facts, and hunches loomed frustratingly large.

I needed to think, so I headed downstairs, stepping carefully through the living room so as not to wake Jesse and Kyle. Jesse slept soundly on the sofa, but Kyle sat quietly still in the dark near the kitchen. I stopped short, creeped out at first, but then realized he sat with a full view of the deck and the front door.

"Hi," I whispered. He turned up his chin in greeting.

"Want some light? It won't bother him." I pointed my own chin at Jesse.

"No thanks. My eyes would have to adjust if I had to go outside. Better this way." His rationale increased my confidence in him. He knew what he was doing.

"Help yourself to anything in here." I stepped into the kitchen where the moonlight streamed through the sliding doors. I pulled out a Romeo and Julietta cigarillo and poured Kahlúa and milk into a highball over ice, stirring with my finger before sucking it clean. Heading out to the deck, I raised my glass to an impassive Kyle. He followed me out to the deck and looked over the low privacy wall to the walkway below. We were above ground level, unlike the kitchen window, but he wasn't taking any chances and I was grateful for his caution. He went back inside to give me some privacy, but I saw him move his chair so that he could keep an eye on me. I raised my glass to him again before sitting down.

Stretching out on a lounge chair, I moistened the cigarillo and spun it slowly between my thumb and index finger while holding a lighter to one end. My dad had taught me how to prepare a cigar before bringing it to your mouth and lighting it with a few pulls. I figured the same went for cigarillos. I took a sip of my drink with a taste of the cigarillo and sat back, mesmerized by the glow of the full moon and its crisp shadows. The airplanes on approach to LAX lined up like stars in a Southern California galaxy.

In my mind I catalogued all the information I knew—the verifiable, fact-based information first. Joey is kidnapped to distract Luis from the deadline he has on a development project. The kidnapper admits to working with Luis's friend, Tony Gonzalez, a union leader. Tony and his sidekick Rudy both disappear after we rescue Joey, and then Tony turns up dead in Griffith Park, possibly from a blow to the chest and a weakened aorta. Carmen, a black belt in Taekwondo, and Luis, a former amateur boxer, are taken in for questioning and released. Someone caught on video, who limps like Rudy but could be hiding a beard like Andy's, stalks and threatens Sydney to warn me off the case. Over dinner, I meet with Luis and Manny Martinez, who is Luis's friend from his boxing days. Leon James, Carmen's rival union boss, is there too, and talks to Manny. Martinez is linked to one of Luis's developer rivals now that the councilman's wife has a cushy job with them. The developers are rumored to be working on a merger. After my dinner meeting, I'm attacked from behind and left unconscious. A prowler comes around after I get home. Then Rudy turns up after a multiday bender. *Did Rudy kill Tony? Did he stalk Sydney? Did he attack me? Did he come around here in the morning? Or was it Martinez? Or James?* All three could have had the opportunity. All three could have had financial motives. *Were they working together?*

So far, most of the facts, or what I had of them, pointed to Luis's friends, which brought me to Jesse's intuition about Andy. And Luis? Could he and Andy be in on this together? My personal feelings for them said no, but my training said I couldn't rule it out. I was about to start considering all the non-factual, woo-woo information when the sliding door opened. Sydney, in her red terry cloth robe, joined me on the deck. I put out the cigarillo and sipped the last of my Kahlúa. She frowned and shook her head at both.

"It helps me think," I said.

"Babe, are you serious?" Then, containing herself, she said in a harsh whisper, "You've just had a concussion. You were hospitalized, for Pete's sake! What makes you think you can have alcohol—and smoke, of all things?" She sounded tired. I was about to tell her I felt fine and that one doesn't inhale cigarillo smoke, which I only had a few times a year anyway, but her tone made me think better of it. She'd been looking after me, worried enough to miss work, and now I was making her worry more. I felt small.

"I'm sorry, love. Really, I didn't mean to make you worry." I felt like crap and probably showed it, because she kind of accepted my apology.

"Fine, no refills." She brought her arms across her chest, her lips tight, still not happy.

"Okay, Doctor," I said. We didn't argue much, but when we did, we both wanted to move on quickly. Our friends thought we argued more in private, but what was the point? Wasted energy, Sydney called it. I had to agree.

"Well, what did it help you think?"

"Come sit with me." I patted the lounge chair next to me. The cushion was slightly damp from the night air. "I'd like to run it by you." Sydney tightened the sash around her waist and sat cross-legged, facing me. I listed the facts as I knew them first.

"Then we get to the juju stuff. It's all a jumble. Some of it makes sense only after the fact, and some of it doesn't make sense at all. I don't see how I can rely on any of it other than as minor 'gut feelings.'" I made air quotes.

"Maybe that's all they're supposed to be."

"Maybe that's all they *can* be," I agreed. "First, we have my dream about Joey, and the anxiety and vertigo I feel about it. Jesse has similar feelings and appears to see, or feel, what Joey feels—the fear, the UFW flag—again, after the fact." Sydney made a small sound of assent, so I continued, "Then we have my dream about the *birria* place. No anxiety, no warning. In fact, it felt like it was supposed to be a helpful omen. Only, I end up being attacked. See what I mean? Unreliable."

"And what do you feel now?"

"Well, Dr. Freud." I leaned back on the lounge chair and crossed my ankles, exposing my highlighter-yellow, furry socks. Sexy. That's me. "I'm not feeling so hot about Andy at the moment, but that has more to do with Jesse's premonition about him—and Luis's bad track record when it comes to his friends. Now I think they both could be suspects too. But why? I don't see Luis having anything to do with kidnapping his own son. Could it have been part of a larger plan gone wrong? Like maybe Tony got too eager about something? I still can't get my arms around a motive for Andy either. I can see the money motive for Tony Gonzalez and his sidekick Rudy, and for Manny Martinez too. It usually comes down to that: money, or passion, or something like that, but I need to know more. I don't think that Tony acted alone. He had help from that Gary O'Neil guy. Maybe others too. Could James have anything to do with it? And there has to be some connection with Barrio Homes or Casas, but I'm missing that piece of the puzzle."

Sydney pulled up the collar of her robe and brought her bare feet under her.

"Temperature's dropping," she said. "Why don't we go inside. I'll make some chamomile."

I agreed it was getting a bit chilly, so I gathered my things and got up with her. From the kitchen, we could see rumpled sheets on the living room couch. Jesse had gotten up. Sydney placed tea bags in two mugs and filled them with water from the Insta-Hot tap. She passed one to me as Jesse approached from the hallway bathroom.

"Damn, you guys get up early. It's only three thirty." Then he looked over to me and asked, "Another dream?"

"Nope. Just thinking," I said.

Sydney raised her mug to Jesse and to a silent Kyle in offering, but both declined. I filled Jesse in on my current inventory of facts and juju clues.

"I don't get why Andy would be involved either," he said. "But I can't shake that feeling about him. I didn't get the same feeling with Luis."

"And where does that leave Manny Martinez?" I asked. "I don't like the guy, and he may have a financial motive with his wife working at Barrio Homes. And maybe more to lose as a politician if he's doing something slimy. He certainly had the opportunity to attack me Tuesday night. And for all we know, he could have been the prowler."

"Leon James could have too," Sydney said.

"Did Martinez know enough about me to stalk me too?" Sydney asked. Neither Jesse nor I knew the answer to that, but Martinez knew we were married from seeing us—more like avoiding us—at Ochoa family gatherings.

"Why don't we try sleeping on it some more." Sydney yawned. "I can still get a couple of hours before I need to get up." We all went back to bed, but I couldn't sleep. I spooned with Sydney for a bit, still trying to make up for upsetting her. Then, to let her sleep, I turned around, our backs leaning against each other. My mind continued to search for motives and connections among those I thought were involved, but I still hadn't come up with anything new by the time Sydney got up a little before her six o'clock alarm. I went downstairs to make some coffee, but Jesse had beaten me to it. This time, Kyle joined us. He took his black, no sugar, of course. We sipped in sleepy silence while Sydney showered for work.

"Okay, you three," she said when she came downstairs. "Can I count on you to stay put today? Duc's taking me to work before getting some shuteye." Then, to Kyle, she said, "You'll catch some Zs here, right?" Kyle shrugged, not seeming to need any sleep, but I hoped he'd at least nap a little. "Please make sure they don't go anywhere."

"No worries," I said. "I can make calls from here today."

Sydney checked the bandage on my head. "Leave this on today. How do you feel?"

"Good." I looked her in the eye, my own stinging from lack of sleep. But other than that and a slight headache, I did feel fine, and I wanted her to stop worrying about me.

"I'm gonna tell Chief Johnson that Kyle and his partner will have our security covered starting tomorrow," she said. *Was it almost Friday already?* Sydney tipped her head to Kyle, who did the same.

"Good idea. Duc's been great. I'll get him something nice for his trouble." When Sydney looked a warning at me, I added, "Not today."

"No worries, Syd," Jesse said. "She won't go anywhere. I'll make some *huevos con chorizo* for breakfast again. She won't be able to resist." He smiled back at me.

I wasn't hungry, but he was right about my favorite breakfast. When Duc came to the door, looking brighter than I would have after an all-night stakeout, I kissed Sydney goodbye. Then I called my dad before he left for work to let him know that I was fine, and that Jesse was still with me. Neither of us wanted him to worry.

Kyle joined us for breakfast. As we were finishing up, I got a text from Sheila. She had attached two photos of a document. The first picture was the title page of a "Memorandum of Understanding." The second was the signature page. It was signed about six months earlier by someone from Barrio Homes and someone from Las Casas Builders, as well as Andrew

Stewart and Antonio Gonzalez. *Wait. Andy and Tony? So, they are in this together. And the developers?* I got a sick feeling in my stomach at the thought of Andy having anything to do with Joey's kidnapping, but the nausea went away with an angry rush of adrenaline and blood that made my head throb at my wound.

"Holy shit!" Jesse said when I showed him the text. "I knew something was off about him!"

I called Sheila right away.

"I'm emailing the document to you now," she said without her usual friendly greeting. I put her on speaker. "I'm worried about you, Yolie. Isn't that Andrew guy the one I met at Joey's party?"

"Yes, Joey's godfather. I'm starting to worry too. But Jesse is with me, and Carmen got us a bodyguard, and the hospital assigned a guard to Sydney too. We're good."

"Oh, I'm so glad to hear that."

"So, how'd you get this?"

"Well, Jane did, but she said it might be better not to ask her how. So, I didn't. You know, gift horse and all." I could hear the smile in her voice and understood her position. I wouldn't have asked about possibly illegal hacking either. The document might be excluded as evidence eventually, but I was more concerned about stopping a threat than getting a conviction at the moment. I'd let the cops figure out how they could come across it on their own via "inevitable discovery" for the DA.

"Got it. So, tell me about the document."

"It's an MOU between the developers, the union, and Andy. It reads like an agreement for work on a joint project. It's not the rumored merger, but it's definitely a partnership. And it's for a good amount of money. The union workers get the city's designated living wage plus an additional percentage for journeymen, all indexed to any future living-wage increases the city may adopt. But here's the kicker. Tony and Andy split a bonus of a hundred grand when permits are secured, plus a percentage of the rental income for the first five years. The hundred K doesn't sound like much, but the rental income sounds like it could add up. Is that a normal arrangement?"

I looked to Jesse for his opinion.

"The living wage stuff is almost standard now. I don't know if the bonuses are high, but they're not unusual. A cut of the rental income sounds fishy, though. I've never seen that before."

"And it sounds like a good chunk of change," I agreed. "Makes you wonder if there's a similar arrangement for the Metro project."

"You know," he said, as if thinking aloud to himself. "The bonus for getting permits is usually for controversial projects that require a lot of community outreach—the kind we're always involved in." Then, turning back to me he added, "Maybe they were trying to secure Tony's help with union support? But I don't think Andy does community outreach work. I thought he only worked on legal stuff. Luis would know more about that."

"Let's look at the document," I suggested. I opened my laptop on the kitchen island. "Where's the project?"

"Boyle Heights," Sheila said.

"Wait, not the same project Luis is bidding on, right?" I asked. "Wouldn't that be a conflict of interest for Andy? He's Luis's attorney. He wouldn't be that stupid, would he?" I brought up Sheila's email and we scrolled through the document.

"It doesn't list an address," Jesse observed. "And the project name is different from Luis's competition."

"What kind of project is it?" I asked. "And where is it?"

"Likely subsidized family housing, maybe a mixed-use project with some retail on the ground floor. That's their bread and butter," Jesse said. He pointed at the screen. "Here. Northwest corner of Soto Street and First Street. Isn't that across the street from Luis's project?"

"So that wouldn't necessarily make it a conflict for Andy, right?" Sheila asked.

"Maybe not technically, but is it something that's already public?" I asked. "Would it affect approvals for the Metro project?" I knew I was close, so close I could almost taste it. There had to be a connection here. I just had to figure out what it was.

"It would need to be considered as part of the environmental impact report," Jesse said. "But I haven't heard about it. It would be worth looking up property records to see if someone's been buying in the area."

"Jane and I can do that," Sheila said. "But is this really something to kill over?"

"There's one way to find out," I said.

CHAPTER TWENTY-THREE

Thursday, noon

The more I thought about Tony and Andy's arrangement with the developers, the more I felt like I needed to take a shower. Keeping the bandage on my head dry made it feel more like a sponge bath, but then I put my plan into action. If it worked, Andy would arrive with Luis. If he did, I'd be able to confront him. And if I was right, he wouldn't be able to deny working with Luis's rivals. But would he admit to anything else? Was anyone else involved? Could it be Martinez or Rudy instead of Andy? Could Leon James be in on it? Was Andy working with them? Before calling Luis I cleared my throat to dismiss my doubt. It was too late for doubt. I filled in Kyle, who had been playing solitaire on the coffee table, then I sat on the couch with Jesse and dialed.

"Luis, I have something you'll want to see about your competition," I said as soon as he answered, left knee bouncing up and down.

"What is it?" He sounded intrigued, just as I'd hoped.

"I'll have to show you."

"Oh, come on, Yolanda. Just tell me."

"No. Really. I'm not sure what to make of it, and I don't want to be wrong," I said truthfully. "I need your help figuring it out."

He gave an exasperated sigh before giving in.

"Okay, but I'm a bit busy right now."

Don't bail on me.

"That's okay. Can you come by after work tonight, around seven thirty?"

"I don't know…" Luis hesitated. Jesse glanced at me, a worried look on his face at Luis's hesitation, but I winked at him.

"Please?" I said into the phone. "Or do you think Carmen would know enough about your business to ask her?" I hated to pull the Carmen card, but he'd left me no choice.

"Fine," he said. "You don't have to hit below the belt, you know."

Jesse smiled and gave me a thumbs-up.

"Sorry," I said into the phone, not meaning it. "You'll be here at seven thirty, then?"

"Yeah, see you then. Gotta go." When I hung up, I took in a deep breath and let it out slowly. I hoped he wouldn't cancel.

"Why didn't you ask him to bring Andy?" Jesse asked.

"Oh, Andy'll come. You can bet on that." I knew Luis trusted his best friend, and any news about his "competition" would be something Andy would definitely want to know about. Luis would tell him about my call like he'd probably told him about our dinner meeting, and Andy wouldn't be able to resist inviting himself. He might be even more interested in coming than Luis. At least, that's how I hoped it would play out.

"You know, neither of us have had any juju messages about this plan," Jesse said. "I mean, I had that odd feeling about Andy, but nothing since."

"I know, but it feels right. Doesn't it?"

"I guess so. Maybe it means we're doing the right thing." It came out more as a question than a statement.

"Like maybe we don't need help on this one?" I leaned forward on the couch and rested my elbows on my knees.

"Yeah." He stared at the black television screen. We'd turned it on earlier, but I had to shut it off when the news coverage turned to more xenophobic incidents across the country.

"I think I know now why you had the dream about the *birria* restaurant," Jesse said.

"Oh? Parking karma?"

"No. The cook," he said slowly, as if it was only now coming to him. "He helped you. Stayed with you until the cops and the paramedics arrived. I think it was a helpful hint after all."

I thought a moment, trying on his theory. It seemed to fit.

"You may be right. So, you think it was a message to be near someone who would help?"

"I think so. The messages you get seem to be about keeping you safe."

"Would've been more helpful if it had been a warning instead," I said. "See why I have trouble with this stuff?"

"Maybe it's cuz you haven't been paying attention to warnings. You didn't with the dream about Joey, you know."

I gave him a side-eye.

"Or maybe you were just supposed to meet with Luis and Martinez."

"I don't know." I rubbed my forehead where the bandage made it itch. "But I should get something for the cook, to thank him."

Jesse had stopped listening, lost in his own thoughts. I sat back and considered all the help Mom and Bobby had been trying to provide. But now I was on my own. I wanted to believe that they were behind us a hundred percent, that they were confident in our ability to carry out our plan. I could almost hear Mom saying in her accent, "*Ju* got this!" like she did when Jesse and I played sports. I smiled at the thought and hoped I was right.

Then I called Sydney to fill her in.

"Are you sure about this?" she asked. "I don't want you to put yourself in any danger."

"I won't, I'll have backup. Kyle is here, and you and Duc will be here tonight too."

"Shouldn't Detective Lan know about this and be there too?"

"Way ahead of you. Lan is my next call," I assured her. I didn't tell her that I'd left Lan for last because I didn't want the detective talking me out of it. "See you tonight. Love you."

Seven thirty could not come fast enough. I should've been working on intake interviews with new clients, but I couldn't concentrate long enough to get anything substantive done. Instead, I made appointments for the next day.

"You know, you're supposed to be resting," Jesse said as he watched me pace back and forth between the couch and the laptop. But he wasn't so still himself; his knees bobbed up and down as he turned on the TV and cracked his knuckles before flipping through channels again, unable to focus long enough on a single show. Kyle was the only one who seemed unconcerned, sitting so still that he could have been sleeping behind his sunglasses.

Jesse and I went over the Memorandum of Understanding several times, as if it could tell us more than it already had. But other than noticing a "CONFIDENTIAL" watermark on the document when we printed it out and confirming that the signatures were dated six months prior to the kidnapping, we got nothing. We finally gave up because it was only making us nervous. I considered calling Carmen but decided not to alarm her. She'd been through enough. I'd fill her in later. Jesse and I talked about food instead, trying to recall Mom's recipe for *pozole*, our favorite pork and hominy stew, but that only served to make us hungry and dissatisfied with the salad we had instead. Kyle liked it just fine. Sydney and Duc got home a few minutes before seven o'clock.

"Where's Kyle?" she asked after giving me a kiss on the cheek.

"Right here, Dr. Garrett." Kyle entered from inspecting the patio deck. "I'll be right at the top of the stairs."

"Where do you want me?" Duc asked.

"How about on the deck, behind the barbecue grill?" Kyle walked Duc to his position.

"Thanks, guys." Sydney sounded relieved. Turning to me, she asked, "How about Detective Lan?"

"She's on her way." Sydney looked down at my legs. I stopped rocking on the balls of my feet, a nervous habit at times of stress that she knew well. I tried willing away the tension.

"I hope she gets here soon." Sydney bit her lower lip to calm her own nerves. "What if Luis and Andy get here early?"

A couple of minutes later, Detectives Lan and Conroy arrived. My voice took on a deeper register when we went over the details of my plan. It wasn't the "bossy cop" voice that Carmen and Jesse teased me about, but the "Yes, Officer" tone that Sydney said was my version of her "Doctor Garrett." I knew what I was doing and hoped the detectives wouldn't mess with my plan.

"Sounds good," Conroy said, much to my relief. I turned to Lan and nodded a thank-you, figuring she had talked him into it when they'd agreed to come. They talked logistics with the bodyguards for a bit before Lan took up her position with Kyle at the top of the stairs, Conroy heading out the front door, out of view.

Then we waited. And waited. At seven thirty, I hoped Luis wouldn't cancel and resisted the urge to text him. Seven thirty became seven thirty-five, then seven forty. I was about to phone Luis when Lan shouted from upstairs, relaying Conroy's radio message that two men were approaching. Jesse jumped at her announcement. He jumped again at the sound of the doorbell.

"Chill, dude," I said. To anyone who didn't know her well, Sydney looked like her normal, serene self, but I could tell from her barely noticeable, deep breathing that she was centering herself. She stood motionless, unable to sit, but then she leaned on the back of a barstool at the kitchen island and assumed a more relaxed pose when I went to the door. Jesse took Sydney's cue and leaned back on the couch, pretending to watch TV.

"Come in," I said to Luis and Andy, opening the door. They both looked like their everyday selves in nearly matching, navy-blue suits. The tailoring flattered them. I could smell Andy's cologne—the one I'd always liked. We hugged at the door as usual. Nothing about them indicated any concern. That somehow made me feel better about Luis but more nervous about Andy. Like maybe this might not be so easy. They entered and exchanged greetings with Sydney and Jesse. I tried unsuccessfully to ground myself, and still the adrenaline pulsating at my head wound. I wished I could go into this encounter without my head bandaged, less vulnerable-looking. Jesse tried to appear disinterested in the men and more engaged with the *Star Trek* rerun he had on at low volume. I had to smile at that and found that it helped me relax a little.

"No bodyguard?" Andy asked.

"The cops found Rudy behind a bar in Lincoln Heights," I said, evading the question. "He's not a threat anymore."

"Good," Luis said. "Hopefully the cops will focus on him now."

"Hope so," Andy agreed.

"So, what did you want to show us?" Luis asked.

"Well, it's something I really wanted to discuss with you, but Andy may as well hear it too." Neither of them said anything, but they glanced at each other and back at me. I took another deep breath, bracing myself for Andy's reaction. "Well, here goes. Andy's been working with Tony Gonzalez, Barrio Homes, and Las Casas Builders." I spoke faster than I'd intended. Andy frowned and jerked his head back slightly with a half-smile as if to say, "That's it?"

"What is this?" Luis asked, looking from Andy to me and back. But Andy just looked at me with a questioning frown. He was waiting for me to show my hand. I obliged.

"I think Andy may want to explain how he's come to work with them on a project across the street from your own," I said more slowly. "And maybe how he stands to benefit from it." I looked Andy straight in the eye.

"Whoa." He raised his hands innocently. But his eyes shifted quickly between me and Luis.

"What are you talking about?" Luis asked. "Andy works with me. He doesn't need to work with those guys." He glanced at Andy for confirmation.

"Right," Andy said, but he sounded less confident now.

"Maybe I should show you." I moved to the laptop and tapped on the space bar to call up the MOU. Luis and Andy followed, and Jesse came up behind me. Sydney slid back to make room for us. Their proximity made me feel safe and increased my confidence.

"What is that?" Luis asked. We all leaned toward the screen.

"An MOU between Tony Gonzalez, Barrio Homes, and Las Casas Builders. And Andy," I said. "It's for a project across the street from yours. It might explain why things didn't end when we rescued Joey."

"Wait!" Andy exclaimed. He raised his hands, palms out again. "I had nothing to do with Joey's kidnapping." Then he pointed at my computer, keeping his distance from it. "And that—that's a confidential document." He looked back at me as if wondering how I'd gotten it. "It has nothing to do with the Metro project." He recovered some of his composure. "Luis's right, I don't need to work with those guys."

"But you *are* working with them," Jesse said from behind me. Luis continued to scroll through the document.

"I stand to benefit from both projects," Andy asserted. "Nothing wrong with that." He was talking to Luis, palms up again, but Luis kept his eyes on the laptop screen.

"Maybe not," I said. Sydney edged, ever so slightly, behind Andy. I could tell that his hand motions were making her nervous and she wanted to be close in case he reacted badly to my version of events. "But you needed to talk to Tony, or maybe he needed to talk to you, after the kidnapping. He was on the run and needed to turn to someone who might help him escape, or maybe negotiate a surrender—someone like a business partner, someone like a lawyer, someone like you."

"You're crazy." Andy gave a cocky smile, but his eyes shifted between me, Luis, and Jesse. I'd seen perps give that same smile hundreds of times when I was on the force. It always meant they thought they were too smart to get caught. It usually meant they were guilty of something.

"You signed an MOU with them?" Luis said, still stuck on my first revelation. His shoulders slumped, and he shook his head slightly, turning from the laptop to Andy. A part of me felt sorry for him, but another part of me rejoiced that he wasn't in on Andy's deal.

"That doesn't mean anything," Andy said. "I was gonna tell you, when I actually started working on permits, but so far all we have is the MOU, not full property control. The project may not even come to fruition." He was talking fast now. "C'mon, bro. Can't I get some? This is just my chance to create my own portfolio." Playing second fiddle to his buddy had gotten to him. I saw that now. But he was a lawyer, not a businessman like Luis. Probably thought he knew more than his friend and boss, deserved more. I shook my head in disgust.

"What about Tony?" Jesse asked.

"What about him? I didn't have anything to do with him or his death." This time, Andy's head turned along with his eyes between Jesse and me. I could tell he was feeling trapped. Sydney must have sensed it too, because she eased one leg back, a slight bend to her elbows. She still looked relaxed, but I knew she was on full alert.

"Are you sure you had nothing to do with Tony?" I asked Andy, working off a hunch. "His phone was never found, but maybe I can ask Detective Lan to search your car or home for it. Or maybe just search your phone for calls or texts from Tony after Joey's kidnapping. And maybe some of your shoes for mud." Andy's eyes grew big. His upper lip curled, an angry realization coming over his face. He lurched toward me, but before any of the rest of us could react, Sydney stopped him in midmotion with an elbow strike to his right shoulder. A sickening crack preceded a high-pitched squeal as he fell to the floor writhing in pain. Kyle and Detective Lan bounded down the stairs, and Duc appeared from the deck. Andy screamed in pain again. Sydney was still in her sparring stance but relaxed when our eyes met.

Andy wasn't going anywhere. Lan spoke into her radio and Conroy came in the front door in two seconds.

"It was an accident!" Andy shouted, seemingly alarmed at all the muscle descending on him. He rocked side to side on his back, gripping his shoulder. "He came at me," he said with a grimace. "When I told him I couldn't help him negotiate with the cops, especially after he took Joey. All I did was block his chest with my elbow. Ahh!" he yelled as he absently tried to lift his injured arm. "He just fell. I was gonna help him up, but he was out cold. I was gonna call 911, but he had no pulse. You gotta believe me." His eyes pivoted from me to Luis and Lan before looking away, defeated. "It was an accident." His confession ended with a moan and clenched teeth.

"But you were afraid that no one would believe you, especially if we discovered the MOU, so you stalked Sydney and attacked me to get me off your trail. And you came by yesterday morning to do more, but something, or someone, spooked you." I looked down at him. If he'd been upset and off guard enough to come at me, and to admit striking Tony, his pain-addled mind may have him admit to this too.

"I'm sorry," he apologized—a bit too late. "I panicked. I'm sorry," he repeated, looking up at Sydney. Adrenaline pulsated under my head bandage again at the thought of him threatening Sydney. Her own hands opened and closed into fists, likely feeling the same anger at him for coming after me. Neither of us spoke as Andy turned to look up at Luis. "But I didn't have anything to do with Joey's kidnapping. I swear. I didn't know Tony was going to do that."

"We'll see about that," Detective Lan said. She and Kyle helped him up, and Conroy approached with handcuffs. "Andrew Stewart, you are under arrest for the murder of Antonio Gonzalez and the assault and battery, and attempted murder, of Yolanda Ávila. You are also under arrest for stalking and making threats against Dr. Sydney Garrett, and conspiracy to kidnap and falsely imprison the minor Joseph Ochoa."

Andy's face contorted in pain again when Conroy cuffed him. Tears welled in his eyes when Lan read him his rights. I was pretty sure they were more about his sudden downfall than any physical pain.

"I'm sorry," he kept repeating as Conroy led him away. When they got to the front door, Andy stopped and turned to Luis. "You gotta believe me, bro, I didn't know about Joey. I would never do anything to hurt my godson."

Luis barely looked at him. He turned away and slumped on the nearest barstool, his elbows on the counter, his head in his hands. Sydney and Jesse placed a hand on each of his shoulders. There was nothing we could say. His best friend had betrayed him and may have inspired another friend to kidnap his son. Yet another friend kept information from him about his wife working for a rival. Andy had killed Tony—accidentally or not. And he'd continued on a downward spiral, stalking Sydney and attacking me. It had to hurt. It had to make him question his judgment. If anyone knew how bad that felt, it was me—not about my own friends, but about the juju. Detective Lan came over to me and shook my hand.

"Thank you. Hell of a job," she said. "The guys may never say it, but you can be sure they agree."

I thanked her, relieved by the vindication and proud of the outcome. Helping Carmen and Joey was just the beginning. *I can do this.* I knew all along that I could handle more than insurance fraud cases, but now I had proof.

A judge or jury would decide Andy's fate, but Sydney and I were safe again. I went and hugged her now. I'd welcomed Lan's comment about Andy's arrest. A detective's track record is the most important thing in establishing a good reputation. And a good reputation opens doors for a private detective on other cases. I took a deep breath, this time to soak in the realization that things were going to be all right. I could pursue the work I loved, maybe even work with the juju without it getting in the way. Jesse joined our embrace. Duc and Kyle retreated to the living room to give us some privacy. We all turned to Luis, who stared blankly at his hands.

As good as I felt, I knew the road ahead for him would be rough.

"How?" he said, more to himself than to any of us. He ran his hands through his hair. "How could I have been so blind? So stupid? Carmen's right. I've gotten so into my own shit that I've stopped seeing others."

Jesse walked back to him and put an arm around his shoulders.

We had no answers for him, but I hoped his new introspection meant that he could make up with Carmen. His friends had betrayed him, and one had kidnapped their son. I knew Carmen wouldn't let him off easy. He'd have to work hard to regain her trust after the danger he'd exposed them to. For Carmen and Joey's sake, I hoped he would do whatever it took.

I was sad for him, but then I was confused by another feeling. As Sydney continued to hold me in a warm embrace, I somehow felt lighter, like a burden had been lifted, but I felt teary too. It had nothing to do with Andy's arrest. I was relieved that Sydney and I were out of danger, but that wasn't why tears welled in my eyes. I shuddered in Sydney's arms and she held me tighter.

"I don't know why I'm crying." I sniffled. "I've never cried so much as I have the past few days…"

"Shh. Shhh." She continued to hold me, rocking me softly. Then I understood what had triggered the tears. It wasn't about Andy's arrest, or Luis's struggle, or the danger Sydney and I had faced. It was about that weight I'd been carrying around in my gut. The one that held on to guilt and blocked out grief, the weight from believing I couldn't trust myself, that what had happened to my mom was my fault. The more I sobbed, the lighter that weight became. I knew what it was now. The juju was Mom and Bobby looking out for me. That realization released a flood of pent-up grief, and waves of emotion rolled through me.

Images of Mom and Bobby came to me. I saw their pictures on *Nina* Mercedes's altar,

Mom laughing and Bobby strutting. I smiled and cried all at once and shook my head at the incongruity of it all. *Was that what grief felt like if I stopped blocking it with guilt?* Both would always be there, but now I could push the guilt a bit to the side. I could grieve, missing Mom and experiencing all the emotions—joy and sadness, love and regret—that came with her memory. And I knew, whatever came next, I could handle. Sydney held me tight, her cheek smiling against mine.

Bella Books, Inc.

Women. Books. Even Better Together.

P.O. Box 10543
Tallahassee, FL 32302

Phone: 800-729-4992
www.bellabooks.com